Book of Birds

Book of Birds

ISBN-13: 978-0-9979491-0-0
ISBN-10: 0-9979491-0-4

LMBRYSKI.COM

MORANPRESS.COM

To Rooslana —

Book of Birds

A novel by

L. M. Bryski

Hopefully this book makes scents to you :)

L Bryski (Lisa)

Moran Press
Blackstone, Massachusetts

For my family.

1

I don't advise losing your parents when you're young. Sure, you get out of their expectations and chores and all, but you also lose your place in life. You lose the knowing that whatever you did that day, you still got a kiss good night. At least, that's how Mam did it.

Dot and I had a place to go when Mam died. It was easier on us than some. I heard about the war and all, where my Da got killed helping Britain stay free. Who hadn't heard? It was only a couple years before. Some who lost a parent lost more of their family there, too. We were lucky. We still had Mam's parents.

I bet my grandparents didn't consider themselves lucky. Every last penny they had went to the running of their hotel. They likely didn't account for clothes and other expenses that came with caring for young people. They certainly didn't have enough money to come get us. We had to make our way to Gram and Grandpa's town ourselves.

We took the train after the funeral. The local parish packed us a lunch and put us on board, settling with Gram and Grandpa to meet us at the end of our journey. Everyone deemed me old enough to watch over Dot. For the most part, I did. We sat eating sandwiches wrapped in brown paper and watched fields sweep by. Dot saved her paper, thinking to find a pencil to trace dolls and dresses out. I picked at a scab on my elbow. A few women eyed us and tutted as they walked past in the aisle.

When we got to the station, there was no one to meet us. We were alone for more than a few minutes before a hired car pulled up and its driver shooed us inside for our ride. I looked out through the open window to make sure he didn't leave our suitcase. Dot just sat, trusting we'd get to our grandparents somehow. The dust billowed behind us as we were driven to our new home.

Gram spotted us first and called for Grandpa to come greet us. She wiped her hands in her apron and held one out for our things. I kept hold of our suitcase and shook Gram's hand instead. Grandpa squinted at us from the steps, like he expected we'd be taller and prettier. Gram must have bolstered Grandpa with hopes that we'd be a big help around the hotel, helping in the kitchen until we were old enough to serve in the bar. When we finally showed up, Dot with her little voice and me in my jeans, Grandpa nodded "Hello" and left Gram alone to pay for the ride.

I would have done the same.

Living with old people wasn't a real bonus for Dot and me, either. The hotel they ran was cruddy and worn in spots, like the threadbare sheets Gram used to cover the beds. Dot and I were relegated to a small room to share on the guest floor. At least they had a place for us, I suppose.

The room had a double bed and more space than Dot and I were used to. We each had our own drawer and a place on the dresser for our things. Dot spread her rag rabbit and little tea set out on her side of the dresser. I just put my book of birds on mine.

Grandma tisked and fussed over Dot's hair, saying she needed a haircut. I wouldn't let Gram near me with that comb. I grimaced and moved away when she brandished it above my head. I should have been more obliging, considering she was taking over from Mam. She had raised Mam, after all, and taught Mam ways of minding children. Mam said Gram earned her name "Grace" many times over with how caring she was. Mam mostly said it when she was admonishing me to act like my own middle name. Grace. Same as Gram's. Mam musta regretted not giving it to Dot, instead.

"Don't you have even one dress?" Gram's eyes raked the few clothes I was stuffing in my drawer.

"No, ma'am. I grew out of them." Secretly I was pleased at this development in height. Other developments? Not so much.

"Let's see what you have." Gram took our clothes out for inspection and folded them one by one on the bed. Then she looked me over like I was a pig for roasting. She shook her head and seemed to square herself up.

"Well, it'll have to do for now. You'll need a dress for Sunday, though." Gram lifted my arms and poked me in the waist.

Dot giggled until I scowled her to stop. Gram left my chest alone as she circled me, though she eyed it close.

"It'll have to be my brown one." Gram tilted her head in thought. "Not the best colour for a girl."

"My dress is too small, Gram." Dot leaned in, all hopeful. Her face was lifted like an angel needing adoration. The glint in her eyes was the first sign I'd seen of real Dot since her sulk over Mam. I didn't comment as I used to. I didn't want to scare her back into her shell.

Gram gave Dot a pat on the head as she continued refilling the drawers. "You should be fine."

Dot shoulda scowled but she didn't. Dot knew how to hold her temper when the situation warranted. I envied her that. She grabbed her stuffed rabbit and squeezed it instead.

"Dinner's in a bit, girls. The bathroom's down the hall for you to refreshen."

Gram closed the door in a quiet old lady way. You barely heard the shush. If it had been Mam, there would have been singing in the hall and a bang or two. Hard to see how they came from the same family. Other than their cheekbones and eyes, I can't imagine two ladies more different than Gram and Mam.

I grabbed my book and slumped on the bed. Dot was perched against the bed's edge, picking at the quilt flowers.

"You think we're gonna like it here?" Dot screwed up her face as she picked a long thread and held it high. She was always bothering me when I settled down to read.

"Don't know. Don't care."

"She seems pretty nice. I wonder about Grandpa, though." Dot put a hand on my leg as she spoke.

"Get off." I shook my leg as if dispelling a gnat. "Why don't you go have a tea party or something?"

I'll admit. I was being mean. Here we were, both in a new place and Dot being younger. Mam would have expected me to watch out for Dot, to care for her. Well, I had. Through the funeral and the trip and everything. Even carrying our suitcase up the stairs to our room. Now I needed a break from being Mam.

"Why don't you go find someone else to bother?" I lifted my book higher to block the sight of her. I was worried enough about myself. It was gonna be hard to fit in here when I didn't feel like trying.

I flipped the pages looking for a bird to focus on. Staring at the drawings of sparrows and shrikes, I could still see Dot's pained face. I could picture her all fluffed out and angry, like she was when things didn't go her way.

"Fine, be like that." Dot laid her soft animal on the bed. "Who wants to be with you, anyways? I'm going downstairs."

"Take your stupid toy with you." I picked up that rag from beside me and threw it on the floor. "Go find yourselves a rabbit hole to get buried in."

Dot's face quivered as she scooped the rag rabbit up. She hugged it tight.

I watched, already feeling sorry for what I'd done. "Dot..."

"*Smelly Elly eat some jelly!*" Dot slammed the door on my apology.

Fine. Be like that, yourself. Now alone, I settled in to read by the light from the window above the bed. I decided then and there she was Gram's problem. I always regret that decision.

2

Next days are usually better after you've had a fight. Minds are rested from the dark of night, and things don't seem so prickly anymore. People forget or make up. Sometimes though, a fight lingers in the air. It's a skunk that drifts in and picks up the heat of your thoughts. You smell it each time you ponder, and your stomach turns at the stink.

Dot and I had a skunk between us. It was there in the bed when we woke. Dot's not a morning riser. She would pretend sleep forever if she could, and wake only with kisses from Mam. Then she would sprawl over the bed, holding her hands up to be lifted.

Today, Dot's curls lay like angel wings over her pillow, while the rest of her snuggled deep in the covers. Even so, I could smell the fight still heavy on her.

"El-len, Dor-othy. Time to get up." Gram's light voice rose over the knock at our door. She had been shushing her steps in the hall for a while now. A boarder or two grunted through the walls as they rose for work.

"It's time to eat." Gram's weight moved off downstairs where creaks followed behind her.

Dot was motionless underneath the blanket, though I thought she listened.

I gave her a tug. "C'mon, Dodderdoo. We gotta get up." No movement, nothing. I would have to relent and speak first. No different than at home. Mam would have told me to.

"C'mon. Time to go."

Dot still didn't move. She lay like the dead, her breathing all deep.

"I'm sorry about your rabbit and all." I sat up and lifted the yellowed curtain beside me. "Looks like a nice day."

The birds outside had been going on about how beautiful the world was. I was anxious to go see where they nested, though it was early autumn with no eggs to find. Still, I was curious and itching to explore. So I left Dot. She'd have to fend for her own way to breakfast.

Grandpa was sitting in the bar when I came downstairs. You could peer straight into the barroom from the hallway. Grandpa stared a moment before turning back to his coffee. I thought I saw him raise his eyebrows in greeting. No matter.

A man leaned out from behind Grandpa for a look at me. He showed dirty, brown teeth as he flicked cigarette ashes to the floor. He lifted a glass and took a swig before grinning again.

Grandpa looked up, so the man arched forward to talk again.

"Good morning. How did you sleep?" Gram caught me as I turned from the doorway.

"Pretty good." I could smell bacon on her, so I let her give me a hug.

Gram frowned at my jeans then peered over my head. "Where's your sister?"

"Still sleeping."

"Well, go tell her it's time to wake up. We can't wait for late risers. I've got to get breakfast done so we can start preparing lunch." Gram gave me a turn and a swat on the bum. "Go on. Get her."

I find it best not to disobey the cook. Even Dot knows the wisdom of that. You do so at peril of starvation or worse: suffering through meals of bland food.

Gram ushered Dot and me to one end of the table away from the boarders. They paid us no mind as they scooped eggs and bacon rounds as fast as their jaws could chew.

"No eggs for me." Dot scrubbed her eyes as she shifted in her chair. "They make me feel all scootchie."

The table was higher than home. Dot looked like a floating head when she put her hands down. I smiled at the thought. Dot pouted in return.

"Dot don't like eggs, Gram." It was me who loved eggs. I had a whole page of them in my bird book, all different types and sizes. I hoped Gram kept the eggshells. I wondered if they were brown or white or speckled.

"You don't want eggs, honey? How about a little taste?"

Dot let her half-undone braids swing out with her emphatic "No."

Gram gave a sigh like she fed picky eaters all the time. Mam never liked eggs, and Dot's tastes took after hers. Gram held the pan up and looked at me. "Ellen? Shame to let them go to waste." She added Dot's eggs onto my dish when I nodded back.

Breakfast was good. I've been tasting Gram's baking all my life without even knowing it. Mam's butter biscuits sat on the table next to a small pot of jam. Even Dot couldn't resist those.

"Thank you for feeding us, Gram." Dot was first to rise and pick up her plate.

I said nothing, as Dot had beaten me to the punch. Dot was always quicker in doling out her manners. I didn't mind, though. I knew she spoke for both of us. I grabbed my own plate and brought it to the sink.

Gram didn't need much help around the kitchen so sent us looking for wayward dishes.

"Things tend to migrate around here. See if you can spot anything that needs a wash. We'll need it for lunch." Gram tightened her apron and rolled up her sleeves. She plunged her hands deep into the soapy sink water as she nodded us away.

Gram's words were all I needed for permission to explore. Mostly I wanted to see what was outside, but there were mysteries inside as well.

"Let's go." I grabbed hold of Dot's hand and pulled.

"I'm not ready yet. I need a wash." Dot shook free and tried to smooth out one braid. A pink ribbon hung wrinkled on the braid's tangled end.

"You can do it after." I wanted adventure. I'd had enough of old people feeling sorry for me and making me sit in reflection. I'd had enough of sadness and funerals. The last week had put the itch in my brain for excitement. No one would spoil it, no matter what.

Dot found a bowl by the back door with ashes in it. I helped her bring it back to Gram who tutted about men and their laziness as she accepted the offering.

I kept pacing the hallway, looking with greed at the front door, eager for escape. Dot paused most in the parlour, staring at the crochet cozies Gram favoured as decorations. God's Eye-patterned crochet squares were laid out over armrests and tables, and under ashtrays and figurines. Gram's colour choices ran through the whole rainbow, but someone musta made a fortune off her passion for purple yarn.

Dot held a purple and red square up for me to admire. "Maybe Gram could teach me how to make one." Dot had always wanted to knit, but Mam had no patience for it.

Me, I found the parlour boring. No books there. Besides, I had spent enough time in a parlour, praying over a casket.

"We should check the front for more dishes." I was hoping for an easy sneak outside.

"I'm not going out. I'm staying right here." Dot dug in her heels right by the stairs. "And I'm telling if you go. We're supposed to be helping Gram." She was on to my plan though I hadn't said a thing.

I wondered if most sisters were like that, knowing without words and stuff.

"We're done helping Gram. We've checked the whole place unless ..." My eyes turned to the doorway with the smoke-blackened barroom behind it.

"Not there." Dot hunched and shivered, wrapping her arms around herself. "It's too dark."

The bar was quiet when I peeked in. The loamy smell of man talk still lingered despite no one there. It clung to my shirt and made me taste my lips.

"Elly, don't."

Only a few steps took me to where Grandpa's coffee cup lay on the table. The strange man's glass kept it company, wet ring surrounding its bottom. An ashtray stood nearby, smoke curling from a cigarette that poked out from its frame.

"Elly." Dot hissed at me from the doorway, but I was determined in my course.

I picked up the cigarette and took a pull.

"Elly, no!"

My throat burned. A cough shuddered through me, and I gave a big retch.

Ya-ack!

Not bad.

"You like that?"

In the doorway, the strange man had both hands on Dot's shoulders. He showed his teeth as he did before.

Dot froze like she'd spotted a snake.

"I was just getting the glasses." I hurriedly tucked the cigarette back in its ashtray and reached for Grandpa's cup.

"I can see that. But did you like my smoke?" The man smiled at me.

"Uh…" I was mesmerized, just like Dot was. I couldn't move or give more sense to my words other than a small grunt. Even that was an effort. I stared at the man as he wiggled his eyebrows and pursed his lips.

The man's lips had tasted the cigarette last. His brown teeth. I stifled another retch.

"Do you want to try a fresh one?"

"Huh?"

"Cigarette. A fresh cigarette."

I was tempted. I looked to where the old cigarette sagged in the ashtray, then back again.

Dot looked wide-eyed, mouthing a plea for saving as the stranger nudged her forward into the barroom. Their two bodies blocked the doorway. No way he was letting us loose without some hassle.

"I gotta go help Gram." I stood as tall as I could.

The stranger grinned wider.

"Mr. Harner, what's going on?"

We all looked back to see man in a suit. Grandpa stood at his side, face red and silent.

"I said, what's going on?"

"Nothing, Mr. Dionne."

"Why are these children in the bar?" The man pushed through and eased Dot out of Harner's way. Mr. Dionne laid his own hand on Dot's head. "What are you doing here?"

"Just a bit of fun." The man showed his brown teeth again, then seemed to think better of it.

"Young girls like these… They should be in school." Mr. Dionne gave Dot's braid a tug and motioned her off.

Dot scurried beside me and grabbed my hand. I let her. I would have grabbed her hand first, but I was bigger.

"Why aren't they in school?" Mr. Dionne looked at Grandpa.

Grandpa didn't say anything. He just gave his neck a rub.

Mr. Harner took this as a release. He disappeared out through the hall. The front door squeaked open and swung shut. Good riddance. To him and his teeth.

Grandpa cleared his throat. Dot and I waited to hear what he sounded like.

"Grace?"

Bangs could be heard from the kitchen beyond. They stopped as Grandpa called.

"What is it?" Gram sounded none pleased, although I could tell already she held that in a lot.

"Come on out here. We have a guest." Grandpa's voice was low and growly. He motioned Mr. Dionne to follow him into the parlour. Dot and I trailed behind.

"Nice to see you, Mr. Dionne." Gram came into the parlour all smiles and friendly. She smoothed her apron as she stood in the hall.

"Ma'am. I see your granddaughters have come. It's a pleasure to meet you, girls." Mr. Dionne mocked a small bow. "Girls, this is Mr. Luc Dionne. He's superintendent at the school." By Gram's tight raised tone, we knew he was important.

"Pleased to meet you," we both murmured.

"Mr. Dionne wants to know why the girls aren't in school today." Grandpa lowered his chin and gave Gram a look over his glasses.

Gram reddened but held her ground. "We talked about that. The girls stayed home to get used to the place. They'll be in school tomorrow. They have some books already from the teacher."

My ears perked up at hearing books. I hadn't seen a book around anywhere and was beginning to think I was the only literate one in the family. Dot was still shaky with the reading.

"Well, that's fine. I'll see you girls on the morrow." Mr. Dionne gave Grandpa's hand a shake as he left. "Come on over later, Carl. We can check on your account then."

"I'll be by this afternoon." Grandpa lifted his glasses and rubbed his brow as soon as we heard the door close.

People in charge of kids generally fall into two categories: those that like us and those that don't. It was easy to see which category Mr. Harner was in. Gram, too. I still wasn't sure about Grandpa. For some reason, I felt Mr. Dionne straddled both choi

3

By the next day, we had a routine. Gram called us from the hall-way. Dot woke second, refused her eggs again, and wanted a wash.

I took my time getting ready. I didn't mind going slow, as I had explored behind the hotel yesterday. There was an old boarded outhouse with squirrels nipping in and out of the moon hole in the door, a big oak that hosted the bird symphony, brown egg-laying hens that ignored their hen coop, and the kitchen backdoor where Gram would call us inside to eat. I also didn't mind dawdling as I was worried about school.

"Hurry up." Dot jiggled up and down on the bed as I dressed. "Gram's waiting downstairs." Younger sisters move too much sometimes.

"What's your rush?"

"I'm excited. Aren't you excited?"

"I guess."

"Well, I am. We get to meet the teacher and play at re-cess." Dot got that cunning look like she was bribing me. "There will be books there."

As much as I don't like sitting in seats, I never mind school as long as they have books. Dot was coaxing me to share in her happy, though. I wasn't in the mood. I'll admit now, I was scared. I protected myself the best way I could.

I lashed out.

"They're not going to like you." I wasn't proud of it but I said it.

Dot pouted her lip. "Says you."

My mock musta hit Dot more than I thought, because she hid behind Gram when we walked through the schoolyard. I saw the usual morning goings-on. Boys were throwing a baseball around. A couple of small girls hung on to their mams. Some older girls stood giggling by the entrance to the school.

One of the girls pointed at us. She didn't bother keeping her voice low as she called out her mock.

"I didn't know they let strays in school. Look at that hound."

She stared right at me to make sure the lob hit.

I marked her as I passed: black hair, green dress, arms cocked on hips, ready to fire another round. Not much changes between schools, no matter where you go.

Gram must not have heard, as Dot was still clutching hard on her hand. Not that it mattered.

The teacher was wider than our old one. She had her hair cut short, and her eyes were hid behind thick glasses. She looked like a fat snail, the way she peered at us. I half expected an antenna to come waving out with her greeting. She stood and looked wider still.

"You must be Ellen and Dorothy."

Dot said nothing behind Gram so I took the lead.

"Yes, ma'am."

"Welcome to school, girls. We're excited to have new students."

I couldn't tell if she really was happy as the fat folds hid her eyes. But there was warmth in her voice, and she had made an effort to stand instead of keeping us waiting.

Gram cleared her throat. "Thank you, Miss Oswin. I hope you enjoy having them in your class."

"It will be a pleasure." Miss Oswin motioned for us to follow as she edged around her desk. "I'm so glad you came early. I have a lot to show you."

The schoolroom wasn't much to look at. Some number charts and a poster of Canada sagged on the wall. I spied a small bookshelf that might give some relief. A few math problems dusted the chalkboard up front. They were easy. But they weren't what made me nervous.

"Dorothy, your desk is here up front. You'll be with the beginner class. I've set out your worksheets for you. We're starting with arithmetic today."

Dot managed a nod, but didn't move from behind Gram.

"Ellen, I've put you here in the middle beside Darlene. She's also in Grade Eight. The older students are working on geography."

I nodded, too. Maps and such were a snap for me. I learned all about them from the bird book Da gave me. It showed habitats and ranges. Still, schoolwork didn't worry me. Students did. That schoolyard teasing was nothing. I was waiting for the bomb to drop.

Gram disengaged herself from Dot's worry and gave us each a kiss. She left with a reminder to head home for lunch. I wished I could, but Mam was dead and our home gone. I didn't consider the hotel my home yet.

Miss Oswin rang the bell for school. She had a good strong arm.

I watched from my desk as the students came in. The boys jostling in line were fun to watch, all spirited like my friends back home. I wanted to join them, but it would have been a rookie mistake.

The pretty girl with the black hair stopped by my desk and scowled. In my mind, a high-pitched whistling sound began.

"Get out of my seat."

I stared back and didn't budge. No good would've come of saying that Miss Oswin put me there. I'd have to settle it my own way if I was to start off right.

"I said, get out of my seat."

"It's my seat now." I could scowl with the best of them.

"Find your own bloody seat." It was a risk, but it's best to fire your cannon early if you want to win.

Black hair girl raised her eyebrows at my cuss, but didn't squeal. I respect that. She gave a look at her partner, who shook her head and sat down beside me.

"Constance, you can take a seat behind our new student." Miss Oswin's voice was a signal to end the battle.

"Better do it, Connie," the girl beside me advised.

Connie gave me the squint eye and sat down in the seat behind. So far my troops had lasted, but I was now flanked on two sides.

"This isn't over, hound." I barely heard her whisper as the teacher presented Dot and me to the class.

Miss Oswin had everyone introduce themselves and got us down to work. She gave Darlene beside me permission to talk quietly to help me along. She shouldn't have bothered. I had more to teach Darlene than she did for me. Dumber than a goatbag. She was half-friendly though, despite my being targeted as the enemy. Still, the sound of Connie's muttering behind us kept Darlene tight in her manners.

The girls weren't what I was interested in. I kept an eye out for the boys: who was slouching the most, who kept dropping his pencil, who smirked when the teacher talked. You can tell a lot about the pecking order of chickens in the coop by their struts. Same with boys in a class. The ones who stretch a rule or two rule the roost. Seems there was no one general I could figure on. Might make it easier to join in on the fun.

One boy about my age paid them no mind and just sat hunched over his books. I notice these things, too. The weak chicken is one to avoid in any schoolyard. You never know when you'll get in the way of a group pecking. Once, he was called on by the teacher and went beet red.

"Stanislaw, can you please tell me what is the name of the river that runs through Saskatoon?"

"South Saska-Saska-uh-Sask..." The boy went even deeper into the trench of his desk, barely poking his head up to deliver his rat-a-tat-tat.

Connie behind me giggled—of course—and made a poor whisper mocking the boy's voice. "Saskuh uh uh Saskuh..."

Darlene wasn't any better. "Stammerslaw." She nudged me to share in the joke. "We call him Stammer."

That cinched it. Two against one is hardly fair in boy wars but when it's girls involved, you know it's bad. I raised my hand.

"Yes, Ellen?" I could see Miss Oswin was pleased that I was already participating. She should know better.

"The river that runs through Saskatoon is the South Saskatchewan River." I made a risky move giving out the right answer on the first day, but I had to put the boy out of his misery.

"Very good, Ellen."

I kept my head down like it was no matter. I almost didn't see the school door open and Mr. Dionne step in.

Connie had her hand up almost as soon as Mr. Dionne motioned the class to go on.

Miss Oswin sighed and waved her to speak.

"And the Qu'Appelle River is just north of Regina, the capital of Saskatchewan."

"Very good, Constance."

An unasked-for fact. I hadn't heard of a student doing that before. Darlene beside me seemed to take it as no matter. I snuck a backwards look to see how this thing could be true.

Constance beamed as Mr. Dionne commented, "Well done, daughter."

Of course.

"Class, we have our superintendent here. Would you please stand and greet him?" Miss Oswin's voice quivered. She was beaming just as hard as Connie.

In unison, except me a second later, the class stood. "Good morning, Mr. Dionne."

"Good morning, Class." Mr. Dionne smoothed his moustache as he peered across the desks. His eyes lit on me, and then he glanced at Dot.

I did, too. I could barely see her at her desk. She hadn't stood with the rest.

"I see we have our new students today. Welcome."

I nodded, uncertain if the students were allowed to speak to their highers even when addressed.

"Class, we're going to have an early recess. You may go." Miss Oswin smiled as the room burst into life. Students still filed out in order despite their eagerness for release.

I stayed last to let Dot catch up with me. I hadn't noticed her at all during the morning due to my own concerns.

Dot hadn't moved from her place. Miss Oswin and Mr. Dionne were both leaning over her as she trembled in her seat.

"Dot, are you ready?" I felt bold because recess was called.

Miss Oswin looked up and wagged her head. Her chins bobbed side to side with each swing. "Dorothy will be staying in during recess. She hasn't completed her work."

Miss Oswin held the paper up for Mr. Dionne to see. I caught a glimpse, too. There wasn't a pencil mark on it. Mr. Dionne frowned and bent to speak with Dot.

I left Dot behind to fend for herself.

4

A new kid at recess is what a trip to Mars must be like: there's no warmth, you're far from help, and you might not survive the landing. Lucky for me, there was a party already waiting my arrival. Unlucky for me, it was headed by Connie. Darlene said nothing, but hung around like she was still deciding who to bet on.

"Look, it's that stray dog again." Connie pointed as she spoke.

"Careful, it may have rabies." A smaller girl piped in, knowing the group could save her.

I didn't answer. Best to keep moving until you find a spot to set down your craft. The taunts still followed, though.

"Look, she's turning tail." Connie flipped her black hair like she was queen of the playground. She probably was. Bad choice, Miss Oswin, of where to seat me.

"Are you girls okay?" A man stood by the corner of the school building. His overalls hung on him like he forgot how to eat.

The girls quieted and shared looks with each other.

"I haven't seen her before." The man pointed at me with some garden shears he held.

Connie spoke up. "She's new. We're just showing her around."

I closed my eyes in complaint, but dared not scowl or shake my head. I wasn't stupid.

"That's nice of you, Connie. Is it recess already?" The man peered at the field where the boys were gathered. One waved at the man and held up a baseball glove.

"Yes, Mr. Oswin. Miss let us out early. My father's here to check up on her." Connie had her eyes on me as she said it. I supposed it was to emphasize how high and mighty her family was in town.

"Well, take care of her, girls." The man lost interest and walked away as he spoke. He went to join the boys. What I wouldn't have given for an invitation to follow.

Darlene gave me the second nudge of the day. "That's Miss's brother. He takes care of the school."

Connie shot Darlene a look.

"Well, she should know and all." Darlene took a step away from me.

"Yeah, you're right. She should know." Connie turned back to me, drawing her eyes over my jeans. "Considering she looks like she belongs outside, working with Mr. Oswin. Who ever heard of a girl wearing jeans to school?" She sniffed the air about me. "And she smells like a dirty mutt."

I tried walking away but the girls followed.

"She's probably just as crazy as ole Oswin, too." Connie's words drew laughs from the girls. She paced beside me and grinned in my face.

That stopped me in my tracks. Connie had crossed the line into taking down grown-ups. This was dangerous territory. She was more powerful than I suspected. I was in big trouble.

Connie waved a hand in my face. "Crazy mutt."

I looked around for saving. The boys were far away and not likely to help a new girl, anyways. I did the only thing I could in a situation like that.

I bit Connie.

Not hard, but still a bite. Then I ran.

The girls were shocked into stillness.

Except for Connie. She yelled and shook her hand out. I suppose she made a fist too, but I was already too far away to see.

I made it to the bushes a long ways away. My jeans may be rough, but at least they let me fly down a field when I wanted. The girls didn't follow. They hung around Connie, far off by the school door. I crouched low beneath the bushes and hugged my knees.

"The b-b-ball?"

I looked up to see who called.

Stammer was standing with his glove. He gave a twitch of his shoulders and pointed behind me. His hair stood up like it wanted to twitch off his head. A few longer locks fell over his eyes, and he pushed them back as he watched me.

"What?"

"The ball."

"Oh." I looked behind where a scuffed ball rested at the roots of the bush.

"What's taking so long?" Another boy called out from first base.

Stammer stammered nothing. He just pointed at me.

"Well, get it from her then." The other boy made no attempt to hide his impatience. Why should he? He was higher on the playground pecking order.

Stammer turned again and held up his glove. "The b-ball. Can I have it?"

I don't know whether it was the open glove or that someone was looking me in the eye. I didn't hide the ball like I initially wanted. After all, I'd put myself out for him already. I picked the ball up, stood, and threw it.

Thwack.

The sound the ball made hitting Stammer's glove gave me a great deal of satisfaction. It also reminded me of home. I sat back down under the hedge, a wave of sorrow washing over me.

"Th-that was good."

I looked up to find Stammer standing over me. His glove was empty, and the game continued on behind him.

"So was nothing." Made no sense, I know, but it felt good to be dismissive instead of dismissed.

"N-no. I mean it. You ha-have a good arm." The boy sniffed a couple of times and gave a twitch, but he kept on looking me in the eye.

"Thanks."

"Would you like to play?"

I peered out at the group of boys now gathering their things. Recess was over. I shook my head no.

"I'm St-stani. Short for Stanislaw." The boy stuttered almost every second word. But he was speaking to me and holding out his hand.

"I'm Elly." I reached back.

Stammer looked back to where the boys were heading in.

One raised his arm and yelled out to us. "Stammer. Time to go." Even low ranking boys are included. Boys sure are different.

Stammer grabbed my hand and hauled me up. "C'mon. Race ya."

He was off like a shot, like all those twitches were just coiled up ready to spring. I ran after him, glad to have even a twitcher for a friend.

We were the last at the school door. Mr. Oswin was still there, bracing his garden shears against his shoulder. Stammer went right up to him and pointed back at me.

"Sh-she can throw. Can she join in next time?"

Mr. Oswin examined me with sad eyes. I hadn't noticed how tired his body looked. I wondered if that was part of the crazy that Connie had said.

"What's your name?"

"Elly."

The man glanced at my jeans and gave me a kind smile despite what he saw.

"I'm afraid not. It's a boys team I'm training." He sighed at his words as if he regretted both the question and his answer.

"B-but we're just playing for fun."

"I'm sorry." Mr. Oswin turned and left.

Stammer and I were last to take our seats. I peeked over to try and catch Dot's eye, but she had her head buried in her work already. At least she had picked up the pencil and was printing something out.

"Mutt." The word licked at my ear.

I didn't dare turn. I looked to Darlene beside me, but she avoided my gaze. She twisted her body so that her shoulder blocked me from view.

"Bitch." Connie's hate bit at the end of the word. She added a bark and snickered.

I was gonna pay for my choices.

5

Gram had us home for lunch and was waiting again for us after school. She probably saved my life. I was worried about Connie and her friends. I didn't really think they'd kill me. They're girls, after all. And I can take any girl. But Connie was mad, and who knows what she would have egged the group to do. I didn't even think of Dot being in danger by my actions. Funny how you get caught up in your own small drama and miss the big ones.

"Well, girls, how was your first day at school?"

"Alright, I guess." Dot never made eye contact. She just shuffled along beside Gram.

Dot was never just alright about anything. Dot usually bounced and spun with unbridled joy. She had, this morning. I shoulda paid Dot more attention, but I was also busy keeping watch for an ambush. Connie and Darlene had headed out the door the minute teacher dismissed us.

"How about you, Ellen? Do you like your teacher?"

I thought about Miss Oswin and her size. Then I thought about how she had smiled when I handed in my work. "She's nice."

Gram looked us over as we fell apace to walk back to the hotel. Dot drooped and dragged her feet, keeping her eyes on the path. I kept scanning the trees along each side, vigilant for danger.

"Well, I'm glad you enjoyed your day. You both must be tired, though. I've got soup for you when we get home."

Dot perked up at that. "Can I have some bread crumbs in my soup?"

"I don't see why not. I seem to remember your Mam liking it that way."

The mention of Mam put a little energy in Dot's step. She soon skipped ahead. Still, I saw the group of girls standing on the path before she did. I kept my stride steady with Gram as we approached.

Connie stared at me with a flash of violence before schooling her features. "Good afternoon, Mrs. Johnson." The other girls stood behind, not meeting my eyes.

"Why, good afternoon to you, Constance. How was school today?"

"It was interesting. There was a stray dog outside at recess, but we managed to shoo it away." Connie waggled the fingers of the hand I bit.

Gram nodded. "You can't be too careful. Some of those dogs have rabies."

The other girls giggled until Connie shushed them. Darlene was smiling, but stopped when I saw her.

"I was wondering if Ellen could come play with us?" Connie bit her lip as she said it. Her eyes sparkled with a mischief I don't think Gram could see.

"Well, that sounds like a nice idea. Ellen? What do you think? Do you want to go with Constance and her friends?" I could tell Gram was pleased with my inclusion.

"Elly is coming home with me for soup." Dot's voice piped over Gram's. Dot took a hold of my hand. I swear there was suspicion in her eyes as she stared at Connie. I kept hold of Dot's hand, too. It didn't look good, using my little sister as a shield, but at that point I didn't care. "I'm kinda tired, Gram. I'd really like to come with you."

"Nonsense." Gram took Dot's hand from mine and gave me a little push. "You've been cooped up all day. It will do you good to spend time with the girls. I'll save your soup for you."

Connie smiled her triumph.

I was forced to go stand by Connie as Gram and Dot walked away. Dot kept looking back with wide eyes. I hadn't told her about my run-in with Connie, but I think she suspected. I didn't usually go for the dressy ones as friends. Connie at least waited until Gram and Dot had passed a bend in the path. The other girls crowded in as my family disappeared from view.

"So, mutt. What are we going to do with you?" Connie crossed her arms as she stared.

I didn't give her a chance to figure it out. I ran.

The path was a straight line back towards school. I kept going, as I could hear the whoops and hollers of the girls behind me. Ahead, a lone figure trudged towards me. Leather-strapped books in one hand, baseball glove in the other, hair all spikey like the knowledge of school had scared him.

It was Stammer.

"Whoa, what's your h-hurry? Where are you g-going?" Stammer reached out his glove to tag me as I went by.

I turned and pointed, then tripped over my own heels and fell. I took a hard landing on my backside, and it winded me. Stammer dropped his books. He leaned over, grasped me by the shoulders, and hoisted me up. His face fluttered with curiosity.

I stood stiff, my heart knocking in my chest. "It's those girls." I pointed again up the path where Connie and her tribe came into view. "I gotta go."

Stammer laid a hand on my arm. "D-don't."

Connie was a short shot away. She paused in her tracks at the sight of a boy. The rest of the girls fell in line behind her.

"You l-looking for something?" Stammer took a man stance beside me. His legs practically straddled the path.

Connie took a step forward, but Darlene hauled her back. They looked at each other, measuring up a decision. It was in my favour.

"Nah. We were just following a stray dog. Did you see a mutt come round anywhere?" Connie smirked as her friends tittered their support.

"Well, there's no d-dog here. There's just me and Elly."

The sentence was ripe for picking, but Stammer couldn't see it. I held my breath, awaiting Connie's processing.

Connie smiled. "Seems you got yourself a new girlfriend, Stammer. You better watch, though. She's got some fleas."

"Ah, g-get on with you. Go bake some shit pies or somethin'." Stammer made a fist and raised it in the air. Boy code wouldn't have let him use it, though.

Connie rallied her girls, and they took off back the way they came. Darlene left last, sparing me a kind look over her shoulder. I stood watching, uncertain if I was relieved it was over or upset I hadn't been the one to stop it. Stammer picked up his books and waited to see what I'd do. I waited too, as I didn't know. I thought some gratitude might be a good start.

"Thanks for saving me."

"Aw, you coulda taken them. C-Constance Dionne is too afraid to get her dress dirty." His eyebrows tic'd as punctuation for each word.

"Do you always do that?"

"What?"

"Make moves and such when you speak?" It wasn't the nicest thank you, but curiosity overruled manners.

"I c-can't help it." Stammer glowered and turned to leave.

"It's not bad. I mean, it's not something I seen before, but it's not scary or anything."

Stammer held still for a rare moment and sized me up with his eyes. I held my breath, thinking I ruined another chance at friendship with my boldness.

"I'm g-glad you think so." He didn't look glad, but still he stayed. "You going home? I can walk you. Just in c-case Connie and her friends are waiting."

I was stuck. Going forward was a walk towards Connie and backward to school was a defeat. Only one choice to make. Neither.

"Ah, hell," I said. I jumped off the path and went pushing through the bushes.

"Hey, where are you g-going?" The foliage shook behind me as Stammer shoved through to follow.

"I'm getting out of here."

"You're going the wrong way. The hotel is on the other side."

"I'm not going home." Branches scraped my arms as I pushed further into the bush.

"Then where are you going?"

I stopped dead in my tracks. Where was I going? I leaned against a tree as I pondered this thought.

Stammer caught up. He stood easy, as if moving made his twitches untangle.

"I don't know." It was the truth.

"Oh." Stammer shook a torn leaf free from his book strap and shuffled his feet. His face screwed up like he was scared to look at me.

"You c-could come with me."

"Why? Where are you going?"

"H-home. You could come see my uncle's land. There's an old p-pilgrim's trail that runs through it."

A pilgrim's trail sounded interesting. I could picture the horse-drawn wagons following each other in the tracks, rumbling through the prairie. Maybe even an Indian or two had come across them and shared a smoke and some earth wisdom. What I wouldn't give to meet a real Indian I could stalk with.

"Let's go," I said.

Stammer's home wasn't too far. It wasn't too big, either. In fact, it was kinda small and dumpy. It had a wall of sod and a cracked pane window. The low-lying roof made me think of a fairy tale. I looked around to see if there was a witch nearby. I couldn't see Connie, though.

"What are you laughing at?" Stammer's voice got louder. His face reddened like a hot coal was burning his cheeks.

"Nothing. This where you live?"

"What do you think? I'm showing it, aren't I?" Funny how his tics disappeared when he raised his voice.

I didn't come to make an enemy. I had enough of those for one day. I just gave the truth as I saw it, though.

"It's small, and I don't see how you fit."

Stammer opened the door. "Like this." He didn't invite me in.

When he came back out, his books were gone and he was munching an apple. "Want one?" A small red-green beauty sat in his hand.

Apples taste real good when they're fleshy and fresh. There's a tartness to them. They taste even better when they're being shared. Stammer and me threw the cores in the field as we walked the old trail. My mouth was all sticky from apple juices, and neither of us was in the mood to talk, so we just followed the old wheel tracks in the grass for a while.

"We got to go q-quiet now."

"What?"

"Quiet." Stammer crouched low in the grass and crept to the side where a drove of trees ran through the field.

I shrugged and followed, curious to see what warranted a sneak.

Stammer motioned me forward and climbed through the low brush skirting the trees. My arms were already scratched from earlier, so I paid the pokes no mind.

"Shh. Get down." Stammer suddenly dropped flat.

"What is it?"

"Look."

Through the trees, I could see a small clearing. Two men were conferring with their heads together. A large sod patch of earth was propped up, exposing a room size hole underneath.

"It's my Uncle Ward and Nathan." Stammer stretched his chin in the men's direction.

"Why are we hiding?"

"'C-cause they're at the d-distillery. They don't know I've found it."

Jugs lay at the men's feet, most of them full with a clear liquid. The men filled another as we watched.

"I've only seen it when they're not here. I've never seen the sod lifted. Uncle Ward complains about his back sometimes, and Nathan agrees, saying it's a job for two. Then they hush and look at me, so I know they're talking about the still." Stammer only had two tics during that whole speech. He was focused, like he was aiming to shoot at something.

"Who's Nathan?"

Stammer twisted in the dead leaves and peered at me. He looked like his words were swirling in his head.

"He's our hired hand."

"Oh."

Birds were collecting in the trees as we watched. I twisted my head to try and catch a flash of them above. They were black as soot.

"I think they're grackles." I pointed up, but Stammer kept watching his Uncle piping hootch into the jars.

"They've got the b-best moonshine around, people say. And everyone buys it. Connie's pa has a regular run of it. My uncle makes good money off it, but the police would shut him down if they suspected."

"Definitely grackles. There's at least a dozen of them up there." I tried to sit up for a better look, but Stammer laid a hand on my arm.

"Don't. My uncle will see."

"This is boring. I gotta go." I inched backwards on my hands and knees out of the trees. The grackles took off all at once and circled in the sky cawing. I didn't dare look to see if Stammer's uncle noticed what scared them.

Stammer followed behind. We were just as quiet going back, but now it wasn't a shared quiet. I could feel disappointment seeping off Stammer.

"It was nice to see the pilgrim track. Maybe we can go out again?" I was enjoying it. The wheel tracks led in a straight line right up to the gate of Stammer's yard. I bet you could find pottery or something in the waysides. I wouldn't mind coming back for another look.

"Yeah, okay."

"Maybe see you in school?"

Stammer broke into a grin. "N-not if I see you first."

I headed home with a wave. I hoped he was joking.

6

Dresses itch. They ride up and make me worry I'm exposing my underpants. They don't let your legs move the way they're supposed to. And people always want to talk about them. Oh, you look so nice. Why don't you dress like this every day? Then they complain that I roll my eyes. I don't see how Dot can stand them. Dresses, that is. Or maybe people. I have a hard time with both.

Gram made me show Grandpa how nice I looked. Grandpa just lowered his eyebrow bristles and said, "It looks good." No whistle. No comment about how grown-up I looked. I liked him better for it.

"What about me, Grandpa?" Dot did a little twirl beside Gram.

"Doesn't she look fine, Carl?" Gram took a step back so Dot wouldn't bash into her.

"She looks good, too. It's time to go."

We all filed out behind Grandpa onto the street. Families were either walking or driving in, as it was Sunday mass. I caught a glimpse of Connie Dionne walking with her parents. She took a look at me and lifted her chin. Mr. Dionne greeted Grandpa and gave us all a look over, too.

"It's nice to see you going to church as a family." Mr. Dionne nodded to include Gram in his statement.

"We're blessed to have the girls." Gram took hold of Dot's hand, which made Dot smile.

Grandpa didn't say anything.

The church doors were open in hope of a breeze. The priest was atop of the stairs leading in. His robes touched the ground, and I almost stepped on them as I passed.

"Are these your granddaughters?"

"Yes, Father. This here is Ellen, and the younger is Dorothy. Girls, this is Father Don."

"Welcome to the parish, children. Your grandparents have been telling me about you."

Gram talking about me, I could believe. Grandpa? The priest must be drinking some of that distillery stuff if he thought that were true.

"Thank you, Father." Best move on and get this mass over with.

Grandpa paused inside to let Gram greet a few people, then headed for a row in the middle. We followed.

The Dionnes went to the row in front of us. Connie's head was so high as she walked up the aisle, I think she burned it on the holy stars above.

I never liked church before. It's hot and sticky in the summer, the benches hurt the bones in my back, and I don't like kneeling to pray. I do like the lights coming through the windows and making the walls all colourful. It gives me something to look at that isn't the Lord Jesus strung up on his cross.

I also liked the priest. He had a nice, genuine smile that he would sneak through in some spots of the liturgy. He didn't talk too long about bad stuff that was going to happen to us. He did say Hell a few times. Wish I could get away with that. Still, I got bored and started looking around.

"Stop leaning on me." Dot elbowed me in the side.

"I'm not."

"Girls, hush." Gram flicked her prayer book wider to gather our attention.

Grandpa crossed his arms.

I had to be still until we stood for the final prayer. I snuck a peek behind. Stammer was in the last row on the other side. His uncle sat beside him, while the hired hand stood in the aisle behind. I figured the hired hand didn't have enough status to sit with the family.

"Elly. Pst. Elly." Dot's whisper broke into my hearing.

"What?"

"I need to go to the bathroom."

"You have to hold. We're praying to Jesus now."

"What if I can't?"

"Girls. Father Don is speaking." Gram shook her head a fraction, but didn't look at us.

"Elly, please." Dot's eyes showed the whites like she was ready to bolt.

Always up to me, I guess. Gram's head was low, reading over her prayers, so I gave her Sunday sleeve a small tug.

"Gram, Dot has to go."

Connie turned around and had a look at us. She gave a grin that disappeared when her father shooed her back to listening. She sat still and forward, but I think she had crossed a line somewhere. Her pa's hand snaked out to pinch her neck before stretching across the pew behind her. Connie flinched as he did it. I wonder who else saw the red mark left from his touch.

"Right now?" Gram rustled her book leaves as she whispered. "We're almost done."

I looked at Dot squirming beside me. "Sorry, Gram. Now."

A grandmother's sigh can be just like a mother's. Still, Gram took the inconvenience well. She just delegated. "You can take her out back. There's a washroom there."

"Elly, please! I can't wait."

I gave my own sigh, which earned a cross look from Grandpa. He grunted as I pointed at Dot, then looked down, ignoring us both.

Dot jiggled each step we took down that aisle while the priest droned on. Stammer gave a waggle of his eyebrows as we went by.

I didn't see a washroom in the vestibule, so we just headed out the door. There was nobody outside. There was no washroom, either.

Dot was getting desperate, so I had her go around the corner of the church and pee in the bushes shadowed there. She wet herself somewhat, as the spray for a girl doesn't go where it always should.

"What do I do?" Dot had her bum hanging out while she squatted. Her underpants lay round her ankles in a saggy heap.

"Leave 'em." Best I could think of.

"I can't do that. I only have three pair."

"Throw them in the bush, and we'll come back for them later."

"Elly!" Dot pointed at a woman come walking down the street.

"Do it fast. I'll block you." I stood in front of Dot as she quickly shimmied out of her panties and chucked them at the bottom of the bush. Dot's aim isn't good. This time it worked, though.

"What are you girls doing there?" The woman walked up and peered at us. She wasn't quite a woman. She looked more like a shriveled apple that you wrap a kerchief around and make into a doll.

"We're waiting for our grandparents." Up to me again.

Dot had gone quiet. Big surprise.

The woman glanced up at the church doors, then back at us. "Smart girls to wait out here. You're saved from all that bad singing."

Dot gave a giggle.

I just stared. I didn't think the woman's voice was all that pretty to be commenting. She sounded like a gravel road being mulched up by a tractor running over it.

Through the open church doors, the hymn ended on a sour note. The sounds of people shuffling could be heard.

"You girls with the Johnsons?"

"Yes, ma'am."

"Well, I thought so. You have the look of Grace when she was younger." The woman looked straight at me as she said it. My middle name is the same as Gram's name, but other than that, I never thought much of me being like Gram.

"Frieda Witt, come and join us." Father Don called out as he descended the church stairs. Folks started leaving church, following down the steps behind him, chatting as they mingled. He held a hand out to the woman we talked to.

The woman pursed her lips and looked at the crowd behind the priest. "Not today, Father. I'm not dressed for company."

Father Don extended his hand further. "You are fit for any occasion, Miss Frieda."

Gram and Grandpa appeared, followed by Mr. Dionne and his family. Mr. Dionne frowned at us from the steps as he walked down to talk to the priest.

Miss Frieda stared a moment before nodding at Dot and me. "You say hi to your grandma for me."

"She's right there." Dot pointed at Gram's round hat with a spray of flowers on it. "You can tell her yourself."

But Miss Frieda was already down the street. I don't think Gram saw her, either. Or maybe she did, 'cause she came down to join me and Dot soon after. Grandpa and Mr. Dionne followed in her wake.

"I wanna go home, Gram." Dot had hold of Gram's hand already.

"Well, are you girls ready for Monday?" Mr. Dionne moved in beside Gram and Dot. He reeked some of sweat from praying hard.

Everyone paused, while nobody answered. I looked at him. Dot just hid her face in Gram's skirt. It was a fair question, but I didn't think Mr. Dionne should be talking about school on a Sunday.

Gram finally cleared her throat. "I think the girls are tired. It's been a long week at a new place." Gram reached out a hand to mine, too. I let her. "They've had nothing but good to say about our school, though." The flowers in Gram's hat nodded in emphasis.

"Can we go?" Dot braved a look as she spoke and buried her face again.

"*Ahem*. We should be leaving now, Luc." Grandpa–speaking unprompted–nobody had asked him a question or anything. A Sunday miracle!

Time to go. I spared a look at where Dot's panties lay tucked under the bush. The yellow flowers on it were stained, but still glowed at the base of the black roots. Mr. Dionne followed my gaze and raised a questioning eyebrow.

I couldn't go get Dot's discarded clothes. We followed Grandpa and abandoned Dot's skivvies to their fate.

"Elly."

I looked back. Stammer was running towards us. His black pants had a hole that his knee poked through with each stride.

Connie stood with Darlene by the church and pointed at us as Stammer caught up.

"Give me a second, Gram." My face was burning. I didn't like being watched and wanted to get it over with.

Stammer bent a bit to catch his breath. "Elly, I saw you in ch-church."

"So? Everyone was there."

"I know that. I m-meant that I saw you and wanted you to m-meet my Uncle Ward and N-Nathan."

"Ellen, we're ready." Gram and Dot had stopped to wait. Grandpa walked on.

"I can't right now. Maybe later."

"Another t-time, then."

"Maybe."

Stammer didn't seem much upset. He walked back without sparing me another look. Still, I wasn't sure if I'd played too cagey with a new friend. Connie's pointing hadn't helped.

"Gram, I forgot something. I'll be back in a second." I headed back to the church where I could see Stammer talking with his uncle by the bush where Dot had peed. My face went redder thinking about if Stammer saw.

"Hey, Stammer. *Wait!*"

Stammer and his uncle didn't hear, though. They walked off to where the hired hand rested by a truck.

I'd have to talk to Stammer tomorrow. Explain how I didn't like Connie looking at me. Better yet, I wouldn't. My words sounded dumb, no matter how I tried to phrase it in my head. At least I could get Dot's panties for her.

But the panties were gone. The sound of Connie and Darlene's laughter stung my ears as they walked by.

7

I waited for Connie to show those panties around. I cringed every time I saw her near Dot, but Connie seemed to ignore the lesser folks. At least that was a compliment to me, even if Connie was meaner than a badger.

Dot asked about getting her panties back, but I told her they were too dirty and torn from her throw. No use getting Dot worried about anything Connie could do.

School kept going. Over the next week, I got used to Darlene's shoulder block and Connie's whispered threats. I was safe at recess if I kept to myself. I'd often go to the outfield where Stammer was and keep him company during baseball. He didn't seem to mind, and would talk with me when a younger player was batting. Watching from the underbrush was the closest I got to playing. The boys didn't like me touching the ball if Stammer couldn't get it. Once I did get to throw the ball back to home plate, which got a compliment from Mr. Oswin. Other than that, I was tolerated as long I didn't muscle in.

Connie had everyone crowded around her desk a few mornings later. They made room for me to take my seat, then moved back to see what Connie brought. Everyone was talking in low, excited voices. Miss Oswin smiled indulgently from her desk up front, so I figured it was safe to turn around and look, too. That, and Connie was occupied with being center of attention.

On Connie's desk was a paper flyer. It showed a snarling tiger jumping through a hoop. *Atlas Brothers Circus* was printed out in big balloony letters at the top.

A circus!

"Is it coming here?" Curiosity overruled my caution.

Darlene gave a quick look back at Connie. Connie was holding the flyer for one of the bigger boys to read.

"Just after the weekend. They're passing through to Saskatoon." Darlene pointed her thumb behind us. "Connie's pa made a deal with them to use some of their family land."

At the sound of her name, Connie looked up.

"Maybe they could use a trick dog. Do you know any tricks, Smelly?" Connie stuck her tongue out and panted at me.

Darlene giggled. "How about fetch? She likes boys and baseball."

I wanted to tell them both to play dead.

Stammer soon joined the group. When he read the flyer, he grinned wide and crowed. "A c-circus! I hope they got a m-menagerie. I always wanted to see an elephant."

"I see an elephant right now." Connie leveled a look towards Miss Oswin up at the front of the room.

The kids around Connie sniggered. One boy raised his arm like a trunk and made a small trumpet sound. Another puffed out his lips and cheeks.

Miss Oswin didn't notice. Her fat arms wobbled in their short sleeves as she sorted papers into various piles.

"See? It's right over there with a big heap of shit. Someone should go clean that up." Connie smirked and pointed at me. "You look dressed for shit-shoveling."

Muffled laughs carried Connie forward in her boldness. I didn't dare fire an answering salvo.

"Maybe Miss Oswin's the fat lady." Connie wrinkled her forehead in mock thought. "Or the tattoo lady. We'll have to check her backside when she bends over."

Miss Oswin looked up at that moment. I bet she didn't like seeing students sneaking peeks at her and smiling to each other.

"Class, come to order."

Students were fast in taking their seats. I turned around, but still heard Connie's whispers.

"Does Stammer check your backside, Smelly?"

Darlene giggled again. I winced at the words, then relaxed. Still no mention of Dot. Maybe Connie thought the panties were mine.

Connie didn't let anyone except Darlene hold the flyer at recess. The older girls followed behind, chatting like magpies over a shiny bright button. The younger ones watched, but mostly did their own business. I was glad to see Dot chirping away happily among the smallest girls by the school steps.

The boys grouped around Mr. Oswin with the same excited stir. They were too wound up to play any ball. No one except Stammer noticed when I sidled in. He moved to make space for me to listen.

"What do they want you to do?" One of the younger boys gave Mr. Oswin's sleeve a tug with his question.

Mr. Oswin smiled. "Help them set up their tents and such. They asked for a maintenance man. Mr. Dionne said I'm to bring my tools."

An older boy cleared his throat. "Will there be any other jobs?" His voice cracked as he said it, and he blushed.

"There might be one or two still left. I heard they need a barker." Mr. Oswin looked over the hopeful faces surrounding him. "Maybe one of you boys can help."

"Ah, they won't choose us." The oldest boy in class piped up. I'd seen him a couple of times at the hotel, looking for his father. "My da says circus people just hire men to work, not boys. They're too afraid of the town getting mad if someone runs away with them."

I gave Stammer a nudge. "You think that's true?"

"It m-might be." Stammer's shrug turned into a tic. "S-still, it would be fun to get a job there. Get some money and see the animals up close. That would be something."

"I wonder what animals they'll bring. Maybe they'll have that tiger."

"They g-gotta have one. Why else would they put it on the p-poster?"

In my mind, I pictured the tiger leaping around a circus tent. It could be they had a lion, too... or a bear, or even an ostrich.

I firmed up my stance. "I'm gonna ask for a job."

"You are?"

"Yeah. Maybe they need help with the animals when everyone's at the show."

Stammer scuffed his shoe into the dirt as he thought. "Couldn't hurt to ask. I'll come too, then." He didn't shoot the plan down. He didn't even remind me that I was a girl.

I grinned all through the rest of school. I don't know if it's because of the circus or because I had a friend.

Before dinner, Dot found me stretched out on our bed. I had my book open and was reading about how big ostrich eggs were.

"Hurray! The circus is coming!" Dot threw her rag rabbit in the air and caught it with both hands, bringing it close for a hug.

"Uh huh." I was just as happy, but younger sisters, you know?

Dot sat down beside me and peered at the egg page. I shifted to make room.

"You think Gram and Grandpa will let us go see it?"

I hadn't thought of that.

"They just gotta. I wanna see a flying trapeze man." Dot held her rabbit by its ears and gave it a twirl. Its ears corkscrewed tighter with each spin. "He flies through the air with the greatest of ease..."

I hadn't thought of it at all. I sat up and closed my book. "Dot, hush. I'm thinking." I didn't know Gram well enough to tell if she disapproved of circuses. My hope was she didn't give a hoot one way or another.

The rabbit spun as Dot continued her song. "It's that daring young man on the flying trapeze..."

"You think Gram won't let us go?" I put it out there, though Dot wasn't always a reliable judge of character.

Rag rabbit stopped its jig long enough for Dot to screw up her face in consideration. "I don't think so. She didn't mind the church announcing a dance."

Good point.

"I'm more worried about Grandpa."

Grandpa? He never paid Dot and me much attention to worry about. Still, I had to ask. "Why Grandpa?"

Dot smoothed rag rabbit's ears out. "Don't circuses cost money? Grandpa won't wanna pay for it."

Another good point. Still, I had ways around it.

"That won't matter. I'm gonna get a circus job so I won't have to pay."

"You can't do that, Elly."

"Why not?"

Dot looked at me with big eyes. "Aren't you scared of the circus people? The moment you're not looking, they'll steal you away."

"That's just a bunch of made up baloney." Little sisters.

"No, I'm serious. I heard some of the boys talking about it at school."

"I'm not worried. I'm big enough. I could take 'em."

"Not the strongman, you couldn't." She had me there.

I had nothing to say back, so I stuck my tongue out.

Dot had every right to look at me all dubious-like. I don't think anyone could take out a strongman. You'd have to be pretty strong, or hypnotic, or something.

The boarders had been fed, and then it was our turn. We were surprised to see Grandpa at the kitchen table when we came down to supper. True, he was sitting closer to where the boarders ate than us, but it was nice to see him nod and listen when Gram asked if we'd washed.

Dot helped set the table. I served the drumsticks and potatoes. I breathed in the meaty scent of chicken and basil as I doled out the portions.

Grandpa chewed with his mouth open. Now I see where Dot got it from.

While we were eating, Dot gave me a nudge and a hopeful look. I hate being oldest sometimes.

"Gram, did you hear the circus is coming to town?" I tried to act casual as I cut into my meat.

I peered at my grandparents between bites, as neither was answering. Gram shared a look with Grandpa, who shook his head.

Gram cleared her throat. "Yes, I did. Mrs. Dionne stopped by to let us know. She asked if you were going."

"I've never been to a circus!" Dot raised herself to kneel on her chair. She almost tipped her glass of milk in her excitement.

"Dorothy, sit down proper, please." Gram smiled when Dot complied. "Well, I don't know about a circus. I still want to know what the other ladies say."

"Mrs. Dionne thinks it's okay. She's letting Constance go." I was loathe to use the enemy as ammunition, but this was extenuating circumstances. Connie had bragged that she got free tickets.

"What Mrs. Dionne thinks and what I think are two different things." Grandpa raised a fork and jabbed at us. "And I don't think it's proper for young children to see those sort of things."

Dot wasn't set back by hearing Grandpa lay down some law, let alone speak. "What sort of things, Grandpa?"

Grandpa snorted, but took a sip of coffee instead of answering.

"Well, there are things that are too much for young eyes, sometimes." Gram kept watch on Grandpa's face as she spoke. "The circus folk can be an odd lot to look at... and they don't often live with the Lord."

"But..."

"No buts, Dorothy. If you want some amusement, you can help me with the dishes."

Gram musta seen my scowl.

"You too, Ellen."

I didn't answer. I have some Grandpa in me, sometimes.

"Ellen?"

Dot gave me another nudge.

"Yes, Gram." I hid my sigh.

"There are more important things in life than circuses." Grandpa's eyes glinted over his half moon glasses.

"Like the pie I made special today." Gram laid a hand on Grandpa's shoulder as she spoke.

Grandpa grumbled and shifted, then he laid a hand on hers in return. "Like your pie." I could tell the moment for discussing was over. Grandpa was all closed up again, and Gram was fussing over the dessert.

Disappointment soaked through Dot beside me. Her eyes moistened over her pie slice. My eyes held more a burn of defiance. I kept my gaze low over each bite, mulling over my thoughts. This didn't affect my plans. I was still going to work for the circus. I only had to figure out how to get a job and then how to hide it.

8

The circus train pulled into town long before dawn. Its rumbles shook the bed as Dot and I lay cosied under Gram's quilt. Usually, trains raced through on their way to somewhere else. I could tell it was the circus train, as the rumble slowed and got louder, before it finally shushed itself in a breath of steam. Even the night air tasted of hot coal-black engine. I stayed awake after that.

Dot sighed and cuddled in closer to me. She called out once for Mam, then was quiet.

I just lay there plotting.

Gram needed convincing to let me go to school early. I told her I was meeting someone to practice a poem for class. Dot knew I wasn't telling the truth. I think Gram suspected, too. I didn't care.

"Here's your pail." Gram handed me a large tin can to carry. Its handle was a string through two holes at the rim. It was full of food. I could see wax-wrapped sandwiches at the top.

"Thanks, Gram."

"I won't be able to bring you home for lunch today. Some ladies are coming this afternoon."

I hefted the pail, feeling its weight, and wondered if it would slow me down. It would. "Can you bring it with Dot, Gram? It'll be hard to watch it and work."

Dot reached a hand to me. "I can take it. It's no matter."
Nice of Dot to offer. I didn't appreciate the gesture as much as
I should.

"That's real nice of you, Dorothy." Gram gave me a
look, like it was my turn to speak.

"Thanks, Dot." I mumbled my words. I was busy thinking
of tigers.

"Can I come, too? I can keep track of our pail." Dot
pulled big eyes at me as she spoke.

Little sisters. Always wanting to join in.

"Ellen says she's got work to do." Gram gave Dot a pat
as she guided her back to the kitchen. "She won't have time to
watch you as well."

I could see Dot droop as I left. She looked like a flower
whose stalk wasn't strong enough for the rain.

Stammer was where we said to meet. You could barely
see his crouched form dark against the prairie sky. He rose with
a tic and a stretch.

"What t-took you so long?"

"I had to eat breakfast. Gram insisted."

'Oh." Stammer looked lean and hungry. I almost wished
I'd brought the pail after all. He could have helped lighten its load.
Stammer's nostrils flared like he scented clowns already. He
turned and started loping through the long grass. I had to rush to
catch up.

"Are they close?"

"N-not far. They're off the m-main road and through
those trees."

"Did you see them?"

"Yeah, I did. F-Father Don was there, too."

"Father Don? What the hell is he doing there?"

Stammer didn't answer.

A priest outta church is like a seeing a badger outta its
den. You gotta move slow and polite as you let it go on its way.
A priest at the circus, I couldn't begin to figure. It pricked my

mind like the prairie burrs catching at my clothes. I stopped to pick one off the side of my sock.

"I don't want Father Don to spot us." He was a nice priest. He'd see us no matter as Sunday always comes, but no need on a school day, and especially not here.

"He's p-probably gone by now. Hurry." Stammer reached the trees before me. The trees were fewer here than at Stammer's property. Most of them were weedy like someone had strangled them before they could grow. They didn't smell like trees, though. They stunk like their insides were rotting, instead of being full of sap.

"Phew. Connie must hide her carcasses here."

Stammer grinned as he ducked through the copse. I followed.

I don't think I've ever seen that many colours in one spot. A rainbow had come to life. The Big Top spread out as if the sky had burst over our land and was pinned to the ground. Painted wagons and cages rested in its shadow. The wagons stood side by side, flanking a wide path already worn in the grass. In the space between the wagon rows, people moved as they prepared the site for mere humans. Their work clothes were more fancy than any Sunday I've ever seen. Peacock people.

"Holy Margaret." I couldn't think of anything else to say. Stammer nodded.

A woman inked from head to toe stood beside another woman with a beard. They looked all easy with each other, like they were no big deal to look at. They waited at the edge of a gathering by one of the wagons.

Stammer pointed towards the Big Top. "I saw Father Don over there last."

"What was he doing?"

"Flinging water at the tent. I think he was blessing it."

Priests are weird. "Why bless a tent?"

"Hell if I know." Stammer stood and brushed off his pants. It didn't wipe the dirt from his exposed knees. "If we're g-gonna do this, it's now. Else we're missing school for no good reason."

"I kinda hoped we would miss some school." I stood, too.

Stammer grinned. "L-let's go get some work."

"Not that way, though."

Stammer nodded. Priest that way. He headed instead towards the crowd.

The back end of the crowd turned as we approached. More than one strange face marked us. I slowed in my tracks. Grandpa's drinking friend was there, too. A faint smell of barroom smoke wafted from him the nearer we got. I stifled a gag, remembering how slimy his hand looked holding on to Dot.

"Well, well. Two young pups come to join the circus." The man waggled his eyebrows as he leaned towards us.

"Shut up." Stammer walked by the man like he was a pile of shit to avoid stepping in.

"Who's that?" I whispered my question as I didn't dare speak louder. The nape of my neck crawled as I walked by the man. I felt a sharp pinch on my backside and whirled to see what wasp stung me.

The man laughed loud, causing the circus people around him to shush.

Stammer spared a glance at the man. I shared it, too, and regretted. The man was still looking. He thrust his hips out and gave me a grin.

I reddened, but I didn't know why.

"B-Billy Harner. He buys hooch from my uncle." Stammer made a face. "He tries to cheat all the time. Pretends we gave him a bad batch and demands his money back."

I looked again. Billy Harner pursed his lips and mocked a kiss. My shoulders hunched, and I tried to make myself smaller. Tingles ran down my stomach towards my legs. It wasn't a clean feeling.

Stammer pulled my arm to get me in motion again. "C'mon. We g-gotta find someone to ask."

Some of the circus people were lined up beside the largest of the wagons. They stood quiet, waiting with their hands folded. A dwarf saw us looking, and motioned us to step in front of him.

I could smell the coal smoke around us as we stood. The wagon had a wide hitch and was painted in green and blue colours that outdid the grass and sky. Big letters blazed out from its side. *Atlas Brothers Circus*. I wondered how big the horse was that brought it to the field. Maybe it was even the first wagon pulled off the train when they came last night.

"This m-must be for the Ringmaster." Stammer nudged me forward to keep up with the line. Circus folks crowded round. Except for their bright clothes, most looked like regular townspeople.

"You wanna ask first?" My legs were trembling. I hoped Stammer said yes.

"You're ahead of m-me. You go first." Stammer musta felt some trembling, too.

"I can't do it."

"You h-have to. It's your t-t-turn next."

"No, I can't. What do I say?"

Too late. It was my turn. The man in front murmured and left, leaving me exposed to the Ringmaster. I heard Stammer gasp behind me.

It was the Ringmaster of God.

Father Don stood in front of me, all gowned up like Sunday. He held his chalice in one hand and the Lord's wafer in the other. He widened his eyes, but continued in his role.

"The body of Christ." He gave me a small smile with the wafer.

"Amen." I held up my hands and accepted his offering. Some habits are ingrained, no matter how scared you are.

Father Don nodded as I moved away.

Stammer soon joined me.

"W-we're in sh-shit." His tics were rising, and they made Stammer bounce on his feet.

"Probably. If we are, we might as well make it worth our while." I pointed out a cage to the side of a smaller tent. "Maybe your tiger is in there."

Tell a boy he can see a tiger and you've got him hooked. I didn't even wait for his reply. Stammer followed me this time.

The big cage was empty of living beings. The straw inside was dirty and full of scat. Stammer and I leaned our heads against the bars to see if we could make out what kind of animal lived there. We wrinkled our noses at the rotten, meaty smell.

"H-how about there?" Stammer pointed to the large wagon beside us. Garish reds and greens striped its flank where the word "Menagerie" was spelled out. The door was half open. We could hear chattering come from inside.

We took a gander at the pathway behind us. No one paid us any attention.

The door opened the rest of the way with a creak. The wagon's inhabitants went dead quiet as we peered in.

There were cages. Cages upon cages upon cages. Rows of them set to each side for people to come and see. A monkey wrapped his tail around the bars of his cage. He reached a hand out, begging for a treat or release. Stammer stepped inside the wagon and reached a hand back.

I paid the monkey no mind. There were birds in this wagon. All birds that I'd seen in my book. I could list them like they were cousins of mine: Parakeet and blue jay, weaver and sparrowhawk, robin and finch. They stared back in silence as I gawked, taking them all in. A jet-black bird by the door was the first to speak. His feathers glistened in the faint light. He had a blood red drop of an eye that watched me as I followed Stammer in.

"Groak." The bird hopped up and down in his cage. It was too small for him to do anything more. He stuck his beak out through the bars and gave another croak.

"A drongo!"

"Elly! L-look at this monkey. He's s-so small... A what?" Stammer must have glanced at me, but I wouldn't have known. I was too transfixed by my bird book come to life.

"A drongo! From Australia. This bird right here." I leaned closer to the cage and touched a finger to its beak. It didn't snap.

"Groak." The drongo pulled back and started worrying his feathers, as if he hoped I would invite him out for dinner.

Stammer stared a moment. "It's a b-black bird. We got dozens of those here."

"Not this one. Look at his eyes."

I don't think Stammer could appreciate the finer points of a bird from the other half of the earth. He did make an attempt, though.

"N-nice."

The light in the wagon blazed all sudden. A form filled the door behind us.

"What are you doing here?" The voice spoke gruff and loud. Two hands reached out and nabbed Stammer and me by our shirts.

"Ow!" Stammer was wrenched back first. My body followed. We stumbled into the daylight, blinking in its brightness.

"I said, what are you two doing here?" The man locked his arms, holding us in front of him. His red jacket strained, exposing frayed cuffs.

Looking for jobs. Looking for tigers. Looking for fun. Stammer and me looked at each other.

"Nothing." Best I could do.

"You thinking of stealing something?"

"N-no, s-sir." Stammer stuttered a few more sounds then stood quiet. He bent his head, like he was awaiting an axe.

"I oughta have you arrested for trespassing." The man pinned us with his glare.

Holding still was hard. My feet wanted to run.

"Hey, Mr. Atlas. Whatcha got there?" An even louder voice boomed out.

Walking toward us was the biggest man I ever saw. He had arms like trees and carried a long hammer over one shoulder. The ground seemed to buckle beneath each step he took closer.

Beside him was our school's maintenance man, Mr. Oswin.

I should've run.

"Two kids I found in the Menagerie." The red coat man let go of our shirts and gave us a shove. "I'm thinking of caging them as part of the show."

"Aw, don't do that." The big man nudged Mr. Oswin. "You know these kids? They look like they might be yours."

Mr. Oswin laughed and flushed pink. "They're not mine, but they are from our school."

"Well, they might not graduate if I call the cops on them." Mr. Atlas crossed his arms as he spoke.

"Go easy on 'em." The big man rested his hammer on the ground. "They're just curious, is all. If you chase away all the kids, who's gonna come see us at show time?"

This paused Mr. Atlas.

"I can vouch for these two." Mr. Oswin had lost his flush and spoke smoothly again. "They're good kids. They don't give any trouble."

Mr. Atlas stared at us from under lowered eyebrows. "Alright. You kids can go. But I don't want to see you here until the circus opens. You hear me?"

"Yes, sir." I didn't dare use the man's proper name, Mr. Atlas. This man ran the whole show, and he had us in his sightlines. We were lucky he didn't feed us to the tigers.

Stammer twitched a tic or two as he nodded.

Mr. Atlas walked away, muttering about the things he did for money.

"Don't mind him." The big man gave us a hearty clap on our backs. I was surprised I could breathe after that. "Mr. Atlas gets mad at everything. Comes from being in charge."

"You kids get to school now. They'll be wondering where you are." Mr. Oswin waved in the direction of town.

"If you really want to see the circus, come back for the show." The big man flexed his muscles.

"C-can't." Stammer finally spoke. "N-no money."

I didn't say that I'd been banned by my folks. Why complicate things?

"Is that so?" The big man shared a look with Mr. Oswin, who just shrugged. "Well, you come ask for me, and I'll get you in free. Look for Samson the Strongman."

Both Stammer and I brightened. Samson looked like a giant who could wrestle down anyone. Getting in to the circus should be a snap. No one would dare say no if we had the Strongman's word behind us.

"Thank you! We will!" What a lucky strike. I couldn't stop the smile that spread on my face.

Stammer grinned wide, too. He twitched a few times as he nodded.

"Get on with you." Samson flicked the back of his hand at us. "Come back later for the show."

Stammer and I ran. We made it out alive from the circus, but we were still in a lot of trouble. We were late for school and had to stay in for recess. Connie made sure to point out that I had a boyfriend who jittered and bugged. Stammer missed playing ball, though Mr. Oswin wasn't around for practice. Miss Oswin gave us more than one heavy sigh during the day. No matter.

At the time it was worth it.

9

If you put your ear to the wall of the school when Miss Oswin was teaching, I bet the only thing you'd hear from outside was her voice. She was good at keeping us still. Mostly.

Sometimes we'd get going with a murmur that, if Miss Oswin didn't look up sharp from her desk, would build until we all talked just to sneak some sound in before we were shushed again. Dot never joined in, as far as I could hear. Stammer, neither. I don't think either one trusted their voice.

No amount of shushing lasted on the day the circus opened. Miss Oswin stopped trying and let us murmur away. Mr. Dionne had given us the afternoon off, just in time for the circus parade and opening. I think it was to raise the admission numbers. Maybe he had a cut of the profit. Who knows? I wasn't complaining.

"Cotton candy." Connie's voice scratched at my ear while she sat behind me. She wasn't talking to me, though. I was just in the way between her and Darlene, as usual.

"Yummmm." Darlene leaned into my space to hear better.

"Root beer float."

"Yuuuummm."

"Corn dog."

"Constance, do you have something you want to share with the class?" Miss Oswin had caught on to the clandestine meeting. I hoped she hadn't picked it out from my face. No matter how bad you hate, you don't squeal.

"No, ma'am. I was just coughing."

"Well, cover your mouth when you do." Miss Oswin returned to writing numbers on the board. I could spy Dot ahead, scribbling diligently in her notebook.

Connie gave a sniff. "Whale meat."

"Yechhhh!" Darlene's voice sounded out, just as one of those lulls in people's chatting happened. Darlene clamped a hand over her mouth and bent over her books.

Miss Oswin turned a second too late. Her gaze scanned our corner. I don't know what Connie was doing, but I forgot to duck with Darlene.

"Ellen? Do you have something to say about this math problem?"

Connie giggled behind me. I felt a pencil poke into the back of my neck.

"No, ma'am. I was just clearing my throat." I held my breath after I said it. It echoed Connie's excuse too closely.

Dot chose that moment to drop her book.

"Sorry, Miss Oswin." Dot stood and faced me before picking the book up and sitting again.

"Nice one, Smelly." Connie poked me again with her pencil, this time with the eraser end. I counted that a small triumph.

Miss Oswin rang the bell long and hard at the end of the morning. Her face was squinched. She wanted out, too.

We all piled out of the school. For once, Connie and Darlene didn't try to avoid me. I found myself in relative ease behind them.

"Did your da get the seats?" Darlene looked eager.

"We sit right in the front row." Connie flicked her ponytail out of her jacket as she walked. I held off an urge to pull it and run. I was getting good at holding things in. Someone else wasn't. Another bruise showed on Connie's neck beside the one from church last week. The urge to pull changed into a touch. "Quit it!" Connie swung around and glared at me. I didn't know what to say. I felt like I'd touched a secret. "Stop bothering us." Connie flicked up the collar of her coat.

"Yeah. Stop bothering us." Darlene did the same.

Both went off with their hair swinging. So much for the small step forward.

"You c-coming? The p-parade's about to start." Stammer stepped up beside me.

"I gotta wait for Dot."

"S-she can't come with us."

"If I let her go home, my grandparents will know that school's out." I think that's the real reason people let little sisters tag along.

"You d-didn't tell 'em?" Stammer looked surprised. His eyebrows stayed up instead of twitching.

"No."

Stammer paused his words and really looked at me. I mean, really looked. I didn't know if it was a look of disappointment or awe. I couldn't tell.

"Well, then. I guess the S-Strongman will have three kids to get in."

I let out a breath I didn't know I held. I was going to the circus with Dot. I just hoped Stammer would stick with us, too. He grumbled at first when I led us down the road far from the hotel. I didn't want to be seen by Gram or Grandpa.

The parade was short, but worth it. The acrobats. The clowns. The jumping and jigging. A small brass band led the way of them all.

Candies were thrown on the street only to be scooped up before they finished their first bounce. Balloons for the kids. Stammer and I each refused one. Dot held hers until she forgot, and it drifted away. She had no tears after, though she did hold tight to my hand a while. And there were animals. Cages and cages of animals pulled by ribbon-festooned horses. Festooned. I always wondered what that word meant. With the ribbons streaming in the breeze behind white white-maned creatures, now I saw. Festooned. Now, I knew.

Samson the Strongman was near the end. He walked beside a blue-painted cannon. Every step, he flexed his arms or let out the roar of a Viking. I hadn't noticed Mr. Oswin stand beside us until Samson paused to shake his hand. He shook mine too, gentle this time, and said "Little lady."

Then it was done.

Everyone chattered as they followed the parade to the circus. There were so many people. I didn't recognize most of them. Stammer said they were out-of-towners. I kept an eye out, but couldn't see Gram or Grandpa. I couldn't see many of the ladies, for that matter. The crowd was mostly kids and men.

Dot seemed so little among the crowd following. Her face was pale, and she gasped each time a stranger bumped into her. I almost turned back, but Stammer was there. I didn't want him to have fun, and me not.

Samson made good his promise. I spoke our names and we were waved in. Dot stared up at the man at the gate. You could barely see his eyes through the clown paint.

"Hello, little girl. You here for the show?" The man leaned down and put his face close to Dot.

"*Ellyy!*" Dot clung to me. I had to shake her hand loose. Her grip was so tight.

"Wh-where should we start?" Stammer sounded eager and bounced as he strode.

I looked. The path between wagons was full of people. "Everyone's going to the Big Top. Maybe we should go there, too."

Stammer peered around. "I got no better idea. Might as well."

"I wanna go home." Dot had my hand again and gave it an extra tight squeeze.

"Dot, shush. Just wait. We'll find you some clowns."

"I don't wanna see clowns. I wanna go home."

I know it would have ended there if we had. No way Gram would let me go back. If I'd known the future, I woulda listened to Dot. Right then, I was thinking of the fun I'd miss. That decided me.

"We're staying. So come on."

Dot sniveled but held her peace. For the most part.

We were swept along towards the Big Top. Barkers barked at us from either side. I saw Billy Harner in front of the Fun House wagon. He winked as he called. I don't know, but he may have even said my name.

Dot balked at the Big Top entrance. "N-no way. No way." Big shuddering sobs rolled off her as she stood her ground.

"C'mon, Dot. You gotta." I was frustrated. We were so close to the fun.

Miss Frieda came up behind us. You could smell the smoke on her even before seeing her.

"You kids okay?"

Stammer said nothing. Dot sniveled louder. I rolled my eyes, forgetting Miss Frieda was an adult.

"Whazza matter?" Miss Frieda took hold of Dot's other hand. Dot let her.

Between sobs, Dot managed to get her fear out. "S-scary clowns. Scary clowns."

Miss Frieda gave her a pat. "It's okay, kid. They won't get you. You'll be safe with me." She led Dot in to the tent and we followed.

It was another world inside. There were banners, trapezes, and a brightly painted cannon. Clowns ran chasing each other with buckets, only to throw confetti on the squealing crowd. Everywhere was colour and anticipation. In the middle of it all stood the Ringmaster, Mr. Atlas. His tattered red coat looked new and shiny in the lights. I couldn't take it all in with one look.

Miss Frieda took a sniff beside me.

"Smells like crotch in here."

Stammer reddened.

I did, too.

"C'mon, kiddos. Let's go get some seats." Miss Frieda moved past me, leading Dot to the stands. We were lucky. Second row.

Dot lasted through the Strongman's performance. When he was done though, she started to squirm. "Can we go now?"

They were loading a guy into the cannon.

"I said… Can we go now?" Dot gave me shove from the side.

"In a minute."

Dot fidgeted, then held still. I forgot about her as I listened to the Ringmaster exclaim about danger and terror.

Boom!

The shock wave rattled my teeth. Dot screamed beside me.

The man shot out and went flying like a bird. The crowd exhaled with relief when the man landed in the net, bouncing a few times on his back.

"*Holy Margaret.*" The man was still alive! He swung down to the ground, took off his helmet, and waved to the crowd. Cheers erupted. Boys whistled and girls screamed as the crowd continued to clap wildly.

"Dot's g-gone."

"What?" I could barely hear Stammer over the crowd's noise.

"*I said, Dot's gone.*"

I looked at the empty space between Miss Frieda and me. Miss Frieda was turned away, talking to someone else. I had a clear view of the aisle beside her. I grabbed Miss Frieda's arm to catch her attention.

"Did you see my sister?"

Miss Frieda stared blankly at me. "What?"

Dot was gone. I scrambled over Miss Frieda. "*Dot!*" People shushed me. I didn't care.

Stammer clambered right behind me. "Maybe she went out."

Had to be where she went. She wouldn't have stayed where all the noise was.

I almost missed seeing Dot huddled by the tent ropes at the entrance. She stood as she saw me.

"Dot, don't leave like that."

"*I was scared.*" Dot's wail outdid the crowd's roar behind us.

Baby Jesus. I missed whatever they were cheering for.

"C'mon." Why did I have to take care of her? Why me?

Dot let me take hold of her hand. Stammer paused as if deciding to go back in or stay. I was grateful when he started walking with us through the crowd.

"Let's go home, Elly."

"Not yet." I was mad, and I wasn't finished with the circus.

Stammer said nothing. He just let us play ourselves out.

"We're not supposed to be here." Dot dug her heels in. "If you won't take me home, I'll find someone who will."

I had to stop walking. It was that or drag her.

Circuses are supposed to be fun. They only come once in a long while. Can you blame me for wanting fun?

"Look. I'm staying. You can go if you want." I let go of Dot's hand.

Dot stuck her lip out and tucked her arms under her pits. "I'm gonna tell."

It was the last straw. I looked for escape.

We were beside the Fun House wagon. Billy Harner stood at the door, calling to the crowd. He caught my eye and winked.

"I'm going there." I pointed at Billy's wagon.

Dot said nothing.

Stammer made a face. "You n-need money for that."

I didn't think so. Not with the way Billy started calling me.

"Hey, sweets. Come inside the Fun House." Billy smiled his dark teeth as I approached.

I should have taken Dot to see the birds. She would have liked that. Then we could have gone home.

"You like fun?" Billy waggled his eyebrows as he pointed to the wagon.

"Sure I do. As much as the next person." I felt all adult-like to be talking back to him that way.

"Well, then. Go have some." Billy leaned up and opened the door. I climbed the few wooden steps to peek inside. I could feel Billy close behind me.

"You going or not? I got customers, y'know." Billy's breath came hot on my neck.

I stepped into the dark. A mirror reflected both my distorted form and the outdoor light. My heart started racing, beating a staccato rhythm that had nothing to do with fun. Billy stepped in, too, and closed the door behind us. I could feel his hands on my hips.

"Boo." Billy gave me a pinch.

I screamed full throat. My feet kicked out and my fists went flying. Only twice did I connect with Billy. Most of my fury was spent on the mirrors surrounding me, reflecting me. Billy grabbed me and wrapped his arms tight around my own. I couldn't move. I didn't want to breathe for the smell of him.

Hot wet tobacco grease-gobbed full and mean. Hard lips and face bristle. A tongue deep inside that I tried to bite.

My first kiss.

Somehow I connected with the soft part of him, and he let go with a groan. He still blocked the door, though. I ran the other way, banging into walls and mute-faced mannequins. Fun.

I found a door somewhere as I heard my name called out.

"*Elly!*"

Stammer had followed me into the Fun House. Billy was silent, but I knew he was still there, too. I'd let them work it out between them. I slipped out this back door.

You don't know what you'll see when you come out from danger. It may be safety. It may be more danger. It may have nothing to do with you at all. I saw Mr. Oswin pushed against the back of the wagon, and Samson the Strongman leaning against him. They shared a kiss that looked much better than what I'd come from. They looked like they enjoyed it. I just stood there, wanting to cry my fear out, but more afraid of them noticing me.

Mr. Oswin saw me first out of the corner of his eye and broke away from their kiss. He flushed again, like he did when Samson ribbed him about having kids.

Samson just straightened his costume and crossed his arms.

I wish I'd been kissed like that, by either one of them. Now that I'd seen it, though, I chose to ignore it. I had bigger worries, like saving Stammer behind me.

"*Stani's in there.*" I pointed to the door I just came from.

Mr. Oswin quivered, like some shock had worn off. "What?"

"Stani's still in there. With a man." I felt silly saying it, having just seen them kiss each other. "A bad man. Billy Harner."

Both men shared a look and stepped up to the backdoor.

"Stanislaw? Are you in there?" Mr. Oswin peered in to the dark.

"I'm h-here." Stammer appeared alone.

"Where's Billy Harner?" The anger in Mr. Oswin's voice surprised me.

"I d-don't know. I d-d-didn't see him."

Samson laid a hand on Mr. Oswin's shoulder. "Best let me do it. You know these little ones better." He entered the wagon and was gone.

I'll admit, I didn't think of her first.

"D-Dot." Stammer stammered.

I stared a moment, still caught up in my own drama.

"Dot." Stammer repeated.

"Where is she?" A cold flush swept the heat outta my chest. She had to be where we left her, crying. Mad.

Mr. Oswin trailed us as we went round to the wagon's front.

People of all sorts walked by. Some stopped and looked at the Fun House. Billy Harner was on the stairs in front again, calling to the crowd. Samson came out the Funhouse door and spoke with Billy, who smirked and shook his head.

Dot was nowhere to be found.

"*Dot.*" I called and started pacing. "*Dot!*" I got louder and more frantic.

Dodderdoo.

Dot didn't answer.

10

A book is a comfort. It's a place to hide when things aren't going well. A book is for when you've got no more of your own words, and you want to rest your eyes from all the things the world has to show. Things weren't going well. I guess you could figure by what I've already said.

I adore my bird encyclopedia. My book. I think of Da every time I turn a page. The first page I tend to skip over, though. I don't always like seeing his writing there: love words scrawled out like his letters knew he'd be tucked in a grave. He never came back from the war. Mam hurt because of it. Mam died because of it.

I spent hours poring over the pages he used to read me, the ones with birds from Australia. Africa. South America. Birds of many colours all living together on the same page. I knew that drongo bird because of my book. I knew the specialness of it, even though its feathers were the same as some birds we got here. I saw it in the drongo's eyes. I don't mean the red drop of jelly that he blinked over when he looked at me. I mean the cunning, the seeing. The knowing. Knowing he was alone in his cage, and he was yearning and burning to get out.

My bird book kept all the eagles and hawks separate from the smaller birds. You had to flip to a new chapter to see them, their sharp beaks and their habits. The only exception was the shrike. It was mixed in with the chickadees and sparrows. It had some of the same colour, I suppose. The bookmakers paid it no mind, but I still noticed. I used to think it odd no one could see the predator in midst of the innocents. I don't think that anymore.

It hurt, that moment when Dot went missing. I thought of it over and over. Other people thought of it, too. And asked me 'til I didn't want to think of it no more. But it clung to me.

Samson the Strongman was strong. He found me and Stammer a safe spot with the Tattoo Lady while he and Mr. Oswin looked. She was a real nice lady, a walking picture of kindness. Made us tea and gave us cookies. I couldn't eat. I just let the biscuits alone as I paced in the lady's wagon. They wouldn't let me look for Dot with them. Said I might get lost, too.

Somehow, Miss Frieda found out where we were. She came and sat with us. Made it easier. Held me close, stroked my hair. Comforting. For a while.

Samson returned with Mr. Oswin. The Ringmaster was there, too. He didn't look at all happy. He brought the Royal police and stood far from them while they talked. They don't wear that fancy red uniform when they're just working in the towns. Seems they save that for the Queen and horse parades. No matter. Our leaving Dot would not be any easier by having a red coat standing over us with his worries.

I can't tell you how many times I answered the same questions.

"When did you last see her?"

"What was she wearing?"

"Was anyone else with you?"

"Did anyone else talk to you?"

At the end of it all, Miss Frieda asked the question I needed to hear from the start.

"How are you doing?"

I wouldn't be ashamed to say I cried at that moment. I didn't. Stammer snivelled throughout the questions, while I stayed strong. I guess it wasn't my turn to break.

The policeman drove us home. We couldn't find Stammer's uncle when we got to Stammer's farm, so Mr. Oswin waited with him. I stayed in the car with Miss Frieda while the policeman wandered and looked around Stammer's yard. He muttered when he got back in the car. Pulled his notebook out and wrote a few things. Snapped it shut and kept his lips thin.

The worst of it was telling Gram and Grandpa what I'd done. The policeman was there. So was Miss Frieda, who stayed to see me through. But still, I felt alone.

Dot wasn't there, by my side as usual.

The policeman had us all collect in the hotel's front parlour. Had Gram sit, though she wanted to rush to me at first. Miss Frieda shared a look with Gram that seemed to have miles of speech in it. Shook her head and looked down while Gram stared at me, at the policeman as he spoke.

It didn't take long for the telling. Gram hid her face in her hands, hunched over in a hard chair, with Grandpa all stoic behind her. They didn't look at me. They didn't have to.

They didn't ground me. No hard talk. No loud words. I woulda slept easier if they'd shouted, but maybe not. Grandpa looked his disappointment. I knew him well enough now to see it in his face.

Needless to say, I didn't go to school in the morning. Gram was slow in getting the boarders ready for the day. She sat mostly, waiting for the police to bring news.

I was too restless to sit with them. My bedroom was too quiet, but I had better relief there than watching Gram wither. The rag rabbit stared at me. His button eyes shone in the dust-speckled strips of sunlight. At me. I could feel it through the pages. I shut my bird book from Da, as I didn't deserve the comfort of its words.

Grandpa was in the bar, drinking alone. I could see him through the posts on the stairs as I sat crouched halfway down. No one had cleared the glasses from last night. Gram's voice was silent, but I knew the kitchen now held her. I could picture her wiping and cleaning. Stopping to stare out the window, like she was unsure if she could ever believe in the world again.

The hotel was too silent without Dot, so I left.

I found Stammer outside the school. He was sitting on the steps, picking dried dirt off his pants. He hadn't gone to school, either. I could tell by his strained face, Stammer was thinking of yesterday all over again.

"Hey." I sat down beside him.

Stammer's lip trembled. Mine didn't, but it should have.

"I said, hey."

"I know. I h-hear ya."

Odd I was comforting him, when it was my sister. But he was the last to see her. I hadn't thought of it that way until then.

"They still haven't found her." Obvious. But who doesn't hash over stuff like that?

Stammer looked up. "Th-they've been round our farm. Someone said they saw my uncle there."

"Where else would he be? It's your farm, ain't it?" People make me mad and confused sometimes. Most times.

"Not like that." Stammer's lip trembled again. "They said they saw my uncle at the circus. They said he was with a little girl."

"Oh." I don't know what you say to that. It mixed our friendship up in all the wrong places. The world was picking teams on us.

"The p-police came. My uncle s-sent me away so he could talk to them."

Adults think kids can't handle the seeing. We see alright. Matter of fact, we prefer it. What kids can't handle is the not knowing.

"Well, that does it." I stood and brushed my own jeans off. They needed it since yesterday, but I was kinda busy.

"D-does what?"

"We're gonna go look for Dot ourselves."

Stammer sat up straighter. "Where?"

When a team is down-hearted, it helps to give them a project to do together. I was giving Stammer and me a project. That way, no one could separate us into who did what to whom.

"We're going back to the Fun House. It's where we last saw Dot."

"B-but the circus is closed. Police shut it down yesterday when they were looking for Dot."

"Well, how long does it take to pack an elephant's trunk?"

Stammer managed a weak grin. "A long time, I guess. L-let's go."

The circus was still there. They had the Big Top down and were fussing with its moorings. Nobody had moved the wagons yet. I guess the train hadn't come to pick people up. They were supposed to be here for more than a day.

Only a few people were walking. Most were at the lowered tent or huddled on the bleachers, watching. Stammer and I had a clear path to the Fun House. Nobody cared to check what we were doing there. They were still questioning what they were doing packing up so soon.

The Fun House wagon was deserted. Billy Harner wasn't anywhere near to show us his bad teeth. We tried the door, but it was locked.

"What d-do we do now?"

I thought a moment. "Back entrance. Like we used yesterday."

Stammer nodded. Neither of us relished going in, but it was for Dot.

The backdoor was locked, too. No amount of hammering at the clasp changed the lock's mind. We weren't going in.

"N-now what?" Stammer pointed at the door like it was my fault. It was. I shouldn't have been so eager to grow up.

"I don't know. Maybe you got a plan?"

"W-well..." Stammer looked behind him. "Yes, I do. *Run.*"

The Ringmaster strode towards us. By the frown on his face, I guessed he wasn't too pleased seeing the kids who shut down his circus.

We ran between the wagons back onto the path. A few people looked at us, so we slowed like we were supposed to be there. Still, it wasn't good enough. Stammer was panicked.

"W-we gotta get outta here!"

Am I the only one who wants to spend time at the circus?

"No. I'm staying." I know. I know. I was repeating yesterday, but this time it was to bring back Dot.

Stammer shook his head. "We should leave."

"One wagon. Let's just check one wagon. I need to know I did something to find her." I widened my eyes. I willed my eyelashes longer. Anything. I had to check, but I didn't want to check alone.

It musta worked, as Stammer tic'd a few, but stayed.

"Thanks. I owe you."

"We'll s-settle when we're safe."

Fair enough. Now, which wagon to pick. I spied the Menagerie wagon nearby.

"That one. We're going to check that one."

The door wasn't locked.

Each breath we took was musky this time. The smelly culprit had his mask on and hid deep in the shadows of his cage. A raccoon. I sniggered, as the name reminded me of Connie. The Menagerie had expanded since the last time we visited. I guess city people want to see raccoons. We saw enough of them. Still, I was bothered that a new creature had been captured.

"Dot?" I half hoped she'd answer, half hoped she'd not. I couldn't stand the thought of her stuck in a cage like these. People staring at her, pointing. None of the cages were big enough for humans. I shouldn't have bothered.

"Sh-she's not here. I coulda told you so." Stammer spat on the floor in effort to wash out the trapped fear we both tasted. I did the same.

"Shit." I never swore out loud much. Felt like the situation warranted.

"Wh-what are you doing?"

Latches are hard to move when it's half dark. "What do you think I'm doing? We're busting them out."

I started with the drongo. He flew out and perched on the top of his own cage.

"N-no. Stop."

Next, the monkey. He didn't believe his luck and stayed huddled inside. The raccoon gave a hiss, so I avoided him and went right to the back where the creatures never saw light. I was going to free them all. Each and every one of them.

All except Dot.

"S-stop, before we get in trouble." Stammer shut the monkey's cage door. The monkey immediately sprang to it and started chattering his relief. He looked like Stammer in one of his tic fits.

Too late. I was working on a robin when our own cage door swung open, and Mr. Altas appeared.

"What the Hell are you doing?" His breath stroked fury into the air. My drongo spooked and flew out the open door. I was glad to see it go.

Stammer and I crouched.

"I see you in there." Mr. Atlas squinted his eyes, I suspect to adjust to the gloom.

The monkey gave a screech. I coulda swore he also gave the finger.

Mr. Atlas took a few steps closer to where we hid. "I see you. Come out now."

Stammer stood. I stood too.

And we ran.

We both made it past Mr. Atlas. He swore worse than I ever heard from a grown-up, but his hands couldn't grasp us.

We didn't stop running 'til we made it to school. We shouldn't have bothered. There was new trouble there.

A police car was outside the school. Miss Oswin was on the front steps, talking with two Royal police. She spotted us before we could hide, and she pointed.

For once in his life, Stammer didn't move. Not a muscle.

"Those the same cops that were at your farm today?"

"Uh-huh." Stammer's eyes showed white.

"Well, y'know what you gotta do."

"What?"

"*Run!*" I gave him a shove to set his wheels in motion. Stammer stumbled, righted himself, and dove into the bush.

The police marked him and raced back to their car. No guns out, small mercies. I stood still as the car drove off, leaving a dust plume on the road.

They weren't after me, that's for sure. Still, it was up to me to find out why for Stammer. I took a big breath and made my way up to the school.

Miss Oswin stayed on top of the stairs as I approached. She had a look of pity in her eye. I got used to seeing that look from people at Mam's funeral.

"I'm so sorry, Ellen." Miss Oswin's chins waggled as she shook her head. "How are you feeling, dear?"

"I'm okay." Yesterday, that question did me some good. Today, it was intrusive. "Why are the police here?"

Maybe Miss Oswin was sizing me up. Her eyes searched mine, then she nodded like I had a right to know.

"Stanislaw has nowhere to go. His uncle is... not here and the police say the hired hand isn't family. They came to take Stanislaw somewhere he'd be looked after until his uncle comes back." Miss Oswin blinked a few times before answering. "Somewhere he'll be safe."

It was the closest to the truth I'd heard a grownup say, and more than I could expect. I wished I was in school right then, so I could answer a question or clean the chalkboard for her. Anything to show how much I appreciated her telling.

Stammer was in trouble. I made move to go find him.

Miss Oswin laid a hand on my shoulder. "Your Grandmother has been looking for you. I said I'd keep you here if I saw you."

No matter. Some cages have no bars. Looks like school would be mine for the rest of the day.

11

I didn't have much chance to answer Miss Oswin. She ushered me in and sat me in my usual seat. Darlene nodded at me before turning away again. Connie poked me in the back of the neck with her pencil. Eraser-tip again. You can count on kids to make you feel the same, though everything is different. I appreciated it.

I didn't bring a lunch, so Miss Oswin shared hers. I sat chewing beside her. The classroom looked much different from her perspective. I could see Dot's desk with its chair tucked in place. I guess I woulda seen Dot's face full on if she'd been there. Big sisters are more used to seeing the top of their little sister's heads.

I went outside with the others when we were done eating.

The girls grouped themselves in the usual order: big girls together wandering, little girls huddled by the schools steps. The boys all gathered around Mr. Oswin. The circus was closed, so he'd resumed his duties.

Mr. Oswin saw me edging to the side. I was hoping to make a break for it and go find Stammer.

"Ellen, we need an outfielder. Do you think you can fill in?" Mr. Oswin held up an extra glove. I didn't know he had one.

"Sure." What can I say? Yes. Of course. *Please*.

A couple of the younger boys grumbled, but one of the older ones shushed them.

"You know how to play, I assume?" Mr. Oswin tossed the glove.

I caught it. "Yessir. I was catcher at my old school."

"Well, I trust you'll do a good job here."

I heard Mr. Oswin's stress on the word 'trust.' I pondered it as I made my way to the field. When I got there, I remembered Mr. Oswin's kiss. I'm sure he remembered it, too. I'd have kissed the Strongman if I could. Why couldn't Mr. Oswin kiss him? No matter. Wasn't something to talk about either, considering how grown-ups meddled in things that didn't really involve them. Trust. I nodded to myself and pounded a fist in the glove.

I was in baseball heaven all lunchtime. I didn't mind being outfield. I was still closer to the game than I'd been since coming to live with Gram and Grandpa. I even caught the ball once. And threw it back not too badly.

Soon, Miss Oswin rang the bell for us to come in. What a good lunch break. I could rest my mind off my problems. I'd almost forgot about Dot.

Dot.

"Psst."

It was Stammer.

"Where've you been?" I hunched down to see him hidden in the bushes of the outfield.

"I w-went home."

"That's where the cops will be looking for you."

"N-not that place. I went out in the fields. To m-my uncle's hiding spot."

"His distillery?"

"Yeah."

I stood and pumped my hand into the glove a few times. Stammer was officially a fugitive. It made him kinda exciting.

"Y-you gotta come." Stammer inched forward on his elbows.

"Why?"

"I th-think I found something."

"Is it Dot?"

"I d-don't know, but I need your help."

The lineup for the school steps was shorter now. Only a few kids were still outside, grasping that last bit of sunshine. Nobody looked back at where I stood. Miss Oswin was inside. Mr. Oswin was gone. That decided it.

"Alright. I'm coming." I had to leave Mr. Oswin's baseball glove in the field. I couldn't take it back to the school, as I might get pulled in. Shame, after he was so nice to me.

We took awhile getting to Stammer's farm. Hiding in bushes whenever cars drove by made the journey a long one. Once we made it there, Stammer took the lead and wouldn't let me stop.

"H-hurry."

My legs were tired, though. Poor sleep will do that. It was like I carried Dot all last night. I had. In my nightmares.

"Wait! Too fast!"

Stammer paused while I puffed. His face wasn't even red from the run.

Up ahead, there was a black clot of motion to the side of the trail. Birds. Grackles. Fighting and pecking. Swooping down over the field, only to rise up again.

The grackles were attacking my drongo.

I didn't need to be close to see his red eyes. I could tell which bird was him by the way the others treated him. You could see their beaks diving, pecking at my drongo and his shine. The other birds didn't have feathers so black, so rich and vibrant. They cawed out their anger at his daring to be alive.

I had to stop it.

"C'mon." Stammer was ready to run again.

There were stones on the path. I picked a hand-size one up, hefting its weight. Pulling back, I launched it skyward, so it arched into the murder of birds.

Crack.

The birds rose in a flurry. The drongo rose a few seconds behind. In the grass, one black form didn't rise at all.

Stammer hurried to the motionless bird as the other grackles flew to trees nearby. The drongo landed a few lengths away and began cleaning his plumage. One grackle flew back and joined him. I leaned down for another rock and paused. The grackle mimicked my drongo's preening, so I let it stay unchallenged.

"You g-got it good." Stammer held up a dead grackle by one wing. Its other wing trailed out like black smoke from a plane going down. "You got a mean pitch."

I wish I'd used it on whoever took Dot.

"C'mon." Stammer started us running again. As we paced, I saw two black forms fly over us in the direction we headed. It was my drongo. And the grackle.

This time, Stammer didn't stop at the trees. He barrelled on through to the clearing. A wide, dirty pipe stuck out of the ground, as if the earth had swallowed a house and only its chimney showed. The pipe looked like a tree trunk, if you didn't know what you were seeing. The drongo was perched on top. When he saw us, he groaked, then lifted away.

"H-here. I need your help."

We both peered down the pipe into its darkness. The sides were all licked with a sick sweet musty flavour. My stomach turned at the smell.

"Your uncle makes crap moonshine." Someone had to say it. "I don't know how he's got any customers."

"It n-never stinks like this."

Stammer held my gaze for a long, painful moment. I swear for the first time since coming to this town, my eyes watered. It had nothing to do with the smell.

"H-help me lift." Stammer had hold of a sod of grass. We soon had several flipped over to show a metal box hidden in the earth. Four metal handles, two on each side, stood out from the steel door sheet.

"How big is this thing?"

"I d-don't know. I never been on top of it like this. I only watched before. It needs two people to lift."

He was right. Except it needed two grown men to lift. Stammer and I grunted our efforts but it was stuck. It needed two grown men. That gave me an idea.

12

I didn't think I'd ever want to see the circus again. It reminded me of my foolishness, of losing a big part of my life. Dot. And yet here I was with Stammer, racing to the circus grounds.

I was even the one who suggested the circus. We needed two men to help open the distillery. Two grown men. Or just one really strong one. I knew which one could do it, too.

Problem was, we had to find him. Fast.

The train whistle blew while Stammer and I were running. Meant the clock was ticking on our plan. The next time we heard that whistle, the circus would be boxed up to go. And our plan would go with it. I didn't stop running this time. Not for prairie dog holes nor nettle weed pitches. Now I had motivation.

Most of the people were packed away in their wagons when we jogged up. The dust of the first wagon coated our entrance, leaving Stammer and me looking like ghosts. I coughed, but kept going. Stammer did the same. We arrived just as more engines roared.

We needed Samson the Strongman.

Fast.

"*Help! Somebody!*" I flapped my arms at the wagons as they drove by.

"It's n-no use." Stammer sat down on the grass beside me.

"*Stop!*" Maybe it was the panic in my stance. Maybe it's that circus people truly love to make people happy. The next truck pulling a wagon stopped. So did the rest of the convoy behind it.

Dust scattered and blew as the truck window rolled down. The Tattoo Lady looked out at me, her face a drawn moment of puzzlement.

"Whazza matter, sweetie?"

I could feel the eyes from the convoy on me.

"I'm looking for Samson."

I'll give her this. She didn't pause and ask why. She just pointed backwards at the next car following. "He's in there."

"*Thank you.*"

The Tattoo Lady's truck continued to idle while I approached the car behind. It was small, with no trailer attached. I think Samson recognized me, 'cause the window was already open.

"What can I do for you, little lady?" Samson gave me a nod of encouragement as he spoke.

"We need your help. We found something. It might be important, but we're not strong enough to open it. Can you come?"

Samson squinted, then looked at his driver. The driver shrugged and motioned to the convoy waiting behind.

"How far is it?"

"Not far." I was hesitant to say more, in case Samson refused.

Samson sighed and gave the driver a push. "This ride's taken. I'll meet you guys at the station."

Things must happen like that all the time at the circus. The driver didn't even complain. He just said, "Okay," and left the car.

"Get in." Samson opened the passenger door before sliding over to the driver's seat.

Stammer and I squeezed in beside Samson. He was enormous. His head touched the ceiling. His massive hands engulfed the steering wheel. Stammer and I shared a look.

"H-h-huge," Stammer whispered.

I nodded.

Samson leaned out the window, peering at the trucks behind us. I think he was waiting for the driver to find a new ride. Samson gave a smile, like he was satisfied, and cranked the car back into gear.

"Where are we going, kids?"

Stammer pointed in the direction opposite to where the convoy turned. "Th-that way." We didn't take long to get back to Stammer's place.

Samson insisted we park the car far away from the farm. Maybe he'd done stuff like this before. Now that we were going back to the distillery, I didn't want to. The smell was bad. I fell farther behind, stalling as Stammer led the way.

My drongo was still there, perched on top that enormous pipe sticking out of the earth. He cleaned his beak on the edge, then cawed as he spied us coming. A grackle in the tree cawed back. They both took off when we approached.

We had left the grass sods off. Metal door glinted back at us in the hot autumn sun.

Samson peered into the pipe and drew his head back with a wince. "Whew. That a moonshine still, son? Not a very good one, if it is."

Stammer stood over the pipe like he was ready to strike. "It don't usually smell like that." Not one tic as he said it. I was now figuring when Stammer was mad.

"Well good, 'cause it's a waste of good drink, elsewise."

Samson didn't need to be told what to do. He rubbed his hands and reached for the handles on one side. He motioned us to take the other side to brace it.

I ain't never seen a strong man really lift before. I mean, I saw Samson perform at the circus, and caught a glimpse of his weights. They looked like big black balloons, with numbers written on with white paint. By the look of them, you'd think they're fake, and you could heft them yourself. I felt the heaviness of that metal door, though. It was as heavy as sin, as Gram would say. Samson lifted it like he was raising the dead. Grunts and strains. Face all contorted to scare the devil. But he lifted it.

Samson was the first to look inside. He took a quick look back at me, then down again.

"What is it?" I couldn't wait any longer. I scrambled around, but Samson put a restraining hand out to stop me. He wasn't strong enough for that, though.

I still caught a glimpse. Inside that still, a deep pool of liquid glistened. It swirled with grease stains and flecks of grass. A cloud was reflected in its blue-yellow glass colour.

Dot was there.

13

One thing Christians do when there's tragedy is make sandwiches. Lots and lots of sandwiches. Cucumber sandwiches. Ham sandwiches. Egg salad, tuna fish, cheese. All cut up into little squares, circles and triangles like the Lord is our Geometric Saviour, and we're trimming our crusty sins away.

Dot's funeral had sandwiches. Many people made them. I saw them all working in the church hall before the ceremony. Gram took me for company as she busied herself over the trays. The others tried to convince her to sit, but Gram wanted to keep moving. I took Gram's chair. I was done moving. Each time I did, I lost something. Someone.

I thought about that while we waited through the ceremony. Da was the first. We had just moved to a new home when he was called to fight. That moment seemed far away yet oh-so close. He wrote to us a lot. I think he worried we'd forget him. Young ones, he'd call us. How're the young ones? Always included special words for Dot and me. How he saw a rabbit all dun brown while they were marching. He could see it, he said, 'cause the rabbit sat up straight and looked at him, like it was saying "Hello." Dot had squealed at that one. He didn't forget my birds, either. Always asking which page I was reading. We got his last letter after they told us he was gone. Mam didn't read it to us. I don't know if she read it herself.

I don't remember Da's smile so clear. I just remember his hand as he pointed while reading my bird book to me. Sometimes he'd put his finger out on the page, like he was letting the paper bird perch there. I've tried it a few times, but I don't have the magic he did.

Mam was next. We had moved then, too. We'd been without Da for a year. Dot didn't ask about him no more. Mam was Dot's pa.

Mam said that we needed to go smaller. The apartment we had was too much space for us since Da wasn't coming back. Dot and I didn't mind. We'd already shared a room. Mam said she'd have to share with us, too. We didn't mind that, either.

Then Mam got sick. The landlord gave Mam an extra month.

Turns out she didn't need it.

Mam's friends did all the funeral planning. One of them took Dot and me back to her boarding room to stay until the mourning was done. That room was smallest of all. No bigger than the bedroom Gram gave Dot and me to share. Seems every time there's a loss, my living space gets smaller. I get more cramped with the loneliness and have less room to work it out in.

Gram and Grandpa sent for us as soon as they heard. Turns out Mam hadn't left anyone their address, so they missed the funeral. Seeing as how they couldn't afford to meet our train, and now seeing the state of the hotel, they couldn't have come anyways.

"Sit up straight, Ellen." Gram touched my arm with more than a bit of sympathy.

I sat up. My hunching double in the pew was likely forgivable today, but I don't think Gram wanted the sympathy. I know Grandpa didn't.

We were in the front pew. The unlucky ones on display. Us and our grief. I can't remember ever liking church after having a third sit in those unlucky seats. Maybe it'd be different if I was watching a bride there. Never seen a bride up close. Even for me, that pure white dress would be something. Nobody I knew had one. Not even Dot had a pure white dress. Not even today.

The Dionnes sat behind us for once. Mr. Dionne helped Gram to her seat, then tucked in the pew behind. Mrs. Dionne made Connie walk with me. Connie didn't take my hand like her pa did Gram. Still, she didn't turn away either. Just paused by my side while I took my own seat. Grandpa walked alone.

Connie snuck a peek when I turned around. She made no face to go with the look. Just a stare that was soft. Not prickly like usual. I was a thing of pity in my loss. I think that's what made it all final to me.

I looked farther back, avoiding Connie's eyes. The church was full. Stammer wasn't there with his uncle. Miss Frieda sat in their usual spot. Father Don had welcomed her with a hug, and led her in himself.

"In the name of the Father, the Son and the Holy Spirit."

"Amen."

Gram chose Father Don for the eulogy. Grandpa wasn't going to speak about Dot, now that he had missed speaking to her.

"There is no good in what was done to Dorothy Mae." Father Don spread his hands as he spoke. "There is no good in what we feel today. The loss. The anger. Why?"

Father Don paced for a moment before coming to stand in front of our pew.

"Why?"

The church was quiet except for a few snifflers. Nobody had an answer. I did, though I didn't speak up.

"Why does this happen?" Father Don didn't look at me as he paced. He should have.

Dot's death happened because I let it happen, not because God willed it. I wouldn't drop this one in the Almighty's lap. This one I had to hold close to myself.

"Some may say it's because Evil walks the world." Father Don paused under the cross. "There's no one near who can save us. We are as forsaken as Moses and his people who walked in the desert. We are Moses. We hear the promise each day, and we think to ourselves we'll never see it. Never see it, like Moses didn't see it. Like Moses was blind to the Glory right in front of him. Old in his thoughts. Scared in his heart. He had his eyes closed as he walked, never quite knowing the Holy Spirit walked beside him. We come to pray and to hear, but we don't see."

I think Father Don had most people's attention with that one. He was walking his own thin Lordy line towards a blasphemy. Most grown-ups I know think they see things nice and clear. I lifted my head, though I knew I should keep it low.

Father Don came closer to the front row. He walked slow as he took all of us, his flock, in.

Grandpa shifted beside me, in Dot's spot by the aisle. I hadn't noticed him until then. I was used to him tucked in the middle, like he didn't want to talk to anyone passing by. I felt him breathe through Father Don's pacing.

"Some say it's because we see, but we still don't believe. We hear the words, we see the sight, the Glory. And we mouth the words in return, but we don't believe. Some may be here right now. Watching. Mouthing the words. Seeing all of us together, praying the psalms. And we still don't believe."

Me. Father Don was talking about me. I never once thought of what I do in church as having anything to do with me. I sat in the pew. I sang when told to sing. I watched when told to watch. I stood and prayed, or sat and waited. But I never once felt comfort or love from being there. I only felt flattened by the hard seat. Squished to the side as a body to fill space.

"I can tell you that Dorothy heard. And Dorothy saw. And Dorothy believed."

The congregation let out a sigh, like Dot had just been raised to Heaven. Father Don had proclaimed her above us all in her knowing. I thought about it as he spoke.

"Dorothy Mae believed. I can tell you, she believed. Even in her darkest moments, her coldest fear, she believed. I know. We all know. She believed with each smile she gave. With each hug she shared. With each loving look.

"Dorothy Mae lived as a Christian, a believing Christian. You may say she was too young. She didn't know. But I tell you, she did. She believed. We saw her believe. And I tell you right now. She is in Heaven above us, looking down on us. Telling us that the Evil we hear, the Evil we see, the Evil we know is nothing to be afraid of."

Father Don gave a sigh, like he was almost disappointed he couldn't speak no more. Then, he surprised me by continuing.

"The Evil we know is nothing to fear, because it is the Glory we believe. The Glory saves us in our darkest hour. The Glory holds us when all our strength fails. The Glory of believing brings us to Salvation. Glory to God in the Highest. Glory to God, that we may believe."

No one spoke. A baby cried, but its mother managed to shush it. Father Don climbed back to his pulpit and stood a moment, quiet over his open Bible. He raised his eyes high.

"In the name of the Father, the Son, and the Holy Spirit."

"Amen."

Amen.

The church was quiet for the rest of the service. People shuffled out, tempered by the loss of a child. I'd been to grown-up funerals–Da's and Mam's–and there's more chatting in between the church services and the after-Mass tea. The mood broke once people got downstairs though, and the clinking of teacups and passing of plates took over. Mundane movements tend to enliven people, bring amity to their thoughts, even when they're grieving. Me? I was still quiet, trying to find my peace.

I personally think food should come before the funeral. Get all the talking done, so you can sit in stillness after the sermon. God doesn't like it that way. He wants you to mingle with your fellow man. Let them look you over and murmur something only a grown-up would say to a kid that's hurting.

"You must miss your sister." It felt like Mr. and Mrs. Dionne had come only to taunt me.

"Yes, ma'am." I kept my voice clean, but I wanted to scream at them.

"It's a shame it happened. We so loved Dorothy." Mrs. Dionne clucked a bit. She shuffled her napkin and sandwich to her other hand as she reached for her purse. "Oh, do you need a tissue?"

My eyeballs weren't helping me today. Wetness stung my cheeks as they burned with my desire to run. Thankfully, Connie had left already with Darlene. She couldn't see my discomfort.

Mr. Dionne cleared his throat. "Such a beautiful young girl. I still can't believe we've lost her."

Grandpa's bulk leaned in to the conversation as Mr. Dionne spoke. I felt him near, even with my head hanging low. "I'll need Ellen for a moment, Mr. Dionne. If you can please excuse her."

I trailed Grandpa outside. He paused at the top of the church steps, turned, and waited for me. Someone reached a hand out for him to shake as I stood by. Grandpa grasped it, then laid his own hand on my shoulder to guide me down the steps.

Grandpa said nothing as we walked down the town road, away from the church. I realized it was the first time I'd been alone with him. He wasn't as scary as I would have supposed. He stopped as we got to the field marking the last house.

"It wasn't your fault."

I had to look up at that one. Grandpa had his glasses down low and looked at me over top of them.

"What?"

"I said it wasn't your fault."

"Oh." Don't know what to say to that. Thanks, but you're wrong?"

Grandpa musta seen the disbelief in my eyes. He shook his head, as if to dispel my thoughts from his own head. "I should have given you permission to go instead of sneaking. I should have gone with you."

Sometimes, the world pops you one on the gut. Someone says something you weren't expecting. I wasn't expecting that.

Grandpa sighed. "Well, no matter. As long as one of you is safe." He reached over and gave my head a rough pat.

I always thought if it came down to it, people would prefer Dot over me. I couldn't help but stare. Who had taken Grandpa? Who was this stranger in his place?

"Come on. Your Gram will be starting to worry."

"Is it okay if I stay here a while?"

The sun reflected off of Grandpa's glasses as he held my gaze. "Alright. But don't stay too long. I expect you home by dinner."

Breathing got easier at that moment. I wasn't sure yet what Dot's death would mean for my own independence. Grandpa took some of those nerves away.

"Thanks." I gave him a stiff hug, then turned like I was aiming for the schoolyard.

Grandpa watched a minute until I gave another wave. He seemed convinced and headed back to the church. I was glad he gave me leave to go. There was something I had to do.

14

The fields felt like home now. I could navigate through them using tree clumps and fence posts as guides. Soon, I was on the pilgrim's trail. One way led to Stammer's farm, the other to the distillery.

I stood looking towards where I last seen Dot.

Not Dot, I had to remind myself. Her body.

The wind blew back at me, tossing my hair and ruffling my cheek. The grasses waved and rasped a sad song. The sky was empty.

I turned and walked briskly the other way.

Dresses seem to catch burrs more than jeans do. The prickles poked through where the fabric rubbed against my legs. Kinda like thoughts you can't shake off. You shake them so hard that they bury themselves into your heart, and you spend hours picking at them. Just burying them deeper into you. No matter.

I found Stammer hanging about the yard by his house, crouched over a purring cat.

"Heya." I nodded as I walked through the open gate.

"H-hey. Whatcha doing here?" Stammer nodded back, though he didn't look up.

Fair question. Many reasons. "Came to see you." I reached down to pet the cat, too. It rolled on its back. Dirt clung to its fur as it stretched from side to side under my hand.

Stammer left off petting, but watched for a moment. He dusted his hands off on his pants and finally stood. His eyes widened when he took in my dress. I didn't entirely hate the feeling.

"Y-you come from the funeral?"

"Yup." The cat's tail twitched as I scratched its belly. I could feel the rumble of its purr through my hand.

"I c-couldn't go."

"I supposed that. Not with the police after you."

"I w-wanted to go. I really did."

Someone else telling me that, I may not have believed. Who wants to go to a funeral? From what I knew of Stammer, though, I knew he wished he had come. For Dot. Maybe even for me.

"I know."

"You l-look pretty."

That I didn't expect.

"N-no. I mean it. I mean… you look like you could go to a dance."

"Do I?"

Stammer crouched again to pet the cat with me. Our hands touched as he did it. Neither of us spoke. It was weird, so I stood up.

"Where's Nathan?" I hadn't seen the hired hand anywhere. You'd think he'd be doing the chores that Stammer's uncle couldn't get to.

"He w-went to b-bail out Uncle Ward. He had to go to the p-provincial court." Stammer winced as he said it. I didn't sympathize, though. I didn't know how it felt to have a relative in jail, but I sure knew how it felt to have one die. I thought I had the bigger sympathy draw.

"How come you're here? I thought you'd be hiding in the bush." I looked at Stammer's house behind us. One of the window shutters tilted and waved in the breeze. Maybe it would be more comfortable for him in the bush.

"I was. But the p-police haven't come round for a while. I think they've given up."

We both looked over at the highway nearby. I think we half expected a cop car to come roaring in after just mentioning them. When we looked back at each other, I noticed that Stammer was taller than me. He took a step closer. Uncomfortable moment, considering what I'd come to say.

I gave a shrug that startled him. "Let's go for a walk."

Stammer followed as I opened the gate to his field. He flicked his eyes away from me whenever I looked back. Soon, we were meandering side by side through the same field we roamed before. I think we both knew where we were headed, but each didn't speak for fear of digging up a ghost. I paused to remove a stone from my shoe. Stammer stopped with me, and let me hold on to him as I shook the stone free. He felt warm.

"Why'd y-you come, Elly?"

It was an opener. Might as well be now. "Why'd your uncle do it?"

Stammer froze. His face got all distorted, like I'd stripped some bark off a tree and left the knotholes exposed. "My uncle didn't do it."

"They say he did." I stood as wide-stanced as I could in a dress. Crossed my arms to show I meant it. I wanted answers.

"He w-wouldn't have done it. I know." Stammer picked up a stick and swished it beside him. I could see he wanted to run, but stayed anyways.

"The grown-ups said he did it."

"Wh-which one?"

Now that I think of it, I wasn't sure. I overheard it from the kids, from Connie and Darlene at the funeral. Maybe from Connie's parents, too. They talked like everyone knew Stammer's uncle was guilty. They didn't say why. They just made out that he was bad, and enough said.

Stammer snorted when I stayed quiet. "Thought so."

I wasn't so easy to give up. "But why would people say it?"

The breeze picked up, blowing a few wisps of Stammer's hair around. He looked as if he were electric and would spark off me if I touched him.

"I d-don't know why. Maybe they just don't like that we're here."

My face musta showed my puzzlement. I didn't say it, but he musta known. When I didn't speak, Stammer lifted his arms wide.

"There's some in t-town don't like my uncle." His repeating didn't help. "They come for the moonshine, but else let us keep to ourselves."

"Why?"

Stammer went back to swishing his stick.

"How can I believe you, Stammer, if you don't tell me? What do I say when people talk about him and Dot? Like your uncle's attached to her forever in their heads, and there's nothing I can do to change it?"

When he still said nothing, I turned to walk back. I felt a hand grab my arm and pull me away from my course. If I hadn't known it was Stammer, I woulda shoved hard and run.

"D-don't go. Not yet."

"Tell me then."

Stammer had stepped up close as before. His eyes searched mine as he twitched his head, then settled.

"M-my uncle and Nathan are my family."

"Yeah. I get that." For the most part, I did.

"I'm s-saying they're my family. My parents." Stammer held my elbow to keep me from running.

"Oh."

"It w-wouldn't be like my uncle to go for a girl, let alone a little one."

"Oh." I was low on words as I processed. Then my thinking stopped. Stammer was still close.

"So th-that's why it wasn't my uncle."

Awfully close.

I think the sparks the wind blew into Stammer's hair made their way down to his face. His eyes were sharp as they scanned mine. Then he leaned in and kissed me.

Buttery soft, my toes to my head, scented like raspberries, pine cones, and prairie sky. Lasting forever.

I pulled away hard.

Stammer blushed.

I did, too.

"Elly…"

I could feel my heart pound in answer to the question he didn't ask. My breath was shaky. Words were all jumbled up in my throat. I did the only thing I could think of.

I ran.

Problem was I didn't run so fast as I usually do. And I looked back as I did it. Stammer wasn't following. He watched, then turned the other way.

My stride faltered, and I slowed to a stop.

Stammer didn't look back. I could see him getting smaller as he walked through the fields. Soon, even the top of his head was hidden by the prairie grass.

Every time I ran away, someone disappeared.

15

I left Stammer on his lonesome. I carried on with mine. When your legs tell you to run, there must be a reason. My reason? I was scared. When I felt that drill of blood course through my thoughts, I couldn't help it. But this was the first time I'd stopped. I don't know why. Maybe it was the warmth the kiss had caused. I hadn't listened yet to what else my body was saying. Feeling heat was a new concept to me, but I didn't pay it much mind. Not until later.

Still, I did pause when I got home. I stared out the window at times instead of reading. Maybe because of Stammer. Likely because of Dot.

My ship had lost crew mates before, yet I sailed on. Sure, I missed Dot. I hadn't the heart to move her tea set off the dresser. And I'll admit, I ended up cuddling with that rag rabbit at night. I think it missed Dot, too, and was thankful for the company.

Gram and Grandpa needed me those first couple days. More than I expected. Gram couldn't seem to let me alone in my room. She was always yelling for something or checking to see where I was.

"Ellen, come and set the table."

"Ellen, where are you? The chickens need feeding."

Gram knew I enjoyed those chickens. She even sat on the back step, talking while I spread the feed all neat and even on the ground. Held her apron out for the eggs I dug out of the coop.

Mostly she talked about her day. The things she was making for supper. What laundry needed doing. Gram did a lot each day. I wondered how much more she did when she wasn't slowed up with grieving. One thing about that time with Gram, though. She almost never talked about Dot.

After a couple of days, the talking wore upon me, and I kept trying to go back to my room.

Grandpa surprised me the most. I now knew the sound of his voice. He still wasn't one to holler, but I could tell by the timbre whether he was good-mooded or not. Most of the time, he was not. All three of us were quiet. Even the boarders picked up the hush and kept more to themselves during the meals.

I didn't have to go to school at first. I think Gram and Grandpa forgot. Either that or they were keeping an eye on me so that I didn't take off again. I think they were worried they'd lose me, too. At least, I hoped they were.

The superintendent sure didn't forget about me. Mr. Dionne showed up two days after the funeral, sniffing with his nose in the air like he scented rabbit. I know 'cause I saw him by the front door when he came. He cocked an ear towards the hallway and gave a call out for Grandpa. I was at the top of the stairs when he spotted me. His eyebrows rose, and he smiled up in greeting.

"Hello, Miss Ellen. How have you been faring?"

"Fine, Mr. Dionne."

"I'm so sorry for your loss."

"Thank you, sir."

Mr. Dionne seemed to perk at the sound of my answer. He tugged his tie and leaned an arm on the railing. "We miss you at school. The students are waiting for you to come back."

I didn't know what to say. He hadn't heard that from Connie, so I said nothing.

"You look pale."

Good thing I sat in the stairs' shadows, as I didn't want Mr. Dionne knowing he made me blush.

Grandpa came out of the kitchen and grunted, "Hello."

Mr. Dionne gave one last look at me before turning to Grandpa.

"It's just me, Carl. I thought I'd drop by to see how things are going."

We should really call Grandpa "Grumpa." You can tell he's about to speak by the grunt that starts his sentences.

"That's kind of you." Grandpa ends some of his sentences the same way, too. I think Mr. Dionne knew, 'cause he continued as soon as Grandpa stopped.

"We need to talk about Ellen, though." Mr. Dionne pointed at me as he spoke. "She's missing too much school."

Grandpa nodded and grunted again.

"She's at risk of failing if she misses too much. Besides, it's good for her to be out with others her own age."

"True." No grunt this time.

How odd to hear grownups talk about you. It's as if you're something they're preparing for the cooking pot. I didn't dare go further down the stairs, so I sat down and peered through the bars at them both.

"We had this talk when the girls first came. I didn't think I'd have to repeat it so soon." Mr. Dionne gave another sniff and peered up towards where I crouched.

I moved further back into the shadows.

Grandpa shrugged his shoulders and harrumphed.

"I mean it, Carl. If you're going to be the parent, you need better control. Ellen should be in school now."

That caused Grandpa to bristle. I know 'cause I saw his hands flex before settling into his belt loops. What I don't know is if Mr. Dionne saw it, too. Or if he meant such a harsh salvo, considering we just lost Dot and all.

"I can take her, if that's what's holding you back. If the girl is balking, I can help." Mr. Dionne shifted and licked his lips. I think he finally saw the line he'd stepped over.

Grandpa was silent.

The thought of going to school with the superintendent put a shiver down my spine. I tried to think it over for why. No way the kids would let that one down. Connie could get away with it, being her pa and all. Not me.

"Just have her get her things. I'll wait right here." Mr. Dionne gave his watch a tap. "But have her hurry. I don't have all day."

"I don't think its time. The girl just lost her sister." Grandpa did a pause that Mr. Dionne tried to fill.

"Carl."

"No." Grandpa chopped the air with a meaty hand. "We lost a granddaughter. That isn't something Grace and I take lightly. Especially since we lost their mother not too long ago."

Mr. Dionne tried to hide a scowl, but I saw it flicker before his sympathetic face came on. "I understand."

"It's been a hard week, Luc. We need more time together before Ellen ventures out into learning again."

Grandpa. Speaking up. My muscles loosened, and I began to move again. I stood and went back upstairs. I didn't spare the grown-ups another look.

16

Mr. Dionne's words musta struck a nerve with Grandpa, nonetheless. I was back at school the next day.

Gram didn't walk with me this time. I think it's because of Dot that she did before. No matter. I preferred being alone. Made you look weak to have a grown-up by your side walking to school. The other kids wonder what you need protecting from, and assume it's themselves.

I hung out by the front steps, awaiting Miss Oswin and her bell. The younger girls didn't mind me. They were squabbling about who had the nicest doll. Boring as goat-bags.

The boys were nearby, too. Someone had a pack of baseball cards they'd been given as a present. The boys were huddled around him, cackling in excited voices. Best I could figure, they had a baseball card with a former Saskatchewan boy on it.

"One day, I'm gonna be on a card like that." The eldest boy of our school took a batting stance.

Another boy laughed. "The Negro League'll get their own cards before you do."

That made the eldest boy scowl. "Says you. I'll get my own card. You wait and see."

"Sure you will."

"It'll happen. Soon, you'll be reading my batting average, just like you're reading now. You'll say you knew me as you pick the dirt outta your nails and go back to plowing the field."

The other boy sneered and raised a fist. "I can start plowing right now, if you want."

The group burst into laughter, which scattered the tussle. The two boys shook hands and agreed they'd both make it big.

I wished I could see the baseball card and be part of the talk. I looked at the girls near me, chatting as they combed their dolls' hair. I couldn't imagine a more sap sucking thing to do.

One boy looked at me as I shuffled nearer and gave me a stare. I pinked up and moved away. Farther from the cards, closer to the dolls.

Some dreams are better left undreamed.

Connie and Darlene stood nearby and thankfully left me alone. Maybe it would have been nice to get some attention, though. They were deep in talk, with Darlene giving Connie a pat every once in a while.

The boys started hooting when my back was turned. It made me nervous, thinking I'd done something wrong. Even the girls looked up to see what was going on.

Turns out they weren't hooting at me. They were hooting at someone else.

Stammer.

He was coming through the field, from the direction of his farm. He wasn't even trying to hide. Just kept walking, like he had every right to be there.

"*Stammer. Stammer. Stammer.*" Most of the boys yelled out at him. Their chorus made it sound like a flock of grackles had come to pick him apart. One or two spared me a glance, with smirks to see how I was taking Stammer's reappearance. I didn't know if it's 'cause Stammer and I were friends, or 'cause his uncle was a suspect.

The boys crowded around Stammer, slapping him on the back and calling him a fugitive. Seems like being chased by the police gives you instant boy status.

"Where'd you hide?" Eldest boy looked more than curious. Rumour last week was he was seeing one of the older girls, who graduated and now worked in a store. I wondered if he was trying to find a good place to take her. I shook my head at the thought. Odd direction to take.

"M-mostly around the farm. I g-got places I can go."

"I heard they shot at you."

Stammer stammered, but the other kids kept listening. Their faces were wide and friendly.

"N-no, they didn't. They just d-drove after me, and I dodged them in the bush."

"How come you're here?"

"M-my uncle convinced 'em that Nathan can take care of me." Stammer ducked his head as he spoke.

"Your uncle still in jail?"

"N-not jail. Custody." Stammer jabbed at the boy who spoke. "He didn't do anything wrong."

The boys seemed to take it as natural that Stammer would thrust back. They paid it no mind and kept talking.

A couple boys looked again at me and put their heads together to whisper.

I'll admit, I was jealous. When I first started this school, I felt like Stammer and me were the same level. Neither big on the totem pole, just making our own way through the school day. Today, Stammer had passed me. Boys crowded around him, eager to discuss the doings that made him run.

Miss Oswin appeared at the top of the school stairs and held the bell high. Most of her blocked the door from view.

"Time for school." Nobody likes to hear the sound of that bell, unless they're escaping the schoolyard. Today, like most my days, it was a relief.

"Good Morning, Miss Oswin." Each kid greeted her as they filed past the doorway in the part that remained open. Some of the bigger kids had to go sideways just to make it through.

I was one of the last. With Stammer.

We exchanged a look but no words. He didn't even twitch at me.

I'd seen other kids come back to school after being away. Heck, at my old school, I'd even come back after being sick a day or two. Usually, kids come to greet you and welcome you back. I'd never seen someone be greeted by just one person, like happened to me. And for me, it was the teacher. Pretty low to suffer through. That's how I knew my status.

Connie was seated where my books were from last week. She smirked like she knew she was going to break me.

"You're in my seat." I didn't care no more. Picking a fight was better than not being part of anything.

"It's my seat now. You go sit somewhere else." Connie spread her hands wide over the desk.

I looked behind Connie. One of the boys had moved in to the seat she'd vacated. There were no other seats nearby. Dot's seat at the front was open. That I knew for a Hell-burning fact. No way was I sitting there. Little kids, first of all. And I didn't want to start seeing things from Dot's point of view. I woulda cried. Not a wise move for school. Not like I was making wise moves today, anyways.

"It's my seat and you know it." I wasn't backing down.

Connie made a face that the fight was continuing. Darlene busied herself with drawing on her eraser.

I stood. I daren't lean over Connie, but I kept my shadow across her head. My hands were clenched as I waited beside the desk. My desk.

Miss Oswin noticed. I think the class musta quieted to watch, too.

"Ellen? Won't you take a seat?"

Miss Oswin didn't bother keeping watch after she said it. Her arm was already raised to write a quote on the board. Usually, I'd be watching like a hawk at what she'd write and tasting the words inside my head, but I wasn't even seated yet. I had Connie to thank for a further loss.

Maybe it was Connie. Maybe it was the pity in Miss Oswin's voice. Maybe I'd been pushed against a wall too many times. In recollection, most of the time it was me doing my own pushing.

I broke.

I grabbed Connie by the ponytail and hauled her outta my seat.

"*Owwww!*" Connie's screech was a joy to hear. My fingers grasped tighter, and I swung her around me so I was nearer the seat and she wasn't.

"*Miss Oswin!*" Connie scrabbled at my head and collar. She tried to drag me away from the desk, but I was heavier. I won. I got the seat.

Best I figure, Miss Oswin caught me sitting in Connie's spot, but not my part of the tussle. She stood open-mouthed at the front. I didn't know her mouth was that big. I shoulda suspected, knowing the size of her.

"Constance and Ellen. *What. Is. Going. On?*" Miss Oswin crossed her arms over her hay-bale chest. She woulda stood legs apart, but I suppose they were already as far apart as they could go.

Connie's name was first. That was a good sign.

I looked at Connie. Her lip quivered. Like Dot's would.

"I d-d-d-didn't mean it." Tears formed and welled over her cheeks. Her hands twisted over each other, before she hid them behind her back.

This was new. I coulda swore she had the same stutter as Stammer. I peered at Connie. It was like a sparrow had appeared instead of the grackle I'd been watching. What was going on? I hadn't delivered a real beating, yet she acted like I had.

I think my face registered my surprise.

Miss Oswin stared a moment before speaking. "Constance, please take a seat."

Connie stood trembling. "I can't. There's no seat."

"Well, we'll have to make one." Miss Oswin paused in front of Dot's desk. "Inge, you come sit here by Annie. Jarvis, move forward. Everyone in this row, move one up."

Darlene had no choice but to vacate the seat beside me and move with the rest.

"Ellen, make room for Constance."

My turn to give in. I slid over with much less grievance than I expected. A kid's tears will usually do that to a fight. Unless it's a bully doing the fighting, then it just gets scarier. I ain't a bully, no matter how hard I pulled Connie's hair.

Connie dropped into the seat I'd left. She crossed her arms on her desk and hid her face in them.

Darlene snuck a peek at her and murmured, "It's okay, Con. It's okay." She kept her face blank when looking my way. Guess Dot's death still muffled some hardness that could be felt against me.

Miss Oswin turned back to the board. She finished writing her quote and dropped her chalk on the blackboard ledge. I didn't hear when she started speaking. I was too busy listening to Connie snivel.

Darlene risked another turn, then thought better of it. Connie wasn't gonna get any comfort from her. I thought of Dot and how she shook when her feelings were hurt. Connie seemed more than hurt. She seemed scared. Like I'd held a belt to her, rather than just tug on her hair.

"Hey. Psst." I tried to see under Connie's mop of hair. Her ponytail was snarled, thanks to me.

"Connie." Dot would want me to do this.

Connie took a small peep through a crack between her arms. "Wh-what."

I took a deep breath. It had to be done.

"Sorry."

Connie closed the crack so I couldn't see her eyes no more. She took a shuddering breath, then sat up straight. Her face was ruddy and glazed with tears. Still, she gave only a couple shivers before reaching for the books I had overturned on the floor beside her.

I didn't know what to think. She'd regrouped faster than I expected. What was next for me? A schoolyard beating? I'd seen one of those. They are usually harmless but leave a lot more scars on the inside than you'd expect.

Connie gave me a side look.

I looked back.

She shrugged. "It's okay."

I kept my mouth from dropping. It was hard, though.

"I can switch with Darlene after lunch, if you wanna sit together. I don't mind."

Connie shrugged again. "It's okay."

I left it at that. I didn't push it.

The rest of the morning felt numb, but not as cold as usual. Sure, Dot had been erased from the student ledger. Another kid sat in Dot's seat, now. But I didn't feel the waves of hate coming from Connie. And Miss Oswin had talked more about that quote she put on the blackboard.

> *O time, thou must untangle this, not I.*
> *It is too hard a knot for me t'untie.*

Shakespeare apparently knew all about troubles and how hard it is to get yourself out once you're deep in 'em. Turns out *Twelfth Night* was full of other people's concerns. I found my own relief burying myself in those characters' problems.

I thought about the knot I'd woven myself into: Stammer, Connie, Darlene. Gram and Grandpa were tied in 'cause of me, too. I thought of the people who'd been woven out: Dot, Mam, and Da. Perhaps I would need my own *Twelfth Night* to think it through.

17

On school days, we had an hour for lunch. That's enough time to make it home, eat, and get back to school again. Some people manage to do more than that.

When I got home, Gram wasn't waiting for me in the kitchen. Grandpa was there. He gave me a nod as greeting.

"You hungry?" Grandpa pointed to the table.

I nodded back. "Yes, sir." Best to imitate Grandpa if you want him to keep talking. He seemed to find encouragement in it.

"Well, there's your sandwich." One side of the table had empty plates and crumbs scattered about. The boarders ate earlier than us kids. Than me. My dish sat alone at the far end. On it was a sandwich and potato salad. I could tell Grandpa had served it, as the sandwich was slopped a bit on the side. Gram makes the food sit up straight.

"What they teach you in school today?"

I stopped my sandwich halfway to my mouth. I never been asked a long question by Grandpa before. I snuck a look over my chicken and bread. Grandpa was fiddling with the lid of one of Gram's pickle jars as if he'd never spoke. I decided to ignore it.

"Ellen?"

"Huh?" I almost gobbed out a piece of sandwich. He *did* mean it.

"School?"

"Oh. Yeah." I gave my mouth a wipe with the back of my hand. Grandpa wouldn't mind. Gram would. "We started a book about Shakespeare."

"About Shakespeare, or by Shakespeare?"

"Huh?"

Grandpa gave one of his grunts, like he'd run out of patience.

"Oh. I mean by Shakespeare. It's about a girl who likes someone, and she's in disguise like a boy."

Grandpa nodded as he speared a pickle out.

"But she can't tell the guy, even though she likes him. And the guy likes someone else, 'cause he likes the way girls look and not the girl who's pretending to be a boy."

"Go on." Grandpa put the jar lid down as he searched for another fork.

I made a face, but he didn't see it. I'd had enough talk of school, considering I still had the afternoon to go through. Besides, if Grandpa had opened up asking questions, I had a few of my own.

"Where's Gram?"

Grandpa looked up sharp. His eyes darted from me to the ceiling and back again. "She's taking a little lie down."

"Is she sick?"

I saw Grandpa work his mouth as he chewed on his answer. He seemed to find the right bite of it. "No. She's having one of her spells, is all."

"Oh. Can I go see her?"

"Might be best not." Grandpa moved to place some slices of pickle on my plate. I watched the pickle juice run into the salad. Lunch was turning messy.

"Why not?" Risky to continue, considering Grandpa had already answered more than his fair share of questions. Still, I was curious.

Grandpa didn't answer. He just flicked his eyes to the ceiling again, before settling down to his own sandwich.

We ate quiet after that.

Overhead, a heavy footstep paced through. A chair scraped, then sounded like it protested a sudden weight. Murmured voices could be heard. I picked out Gram's like it was song I'd heard many times before. The other one was deep and rumbly. I had a hard time placing it. It didn't speak much. Gram's did most of the talking.

Grandpa kept to himself while he ate. His head was twisted, though, so his good ear was facing up. Gram had told me Grandpa lost part of his hearing when hunting. A gun had gone off too close when one of his friends was careless. She said it was part why he didn't talk so much, as he couldn't hear the high sounds. Dot spoke in high sounds.

When eating was done, I cleared the table. Grandpa had already left to run the bar. Drinking started earlier these days. Seems there were those in the town who thought Grandpa's grieving was a better pastime to watch than being lonely at home. Billy Harner was one of them. I could feel his oily smile from the hallway each time I passed.

Today, I was surprised to see Grandpa in the bar with just one visitor, Father Don. I never seen a priest near alcohol before, unless it was the blood of Christ. Grandpa poured Father Don a finger's breadth of liquid into one of his finest glasses. Seems to me he shoulda poured Father Don a drink in a glass made outta pure gold. I didn't think the Lord's lips that prayed even touched mortal nourishment, though it did cross my mind I'd seen Father Don eating a cupcake after one of the Sunday masses.

Father Don caught my eye when he lifted his glass for a sip. He gave it a tip as he winked at me.

Grandpa looked up at the same moment and scowled.

"Aren't you late for school?" Grandpa's huff could be felt through the doorway.

"I was going to say hi to Gram." I reached for the stair bannister. The slingshot approach is the best way to race up stairs.

"You have no time for that." Grandpa raised his eyebrows, so I saw his eyes wide and clear. I swear he was asking me for a favour. "Leave your Gram alone for now. She'll see you after school."

The priest just nodded to himself and sipped as Grandpa spoke.

"Go on." Grandpa held my gaze a moment longer before turning back to Father Don.

You know the feeling of a teacher being done with your questions and turning to another student, even though you still don't understand the lesson? I felt the same. I had no choice but to go.

Difficult to say if Life likes to mess around with you more than you expect. You mind your own business, and trouble still manages to find you.

I stepped out of the hotel and right into the path of Connie.

"Watch it." Connie gave me a shove. It felt homey, after the hair pulling we'd both been through that morning.

"I was. You watch it."

Connie glowered under her eyebrows.

I glowered back. I had part Grandpa in me. I also quirked my lips. I had part Dot in me, too.

"Just saying." Connie broke her stare off first. Her ponytail swung with her head bob, and I suddenly felt ashamed of myself. I remembered her shaking. You don't know whether something's a fair fight or not until after it's done. For some reason, I didn't think we had it out fair. I knew I won hard. Time to ring the bell on the fight.

I took a big breath. "You going to school?"

Connie nodded. "Yeah. Where'd you think I'm going?"

"Well, you're on my road, but I think there's room enough for two."

I got a smile for that one. I guess my old touch was coming back.

"Sure, there is." Connie's face lightened. Her eyes didn't seem so dark. "Let's go, then."

"I might take up more than my fair space."

"I won't let you." Connie started walking. When I didn't move, she motioned with her head. "C'mon."

What can you do with a peace offering like that? Accept it.

It felt good to be walking to school with Connie. Who am I kidding? It felt great. We talked a bit, mostly poking with words to feel each other out. I hadn't joked with another kid since Mam died. Dot was never one for jousting. She couldn't see the use. I'm the one who needed it.

The boys were back at baseball when we arrived at the schoolyard. Mr. Oswin had them arranged into the usual two teams. Only exception was Stammer now covered first base. And he was decent. Every throw was bang on. Every catch perfect. He hardly even twitched. He even looked taller up close than when he stood guard in outfield.

Connie and I both stopped to the side of the field near Stammer.

"He's got a good arm." Connie leaned into her words. "And he looks good doing it."

Connie. Girly-girl Connie. Talking about baseball. Didn't know what to make of it.

"Where you been?" Darlene came up close and stood between Connie and me. I moved over to make room.

"Home for lunch." Connie motioned at the boys in the field. "Now watching the game. You?"

"Same." Darlene gave me a quick look over, but didn't question my standing there. I took it to be an okay sign. "Stammer's playing first today."

"Yeah." Connie kept her eyes on the field.

I kept quiet. Seemed the safest thing to do. I wasn't certain of the rules of their friendship yet.

"I wonder what it was like, him out alone in the cold night. Cops after him." Connie spoke to us, though she kept looking at Stammer.

"You ever notice his eyes?" Darlene gave a sigh. I shifted as I listened. I had noticed his eyes. I wasn't certain I liked them noticing, too.

"Yeah. He's like a husky dog. His eyes are so blue." Connie and Darlene shared a sly look that didn't include me.

I stared at Stammer. You couldn't see his eye colour from where we stood. I remembered, though, and the thought hit me right in my throat.

Stammer caught a base hit squarely in his glove. The smacking sound made Connie and Darlene give a little squeal. Stammer shot us a smile before pitching the ball back. His muscles bunched beneath his thin shirt as he swung his arm up and out.

Connie nudged Darlene hard enough to bump her into me. Darlene giggled. I held still.

"Look at the muscles in his arm."

Darlene sighed. "Yeah."

"Wonder what they look like up close." Connie linked her arm with Darlene's. Neither paid me any attention.

"Real close." Darlene chortled as she hugged in tight with Connie.

"Real, real close." Connie and Darlene said it at the same time. They looked at each other and bent over, laughing.

I stayed standing. My face musta reddened, though. Stammer looked over at us and paused. His eyebrows were higher than his hairline. Too bad he was looking at us, as he completely missed the line hit coming at him.

The other boys cat-called as Stammer scrambled to grab the ball and make it back to first. When he returned, the runner was already safe and smirking.

"Oh geez it." Stammer shrugged and tossed the ball back to the pitcher.

The pitcher stole a look at us girls and gave Stammer a grin.

Stammer grinned too, smacked his glove and took his ready stance.

Connie and Darlene put their heads together and whispered some. I heard them repeat "real close" a few more times. Each time they said it, my shoulders sagged. I couldn't wait for lunch to be over so Connie and Darlene stopped talking about Stammer. The bell hadn't rung, but it was time to go.

Miss Oswin appeared at the top of the school stairs as I approached. She rang the bell good and loud. I didn't so much notice her arm-wings waggle this time. She'd been mostly nice, so these things tend to fade out when you like someone.

I waited at the bottom steps for the younger students to pass.

"Connie, Darlene, Stani, please hurry." Miss Oswin held a hand to her mouth as she called out.

Looking back gave me my first pang of pain not related to Dot. Stammer walked towards me. Connie and Darlene flanked him on either side. All three were together, laughing.

18

It was only Grandpa and me going to church on Sunday.

Gram didn't get out of bed for most of the week. I wasn't allowed to walk in the halls upstairs unless I absolutely had to. Grandpa kept me downstairs, busy with chores to keep me quiet. The few times I managed to glimpse in their room, Gram was alone, wearing the same nightie. A couple of dishes were stacked beside her, both with food still sitting uneaten.

On Sunday, Grandpa gave her a holler from downstairs.

"Grace? We got the fundraiser today."

The upstairs was silent.

Grandpa clomped up the staircase, forgetting his shoes. "They'd be happy just to have you come and watch."

I snuck upstairs and peeked through the door. Grandpa was inside the room, coaxing Gram with her best dress. Gram wasn't talking, though. She just lay there and nodded whenever Grandpa said her name. She finally sighed and waved Grandpa off.

"I'll be better tomorrow. Just let me have some peace, today."

Grandpa slumped in a chair beside the bed. He was silent a moment before shaking his head.

"You oughta get up. We didn't lose both of them. There's still Ellen to think of."

I couldn't get a good look at Gram's face, but her next words sent me scurrying away from the door. Funny how words are that powerful.

"I don't know if I could face Ellen right now." Gram? Disappointed? In me or herself? Either way, I didn't want to know. Still, I stayed waiting to see who was stronger, Gram or Grandpa.

In the beginning, Grandpa won. Then Gram did, after.

Heavy footsteps paced the room before Grandpa appeared at the door. He considered me a moment before grunting.

"Go get dressed, missy."

I had to walk by him to get to my room, so I got a good glance at Grandma. She was still in bed, but the bed covers were crumpled by her feet. She swung her legs over the edge as I passed. There she sat.

I paused, but Grandpa gave me a tap on the back of my shoulders to shoo me away. From behind, I could hear him talking to Gram through the doorway.

"At least try."

Gram made it out of the room. She didn't look like she'd make it down the hall. Big tears rolled down her face. A few fell and stained her already-dirty nightie.

A sigh as heavy as a rainstorm poured out of Grandpa. He reached for Gram and held her close. Then he guided her back to bed.

One of the boarders came upstairs and caught the last moments. He'd asked for new sheets for his bed a couple days ago. Grandpa had said when Gram was ready. I think the boarder was wondering if that would ever happen.

The boarder went off to his room, leaving the hallway empty. I could still hear Grandpa murmuring. Gram didn't answer.

No matter how hard it is to see kid tears, grown-up tears are worse to watch. The walls they break through are that much thicker, so the damage that caused them must be disaster, indeed.

Even though it was Grandpa taking me, I still had to wear a dress to church. I didn't mind the colour so much. Brown is good for hiding. The brown birds keep their nests safer, as no one can spot them in the darkness of the trees.

Church was the usual. I sat and tried not to fidget. Grandpa crossed his arms and tucked his chin in as he listened. His occasional frown made the wrinkles of his cheeks deeper. We had a lot more space between us, being the only two in the pew. Yet after communion, we ended up tight beside each other. I liked the warmth of Grandpa's coat.

People nodded as Grandpa and I made our way from our pew. Grandpa paused more than usual to talk with the women. They all wanted to know how Gram was doing. Seems Gram had been through this before, and they were kinda expecting it.

"Don't forget to pass Grace a Hello." Mrs. Dionne had Grandpa's arm in both her hands. She wasn't letting go. "We missed her this morning."

Grandpa harrumphed. "I'm sure the baking will be just fine without her."

"We miss having her apple pie, though." Mrs. Dionne offered Grandpa's arm an extra rub before releasing.

"We'll have some of her pie soon enough." Grandpa gave Mrs. Dionne his own pat. "How's the collection going?"

"Really well. Today should raise the rest of the money."

Grandpa nodded. "That's good. The boys deserve it."

Most Sundays, we ended up in the church basement after mass for tea and socializing. I managed to skip the one after Dot's funeral. Today was Gram's turn to pass, as she hadn't even made it to church. I don't think Grandpa was too pleased to be going to the tea without her. He kept looking at the cross by the altar, as if hoping Jesus would climb down and accompany him back to the hotel bar for a sit and a drink. Grandpa and I attended the tea anyways, after we mingled outside with the others. His boots clumped loud behind me as we went down the church basement stairs.

Stammer was two heads in front of me. You could see the side of his face when the stairs went around a corner. He had shaved off his wisps that were pretending to be facial hair. New shirt, too, or at least a clean one.

"*Stani.*" I said it loud enough for the whole stairwell to hear. People turned to see who made the holler. A couple older women smiled at me. I hate *oh-isn't-she-cute* looks.

Stammer acted like he didn't hear me. He never looked back.

I watched him mingle with the crowd around the raffle table. Connie sidled up and gave his arm a tug. He turned and smiled wide-mouthed. I could tell by his shoulder set that he was holding back a few tics.

Grandpa almost ran into me, stalled as I was on the last step of the stairs. He gave me a push between the shoulder blades to get going. "Ellen, you're leading the parade."

"Sorry." No choice but to go join the churchgoers hovering around the tables. I steered clear of the raffle table and headed for the desserts. Darlene was there, pouring herself a drink of juice from a clear glass jug.

"You want one?"

I shook my head. "No, thanks. I'm not thirsty."

"Suit yourself. It's free." Darlene turned to look at Connie and Stammer. She winced when Stammer leaned in to listen to something Connie said.

"You think he's asking her out?" Darlene kept eyes on the two as she lifted her drink.

"Maybe." Darlene asking me? Huh? "Likely. Yes. I mean, just look at them."

I took my own advice. Stammer had his hand at Connie's elbow and was steering her towards us.

"Shit." Darlene took another swig of juice like she hoped it was liquor.

"Hey, girls." Connie's cheeks were flushed. "I'm supposed to take a turn at the raffle tickets but…" Connie let the words trail out. She shrugged and looked sideways at Stammer.

Darlene thinned her lips and said nothing.

"Would either of you take my spot?" Connie gave a wiggle of her shoulders as Stammer caught her hand and intertwined her fingers with his.

All four of us were quiet as Connie realized Darlene wouldn't speak.

"I'll do it." I'll admit, I was opportunistic. Darlene was always nicer than Connie, but what kid don't seize the day when the most popular girl needs a favour?

"Oh, great. Thanks." Connie and Stammer had already turned to go.

Stammer gave me a look over Connie's shoulder. He suppressed an arm twitch, but I could see Connie shake her hand as if he'd suddenly stung her.

"Great. Just great." Darlene mimicked Connie's voice. She slammed her glass onto the table beside us. "Like Connie's any better than me. You know she was the first to call him Stammer?"

I shook my head and stayed mute. I suspected it best not to get involved in that. You never know when someone will turn on you if allegiances rearrange.

"I gotta go help the raffle."

Darlene squinted. "She won't remember you helping, you know."

Not much to say to that. I just nodded and left.

Mrs. Dionne, of course, was in charge of the raffle table. She'd laid raffle items out in front of paper bags that slowly filled with paper tickets. A big sign hung behind the table. *Charity Raffle*. Big, strokey letters were filled in with coloured paint. Mrs.

Dionne stood just underneath the double f's, so she looked like she had pink and purple rabbit ears.

"Where's Connie, dear?" Mrs. Dionne cocked her head, making her look even more like Dot's stuffed bunny.

I swallowed a mite of bile that somehow gorged my throat. Dot woulda loved that sign. I barely remembered helping make it this week at school. "Connie asked me to help."

"That girl, I swear." Mrs. Dionne shook her head. "Well, since you're here, Ellen, I may as well show you." She hoisted a large roll of paper coupons from the table. "These here are the tickets. You give them one half of the strip, and you keep the other half. Hold out your arm and I'll show you."

I let Mrs. Dionne measure out a strip of coupons on my arm. Her scissors came close to cutting my dress when she snipped the coupons free of the roll. No apology, though.

"How are the sales going, Mrs. Dionne?" Mr. Oswin stood in front of us. He pinked up when he caught my eye. Otherwise, he ignored me.

"We've got enough for the uniforms and a new catcher's mask. Mr. Dionne plans on donating some extra bats and balls." Mrs. Dionne spoke like her husband just saved Britain from Germany.

Mr. Oswin smiled. "The team will be glad to hear the news. I want to thank you for all your hard work."

"Mrs. Dionne had some help, you know." One of the other ladies swept up beside Mr. Oswin and right into the conversation. She gave Mr. Oswin's arm a squeeze.

Mrs. Dionne didn't quite stifle a frown before plastering her own smile back on. "Gertie's right. It takes a team effort to help."

The woman kept looking at Mr. Oswin as she answered. "We are a great team. And Mr. Oswin, my son sure appreciates the time you put in coaching. It's the least we can do to help."

More pink colour appeared on Mr. Oswin's face. I don't think he minded the cause of it, though, as he let Mrs. Dionne reach a hand out to touch him as well.

"You just keep coaching, and we'll make sure our boys can hold their heads high when they're out on the field." Mrs. Dionne took her hand back as she scanned the crowd and busied herself with the baking for sale.

I looked, too. Nothing stuck out. All I could see was Grandpa talking with Mr. Dionne a few steps away. Mr. Dionne caught my eye. He hooked his thumbs in his pants as he talked, while Grandpa nodded in return.

I snuck peeks at Mr. Oswin while he chatted with the ladies. He'd filled out some since the circus and had a haircut. His face no longer jutted angular, with his teeth fighting his nose for protrusion champ title. He looked handsome. Maybe it was 'cause his eyes held a smile now. Maybe his shoulders were held up and back. I saw more than one woman sidle up to join the conversation. Each new one edged in beside Mr. Oswin. I think it made him flush more.

I glanced at Mrs. Dionne as each new woman came up. Mrs. Dionne had the thinnest lips I'd ever seen. She looked like she swallowed them. Her sourness seeped through into the baking tray she was holding. I swear I saw the icing shrivel on each muffin she touched.

"Humph."

None of the ladies looked up at Mrs. Dionne's warning. She finally clapped her hands loud to get everyone's attention.

"Okay, ladies. We're blocking the table. We want to sell tickets, so if you're not buying, please help sell them."

I've seen geese move when a dog approaches. Nobody paid her attention. Nobody moved. Mrs. Dionne ain't no dog.

I had a feeling Mr. Dionne was.

You could feel him coming. A murmur preceded him. The women parted and let Mr. Dionne through. He stared at Mr. Oswin, who hadn't budged.

"Ladies." Mr. Dionne said it to all, but looked at his wife. She blushed and smiled. The women tittered and moved on, leaving Mr. Oswin standing alone with Mr. Dionne.

"Seems like we'll have a good ball team this year."

Mr. Oswin nodded. "I'm pretty proud of their efforts so far. We'll see when we get the team on the field, though."

Mr. Oswin moved off, leaving Mr. Dionne standing alone at the table.

"Ellen." He looked at me and nodded. "Where's Constance? Isn't she supposed to be helping?"

"Constance is coming later. She traded shifts with Ellen." Mrs. Dionne grabbed my hand as she spoke. I'll admit, I cringed. I hate being touched by an adult I don't know.

Mr. Dionne looked around.

"She's probably with Darlene." Mrs. Dionne continued to hold my hand.

I could see Darlene still over by the drink table. She didn't look like she was with anyone. Even the Dionnes could see that. Connie came into view with Stammer. She stopped in her tracks and held a big 'Oh' on her face.

Mr. Dionne went red.

I couldn't process it, as a few girls came up to buy some baking. They were the same age as Dot. I looked over at Grandpa, wondering where he was. He was talking to Mr. Oswin. I wished he would finish, so we could go.

19

While Gram stayed upstairs in bed, Grandpa didn't ask me to do much of the cooking. I didn't offer, either. I only set to clean up any mess in the kitchen that the day left behind. Grandpa was better at cooking than me, but occasionally, he still let me try. Not often, though. Teaching me woulda meant more conversation and more sharing. What we had already, sitting together during mealtime, was more than enough for both of us.

My idea of lunch includes sandwiches. In that respect, Grandpa and I don't differ much. He's good at fixing sandwiches. I want a different sandwich every day, though. Grandpa don't. He's not partial to egg salad, or ham, or cheese. Just chicken. I was tired of chicken by the second day. I know Grandpa never got tired of its bland, predictable taste.

Gram was down for lunch when I got home. I was surprised to see her sitting there, bathed in daylight. Gram looked up as I entered. She smiled a nice Gram smile. It didn't last more than a second, though. Then, she kept watch on her hands folded on the table. She scrutinized them, like she was willing them to start up and move again. I looked like that once at a raccoon I saw dead in the road. I couldn't believe that it was still. Raccoons keep moving, even when hurt. I know as I seen one shot before. I crouched over the coon and gave it a prod with a stick, but it still didn't move. Grandpa was prodding Gram like that. His stick was the words he used. They weren't sharp enough to get her moving, though. That's what I reckoned.

"Well, look who's here, Gram." Grandpa laid a hand on Gram's shoulder.

Gram peered at me again. "Elly," is all she said.

"Hi, Gram." I leaned in to give her a hug and a kiss. I could feel Grandpa's nod of approval, even though he was out of my sightline.

"How was school?" Grandpa called out over his shoulder as he was cutting the sandwiches.

"Pretty good." Odd to have Gram's questions come out of Grandpa's mouth. I still wasn't used to it. It was like he was trying to be two of them mixed together.

"We're still working on that Shakespeare play."

"Oh?" I could tell that Grandpa was really interested. He never raised his voice up a scale unless he was.

"Yeah. Miss Oswin has got us memorizing soliloquys." I left the sentence hanging. I coulda added that Miss Oswin was arranging a school recital, but I wanted to be asked why. Sometimes, I liked seeing if people paid attention that I had more to say.

Grandpa looked up, like he heard my thought burn the air. Gram just stayed put.

"Which one did she give you?" Grandpa came close to the table, holding a plate of sandwiches. He laid a sandwich on each of our plates, then sat himself down.

I eased a chair out and sat next to Gram. "*Twelfth Night* again. I gotta read the part where she's thinking about the ring the woman gave."

I saw Grandpa nod as he picked up his food. "I know that one. It's a good one."

"I don't think I can eat." Gram's words cut through our lunch. She rubbed one of her wrists and pushed back in her chair. "I…"

We waited for Gram to finish her thought. She didn't. Her chair scraped again as she stood and held on to the table. Her morning robe was creased from being worn every day. I wondered how long it took for Grandpa to coax her downstairs.

"I'm not fit for today." Gram's voice wavered as she spoke.

"It'll ease. Give it time." Grandpa kept chewing like Gram was discussing the weather.

"No. Not today."

"Try."

"I said, not today."

Grandpa laid his sandwich down and took a long look at Gram. His mouth worked, then settled into a tight-noosed "Oh." He scratched his chin like he was out of ideas.

Nobody spoke. The air hung thick like when Dot and I had an argument. I heard Mam's voice telling me my responsibility. I gotta speak first.

"We've got a school recital." I had to spread my cards out full, to move us away from the pull of Gram's pain. "It's in two weeks."

Gram stared at the table. I don't think she heard. Grandpa still held his peace.

"I said, it's for a school recital, my soliloquy. I've got one of the bigger parts. We've been practicing." It was as much as I wanted to say.

Still, nobody spoke. Maybe they were thinking over this new threat to Gram's hiding from things. It was a risky throw.

"We'll have to go see that." Grandpa raised his sandwich for another bite.

"I'm going upstairs." Gram stood and shuffled out of the kitchen. She didn't look back to wish me a happy afternoon. She disappeared into the gloom of the hallway.

Grandpa kept chewing.

I don't think I helped.

"Carl?"

We both jumped to hear Gram's voice from the hall. I don't know who moved faster, me or Grandpa.

Gram was holding onto the railing at the bottom of the stairs. She sunk down onto the final step.

In front of her stood a Royal policeman. He held his hat and shifted it, his hands feeling up and down the rim.

"Morning, ma'am, sir. He nodded at us all, then looked down at his hat.

Grandpa's shoulders sagged. "Morning, officer. How can we help you?"

I didn't think the man was here for a drink.

"I've got some news to tell you. You think you could come into your parlour?"

Grandpa moved past me and reached for Gram. When he couldn't lift her, the officer stepped in to help. The two of them managed to raise Gram back up to her full height. Even then, she looked like she'd lost a few inches. I bet I was as tall as her now. Not that it made a difference.

Grandpa and the officer moved Gram to a seat. I trailed behind and stood in the doorway to the parlour. I had time to kill before school. Besides, I was interested. I knew it was about Dot.

They set Gram as easy as they could in the chair. One of her purple crochet doilies got knocked to the floor, and the officer trod on it before anyone noticed. His boots weren't clean, so a patch of mud smeared across the yarn square. I daren't go and pick it up. They mighta noticed me and shooed me away so I couldn't hear.

The front door opened while they fussed with Gram, and Billy Harner walked in.

"Hi there, sweets. You alone?" A fair question, I guess. He said it all nice.

"No. They're in the parlour." I pointed to emphasize my words.

Billy came close and peered into the parlour. He laid a hand on my shoulder as he craned over my head.

Grandpa looked up and saw us.

"Billy?"

"Afternoon, all. I was hoping the bar was open. I could use some company."

"I'm busy, Billy."

"I was really hoping for a drink of something."

I could feel Billy's words over the top of my head. A waft of tobacco tickled my nose.

Grandpa nodded. "Go make yourself at home. You can take what you like, and we'll square up later."

"Thanks. You're a pal." I could feel Billy shift behind me. He gave my bottom a little nudge that made me jump.

"Oh, sorry." His voice had a snort in it.

I held still, wondering what to do.

Billy moved back and went into the bar.

The officer stayed standing in front of Gram. "Sir, ma'am."

Grandpa cleared his throat.

"I don't think I'm strong enough to hear this." Gram reached in her robe pocket. She pulled out a wad of tissues that looked big enough to play ball with. One came loose in her hand, as the rest tumble-wafted to the ground.

"We have to." Grandpa sat down in the chair beside Gram. I think he was tired of standing.

"Well, it isn't much news but it needs telling." The officer took up his hat rim rolling again.

I moved to one side of the parlour door and leaned behind it. I wanted to hear and not hear at the same time. I wanted to see but not be seen. It was about Dot.

"We found your granddaughter's dress."

Gram's sharp intake of breath hid my own.

"Where?" Grandpa was back to single words. I had none.

"There's a small forest by the grounds where your grand-daughter was last seen. We found the dress in the underbrush there."

Gram slouched farther in her chair.

"Go on." Grandpa's voice shook as he said it.

"No more." I breathed my request, but no one heard it. I was too well-shaded in the hall.

The officer paused, like he was taking aim to deliver a final shot. "There was blood on the dress. It matches what we found on the autopsy. I'm so sorry."

Both Gram and Grandpa dipped their heads. I wanted to barge in and hug 'em, but I was the cause. I wanted to run, punch, jump, turn, twist, scream, cry. I wanted to do something, anything, just to make them lift their heads and smile again. But I couldn't.

I stepped back. I'll admit, I was shaking. I don't know what I looked like.

Billy musta seen something, because he was outta the bar again, standing in front of me in the hall. He gave a look behind him, but nobody from the parlour poked their head out.

"You okay?"

I shook my head. A couple of tears fell free.

Billy lifted a hand and stroked my cheek. "Aw, sweets."

I let him for a moment. Then I dipped my head and stepped away. When I lifted my eyes, Billy was staring at me. He didn't smile this time, so I didn't see his teeth.

Dot wasn't alive. She sure wasn't living in that moment I shared with Billy.

Billy raised his eyebrows.

I couldn't stop looking.

"Elly?" Grandpa's voice called out from the parlour. I didn't answer.

I went out the back.

Billy went out the front.

I went and hid in the old outhouse by the chicken coop. I had already been in there alone a few times, when I needed to release my tears. It smelled of me now, though the old shit stink still lingered. Sunrays washed through the moon-shaped window. Outside shadows made the light flicker, and the birds stopped singing. It made me catch my breath, prick my ears. I heard footsteps approach, and the door to my sanctuary let out a creak.

I didn't go to school that afternoon.

20

I have to tell somebody, Dot. There's no one to tell, though. I used to tell Mam these things at bedtime. She'd listen. You'd listen, too. Mam used to tuck us in and turn out the lights. She'd linger for a few moments, hearing our day's last worries. She'd let us talk until we ran out of words, and the only sound left would be our breathing. Sometimes, I'd fool her and start breathing the same as you, since you always fell asleep first. So I could enjoy the silence of her. The peace of us. Together. It wouldn't last long. Mam would give us one more kiss on the forehead before she left. Every night, she left. But she was always there in the morning, and we could talk again. Those moments meant that we were safe, Dot.

I miss you, Dot. More than I ever told you. More than you'll ever know. I'm alone in our room, now. It's cold. You used to warm yourself on me and cuddle up to my back-side as I'd tell you go to sleep. I miss you tucking a leg in between mine. I'd shoo you off, as your foot was cold, and I didn't wanna be stuck in one position the whole night. I miss your little hand reaching out to touch my cheek in the morning if you woke first. It meant you felt safe. It made me feel safe, too. You stopped reaching when Mam died. You just lay there with your hair all jumbled. You'd scrinch your eyes when the light started to hit, but you wouldn't move. I know you didn't wanna wake first. When Mam was alive, you'd get up when I rose and start chirping with the outside critters, singing and swinging that rabbit around. When Mam died, you stopped that, too.

Your rag rabbit misses you. I know that, at least. One of his eyes fell off. It's like he can't see happiness anymore. I think I crushed it off, as I've taken to sleeping with him. I'm not the best bed partner, though: I find him flung wide and clear of the bed most mornings. Maybe he jumps from me, as he knows I'm the one who let you down.

I have nobody to talk to. That's why I'm up now, in our bed. In my bed. Sitting up crouched over my knees. My whole body aches. I feel like I'm bleeding inside. My cheeks sting so bad. I didn't know that tears hurt so much. I thought they were meant to help, to wash the sorrows outta you. They don't.

It's nighttime that's worst, Dot. I can't see or feel you. The darkness is deep around me. It's no good to try and sleep when you'll only get woken by your thoughts.

Not even reading helps. I stare at the words, and they jumble all over me. They grab at me, pinching my soft innards, making me cry out 'cause I can't hold them in no more. I try to forget the words and just look at the birds, but they don't seem alive anymore: they're flat on the pages. Their wings are clipped and they wait for me to close the book, so they can try and re-grow themselves again. In private. Deep down in their private spaces, on my pages.

My thoughts are bad, the waking ones. The sleeping ones are worse.

I'm in a box. I'm pounding on the lid, and you open it. You look at me as I cry. You shake your head and say, "No more. No more." Then you close me up again. I wake shaking.

I didn't mean to close you up in your box, Dot. I left you, and you were gone, and you didn't come back.

Gram and Grandpa don't talk about you around me. At least, Grandpa don't. Gram won't even talk.

Grandpa talks more, though. You woulda liked his voice. It's all deep and growly, like he got pinched or something. I bet when he's not dipped in sadness, there's a rumble to it that would make your heart ease. I know him better now.

I don't know about Gram really, as she's shut in her room most times. I hear her shuffling in the hall at night. I heard her just now. It wasn't what woke me up, though. I could run to her, I guess, but she's got this faraway look in her eyes now. She hasn't hummed in the kitchen for a while. She barely goes there at all. Grandpa does the cooking. He's not bad at it. He's not good, either.

Gram is still out in the hall. I heard her pause at the top of the stairs, then go back to her room. I don't think it was a boarder. We lost another one of them yesterday. He moved on to stay with the family he works for. I don't think he liked the hotel so much, since Gram gave up the cleaning. I saw him wrinkle his nose once, when he walked up stairs. He works on a farm, so I know what he smelled musta been bad.

You woke me up, Dot. I was sleeping and dreaming of myself, and you woke me. It doesn't have to be a give and take, though. Why do you have to sleep for me to be alive?

I'm in the box, and there's a light that shines through a hole in the lid. I can see the moon, but I can't touch it. It can touch me. It hurts me. The moon is hard, and it pricks me and I scream. You open the box, and you tell me "No more." Then, you close the box again. And I'm alone in the box. I'm crying. I can't stop crying, 'cause I won't see you no more.

21

I didn't feel so bad at school next day. Sure, I kept flipping between giddy and self-hate, but what growing kid doesn't? I hugged myself at times to make sure I was all there.

I was still in the hold of my nightmare. I thought of that box a lot. And the moon grabbing me.

It was so tough to concentrate that I missed being called on by Miss Oswin.

"Wake up, Rabies." Connie's eraser tip gave me a poke. She didn't poke so hard anymore. Felt kinda like a tickle.

I snuck a grin back, then sat up straight. Connie's playful actions were louder than the snipe. Anyways, who am I to argue with what people call me? If they knew what I'd done, they'd probably call me worse.

"Yes, ma'am?"

Miss Oswin stared at me before shaking her head. "Ellen, I want you to pay better attention from now on. Please look at your book and read the next passage."

I could tell her patience with me had worn thin. There'd be no more *You-poor-dear-Dot-is-dead* breaks.

I looked down as I cleared my throat. My textbook wasn't even open. I know there musta been embarrassed heat coming off me, 'cause more than one student turned around to have a good look. Behind me, Connie muffled a giggle.

Darlene slid her book over while keeping watch straight ahead. She left a finger on the word I was to start at.

"On July 6, 1885, Louis Riel was charged with treason against the Dominion of Canada. His trial began on July 20, 1885, in Regina, Saskatchewan. He was sentenced to hang on November 16, 1885. With Riel's hanging, the Northwest Rebellion came to an end, and justice was won for the murder of Thomas Scott."

I gulped at the end of my reading. It was a good lesson. There were harsh consequences to stepping outta line.

"We're not called Dominion anymore."

I sat up, shocked to hear Stammer's voice. Not one tic or stutter in it, either.

Miss Oswin raised herself over her book. "I beg your pardon?"

Stammer shifted and let a tic out. "I s-said, we're not called D-Dominion of Canada anymore. This history book, it's out of date."

We all sat stunned. Admittedly, it was a minor point, but who would ever challenge what we learned? Who would argue with a teacher?

"My uncle said we're just Canada now. Or we ought to be."

I couldn't look at Stammer, so I kept close eye on Miss Oswin. She didn't get mad or nothing. I never seen a teacher let a sentence hang like that and not give a cannon blast back.

Miss Oswin leaned back on her desk. I swear, we heard it groan in protest. "I don't think the name really matters so much as the country, Stanislaw."

We thought that was the end of it, but Stammer didn't.

"Names matters, ma'am. They m-matter a lot. Words got the power to hurt or to heal."

Miss Oswin pursed her lips. You could see her debate shutting Stammer down, but his speech sounded too much like a Sunday sermon. Maybe it was the hurt he hid behind them.

She obviously thought better of it. "That was well said, Stani-slaw. I think we'll keep an eye out for the name change."

Sometimes people time their breaths together. At Miss Oswin's words, everyone expelled the same sigh of relief.

"Well, we still have time before lunch, so I'd like the younger grades up at my desk. Bring your spellers. Older grades, do the questions beside the passage in your history books."

Stammer said nothing in return. I supposed he was sat-isfied with Miss Oswin's response. When I turned to catch a better look at him, I noticed Connie. She had her nose buried in her textbook. The whiteness of the pages stood out even more from the flush that heated Connie's cheeks. She wasn't looking at Stammer.

I snuck another peek. Stammer was looking at her.

What?

I musta said it out loud. Darlene nudged me.

"Connie's da don't like Stammer's uncle. Says he's a killer."

"Huh?"

Darlene's turn to blush, as she remembered whom she was speaking to. She persisted anyways. "Everyone knows Stammer's uncle killed your sister."

I swallowed my temper at her remark. I didn't know if Darlene was trying to get a rise outta me or just plain stupid. I chose the latter explanation, seeing as it best fit her case.

I risked another gawk at Stammer. I could see the heat in his face as he tried to get Connie's attention.

I thought of Stammer's confession before our kiss, his secret about his true family. Best to play dumb. "I thought eve-ryone likes Stammer's uncle."

"They like him to a point." Darlene giggled as she spoke. "And that point is the top of a jug of moonshine."

I wondered what set Stammer off to challenge the teacher. Names. Stammer's uncle had a new name. Killer. Stam-mer wouldn't have liked that. He never blinked when the boys called him Stammer. He obviously felt different when it came to family.

Darlene giggled again. She was obviously enjoying herself. "Connie's da thinks criminals run in the family, and that Stammer will turn out just like his uncle. Mr. Dionne won't let Connie date Stammer."

Connie looked up. She glanced at Darlene and busied herself again, erasing what she'd just wrote in her scribbler.

"Connie." Darlene's whisper cut across me.

Connie didn't respond.

"How's your boyfriend? Has he hurt anyone yet?" Darlene smothered a laugh behind her hand.

Connie kept watch on her book, but her forehead creased.

I knew an answer to that question. Who had Stammer hurt? I shook my head free of jealousy and self-pity, and turned back to my work. I kept close to myself until lunch.

Stammer was in the outfield again. Seems his status depended on notoriety. Having a suspected killer for an uncle was the wrong type of infamy. Suited me fine. I got a chance to talk to him when nobody was around. I snuck over and sat in the underbrush next to him.

"Psst."

No response. How much concentration did you need in the outfield?

"Hey." This time I waved from under the shrubs.

Stammer spared me a brief look, then ignored me.

"I wanna tell you something."

Stammer smacked his glove, staying in an expectant crouch. I might as well not been there.

"Stani, please. I got something to say."

"So say it."

I took a big breath. "I was wrong to run."

Stammer shook his head slowly, like I didn't understand a math problem. "It was your choice."

"Can we at least be friends?"

"I guess."

Thwack.

A ball was headed our way. Stammer kept his eye on it as it descended fast. I kept watch, too. He caught it easily and sent it back.

"You mean it?"

Stammer shook his head again. "I said, I guess."

That was all I was gonna get. It was the same feeling as when you're at the end of a book, and the last few pages are ripped out. You're done, but you don't feel finished.

I inched backwards from under the bush. Stammer ignored my movement, keeping his eye on the infield play. It wasn't until after that I remembered, Stammer hadn't twitched once. I don't think that was a good sign for us.

Biggest surprise of the day happened soon after. I found Connie standing at the side of the field. That wasn't the surprise. Darlene was the surprise. She was striding away from Connie, holding her head high, laughing, mocking Stammer as she left.

"Stammer's uncle's in the slammer!"

Connie stood there with clenched fists, body shaking with held back anger. She winced when she spotted me coming to join her.

"Hi?" I was curious. Did the tremors mean a major earthquake or just a few friendship jolts?

"Don't. Just don't." Connie ground her words out and spat them at me.

"Don't what?" Connie didn't look so scary standing alone.

Connie shook her head. "Don't ask me anything, okay?"

That put a stop to my questions. I felt daring, though. She had Stammer, so why'd she need to control what I said, too?

"I wasn't gonna." I paused, as Connie's face remained puckered. My boldness evaporated as I tried to think of something to appease her. "They should put Stammer back on first base. He's good at it."

Hard to keep angry when your desire is spoken loud. That's what I guessed happened to Connie. She forgot herself.

"Oh! I thought so, too! Stammer throws and catches real well. He's wasted out there. Nobody's strong enough to hit that far, except the older boys." Connie sighed. "I wish they'd move him in close again."

Word onslaught. Each word more painful than the last. Connie still liked Stammer.

"Yeah. He's pretty good." I shrugged to defuse any sense of my interest. "Well, see ya."

Connie didn't stop my leaving. She stayed to watch Stammer play.

22

Pound. Pound. Pound.

"Ellen? You done in there?"

Pound. Pound. Pound.

"Ellen?"

You can't really ignore Grandpa when he wants to be noticed.

"In a minute, Grandpa." Even so, I ignored him. I wasn't done, yet.

"Just how long is this minute?"

I had to smirk at that one. Heh. Grandpa. He usually doesn't bother with a snappy comeback.

Grandpa did like to sit a while in the bathroom every morning. It's no matter during the week when no one's around, but it was Saturday. I was mucking with his routine. He was probably pacing in front of the bathroom door with his newspaper.

Pound. Pound. Pound. Pound.

I didn't answer this time. Grandpa muttered a few words before retreating. His bowels could wait.

I leaned to continue my scrutinizing in the small mirror above the sink. The mirror's edges were fogged from my bath, but I could still see myself. Mam wasn't looking back at me, that's for sure. Neither was Dot. My features came straight down the McGuinty line. Da's nose, sharp and handsome, jutted out from the glass. Mam loved that nose. Said it was the loveliest thing-other than his eyes-on Da's face. I wasn't so certain it looked good on a girl. Mam said no worries when I asked her why Dot's nose was small and mine was big. She said it didn't matter the size, as long as it wasn't a nose for trouble.

I think I got one for trouble.

My eyes were all Da, or so Mam said. Same furrow between, same dark brown, like nighttime hitting the earth. Mam said she could spend hours looking in Da's eyes, falling into their depths. She didn't say it to Dot or me. I heard her talking it late one night, when a girlfriend stayed over. Seems saying those thoughts aloud is only safe in the dark. Hearing it comforted me, though. At least I had my peepers going for me.

Dot's eyes were blue. Figures she'd get the sky for her look. She used to be luckier than me. Maybe it's better to have luck doled out in small pieces.

More footsteps sounded in the hall, strong heavy ones. It wasn't Gram. Hers had become halting when she did choose to pace. Mostly, she was in her room. I sat back on the edge of the tub with my towel around my waist. I didn't have a straight clean line down my body no more. Bumps and curves appeared where before I was reed-thin. Things were changing faster than a single day could account for.

No one was in the hall, so I slipped out to get back to my room. I paused at Gram's door, like usual. Gram was not quiet. I could hear her talking.

The door made only one tiny squeak as I eased it open. Gram stood by the window in her nightie.

"Beds, bathroom, kitchen, parlour, stairs." Her voice sing-songed as she listed the house out loud.

I almost spoke out of curiosity, but remembered what Grandpa had told me. Gram needed her time to herself now.

"Beds, bathroom, kitchen, parlour, stairs."

Maybe I'd tell Grandpa about it.

I forgot by the time I was dressed and downstairs. Grandpa wasn't anywhere. Billy Harner was in the bar as I passed. He turned to face me while he took a swig.

"Is Grandpa around?" I wasn't so scared of him now. Much.

Billy shook his head. "He went out back."

"Oh. What for?"

Billy grinned and mimed unbuckling his pants. "He had a little business."

I flushed, but not because of Billy.

"Wanna join me for a drink, sweets?"

"Uhn-uhn." No way I was getting more involved with Billy. And I now had Grandpa to worry about.

"Suit yourself. Offer's open anytime." Billy winked. "God knows you're old enough now."

I didn't give him a reply. He didn't need one. He tipped his glass at me and took another swig.

"Ahhhhh." Billy grinned after he swallowed.

The bastard.

Grandpa wasn't in the kitchen. Here's where my fear kicked in. I looked out the backyard and saw him there. He was just standing with his newspaper tucked under one arm and looking down something in his hand. I needed a big breath to continue, but I had to find out.

"Hey, Grandpa." I eased the back door open all casual.

He looked up from what he was holding.

"The bathroom's free, now."

"I don't need it." Grandpa pinched his newspaper with his elbow and checked that his belt was done up.

I gulped and looked at the outhouse. Our rooster was perched on top with his head tucked under one wing. A couple chickens scratched the dirt by the door. They clucked contentedly as they bobbed their heads and pecked. The outhouse looked the same as usual. Its rotten boards were nailed closely together to make a place to shit in peace. I almost giggled at the thought of it. Outhouse. The door was closed, so maybe I was safe. Maybe Grandpa didn't know.

"Well if you do, I'm all done now." I moved to go back in the house.

"Ellen."

That he called me back was not good. Not good at all.

"Yeah?"

"What do you know about this?" Grandpa beckoned me forward.

"About what?"

"This." Grandpa held out his hand to show me a pack of cigarettes.

Just as I feared.

Grandpa flared his nostrils like he smelled a fart. "I found these in the outhouse. You take up smoking?"

Running would have guilted me, and I wasn't good at dodging blows while staying still. Best ploy would be to play coy, though I was new to that game. Time to learn.

"No. I was wondering if you were, though."

Grandpa glared back. "No. No, I haven't."

Fear probably smells like cigarettes on a young person's breath. I was glad I brushed my teeth already.

I shook my head. "They're not mine."

"They look like Billy's." Grandpa glowered over his glasses. He was quite good at that. I almost caved.

Our rooster chose that moment to crow. He flapped his wings hard as he gripped the roof in his claws. I was grateful for the distraction. It gave me time to think.

"Billy musta used the outhouse." Now that I said it, I knew how stupid it sounded.

"Oh? So, he hid cigarettes here, rather than keep 'em?" Grandpa wasn't buying it. "I'll have to talk with Billy about this." The pack of cigarettes was crushed in Grandpa's meaty hand as he closed his fist around it.

I could feel the past few days rush up into my cheeks. My eyes musta widened 'cause Grandpa gave a little start.

"Well?" Grandpa peered at me from over his glasses.

My toe started dragging in the dirt of its own accord. Hands shake when you don't want them to. I stuffed them in my pockets to hide.

"They're Billy's cigarettes. I took 'em to try."

"I thought so."

Involving Billy had the potential for a nightmare. I needed Dot's spirit to move free. I looked up with as much Dot in my eyes as I could muster.

"Please don't tell him, Grandpa." I don't think he'd miss 'em. The pack was almost done, anyways."

Grandpa chewed over this thought. His face soured, like someone put vinegar in his coffee. "I guess we can do it that way."

I sighed in relief.

"But I'm taking these. And I don't want to see you smoking. Ever."

"Yes, Grandpa." I hoped he'd take my mumble for a response.

"You hear me?"

"I said, yes, Grandpa." I put my eyes all wide again and hunched my shoulders.

Grandpa nodded. "We're done here."

I watched him go back in the house. I hoped Grandpa kept his promise. No way I wanted him talking to Billy about this. No way I wanted to be there if he did.

I opened the outhouse door when Grandpa was gone. The smell of Grandpa's shit hit me full in the face. I closed the door behind me and sat down beside the shit-hole. I could take the stink. I belonged in it.

The cigarettes had been tucked away on the shelf above the seating, underneath some old newspapers. I don't know how Grandpa found them. I'd hidden them pretty carefully.

My knees were still banged up from the last time I'd been in there. Billy had said "Sorry," and given me that pack as an apology.

"It's not like you didn't ask for it." Billy took one out and lit it after he spoke.

True.

But he hadn't stopped when I told him, "No more."

23

"You wanna practice together?"

Huh? Someone speaking to me? Worth a look.

"Elly?"

Darlene was leaning sideways. Her eyes were on Miss Oswin, but her lips were scrinched like she was shooting words at me.

"Yeah?"

"I said, you wanna practice our speeches together?"

I eyed Miss Oswin, too. She was writing math problems on the blackboard. Math. Addition. My life could use some addition.

"Sure."

"You wanna come over?"

My cheeks warmed with gratitude. I was adding a friend. Then the low. I almost said, *After I take Dot home.* Had to shake my head to dispel the pain.

Darlene frowned. "You don't?"

"No. I mean, yeah, sure." In my language, that's as good as a *Hell, yeah!* I snuck a peek to see how Darlene took my answer. She was busy copying down numbers, but she nodded. I didn't dare look back at Connie.

"Wait for me after the bell rings." Darlene gave my elbow a nudge, so the pencil line I made rocketed off the page.

I snorted.

Miss Oswin looked up to survey the class. "And that's how you do the addition with more than one number. Are there any questions?"

Connie musta raised her hand, as Miss Oswin looked over by me.

"Yes, Constance."

"May I go to the bathroom? I have a subtraction to do."

Students can hide giggles so no teacher's in on a joke. This time, we didn't bother. The boys erupted in roars.

Miss Oswin's face narrowed, or gave as close approximation as possible for her. Didn't help, though. It made the girls bold, and they pealed out their laughs. I did, too. Even the little ones joined in. One or two sat on their heels at their seats, bodies twisting with glee.

Miss Oswin picked up her bell and swung hard and fast. *Clang. Clang. Clang. Clang. Clang. Clang. Clang.*

My teeth juddered. I had to cover my ears. The sound hung in the air as us kids quieted.

I never heard Miss Oswin use force before. My old teacher had a ruler that measured his impatience. Miss Oswin was more the level-a-look type. I suspect her being riled up was new for most.

"Constance, come up here, please." Miss Oswin used polite language, but there was no hint of friendly in her voice. More than a few girls shrunk in their seats. The boys peered round and shared grins. This was good. I wished someone had brought popcorn.

Connie stood slow, like she was rising from a movie reel. She moved between students down the center aisle. Her hand trailed along Stammer's desk as she went past. He watched like a hawk who'd spotted a mouse den. The other boys did, too. Darlene hugged herself as she leaned forward. She didn't bother hiding her glee. A few moments passed before Connie got to the head of the class. She stood with hands folded in front of Miss Oswin.

"Constance, there is no excuse for that kind of joke."

"Yes, ma'am."

"It's filthy, and I won't have you speaking like that in my class."

"No, ma'am."

"Do you understand?"

"Yes, ma'am."

"Now, go and take your bathroom break. When you come back, you're not to stir from your desk."

"Yes, ma'am."

"And you will stay in for lunch."

"Yes, ma'am." Connie bowed her head, but even I caught her smirk. Miss Oswin was too close over Connie to see it.

"Would you look at that." Darlene breathed her words as she watched Connie make her way to the back door.

I looked.

Stammer had a hand out low to graze Connie's dress as she walked by.

Miss Oswin went back at the board, writing a new problem for us to solve. Darlene crouched again over her sheet, eraser shavings piled to the side as she struggled with her answers. I felt the same struggle, but about Connie. Last time she was in trouble, I nearly had a patch of Connie's hair in my hands. She'd blubbered like a rainstorm at being caught. Now she was cool as ice. I couldn't figure the change. I looked around to see what clues could be had.

Stammer was leaning on his desk, gazing upward. There was a quirk set in his lips. He musta felt my stare, 'cause he looked my way.

"Hey." I mouthed the word like it was an invitation. Who knows? It probably was.

Stammer raised his eyebrows. I raised mine back. He nodded, then looked down at his work. He avoided my eyes for the rest of the morning.

Miss Oswin rang the bell gentler to call us back from lunch. When we filed in, Stammer was inside, sitting backwards in my chair, bent over Connie's desk. Now that I noted, Stammer hadn't been in the outfield. I was too busy chatting with Darlene to wonder where he got to.

Connie gave me a cheeky grin. "He's in your seat."

You gotta laugh sometimes at the layers that go into words. So I did! Connie cracked up too, leaving Stammer looking back and forth between us.

"Take your seats, please."

That just set us laughing harder. Good thing people were still shuffling about, else Connie and I woulda been sunk for sure.

I heard snorts from Connie behind me over the next hour. Each one caused me to stifle a giggle. It felt good to be a kid again.

After school didn't have that usual lonely feeling. I was walking home with Darlene. Stammer and Connie were a few strides ahead. It didn't matter. Much. I was filed in place with them all, so I'd take what I could get.

"You like paper dolls?" Darlene poked my arm as she spoke.

I didn't, but no sense starting our friendship wrong-footed. "Sure, they're nice."

"I got some I could show you."

Dot had a couple of dolls when we lived in our old apartment. She spent so much time dressing and undressing them that their arms and legs ripped off. Mam let Dot keep those broken dolls, though why you'd want a doll like that, I couldn't figure. Why you'd want a doll at all made no sense to me. Dot had left them when we moved. Best guess I had was their damaged bodies were a reminder of our loss.

"Sure, that'd be nice." Anything would be nice, just to be included.

Darlene perked up and started describing her favourite doll clothes. My eyes glazed over, but I managed to nod at all the right spots.

"They're gone."

"Huh?"

Darlene gave me a nudge in the ribs and pointed ahead. "Connie and Stammer. They were here a minute ago. Now they're gone."

We had just come out of a curve in the path. The trees on either side hung over us, like we were being marshalled through a sword salute. Stammer and Connie shoulda been right in the clear in front of us.

But they weren't.

"Where'd you think they got to?" My curiosity was burning. What Houdini trick was at work here? I sniffed the air, hoping to flush out the scent of Stammer. Nothing but pine cones and sap.

"Oh, this is gonna be good." Darlene crowed as she hung onto my arm. "You know where they're going, don'tcha?"

No, where? Dammit. Tell me. Don't make me ask.

"No."

Darlene sphinx-smiled at me, but held onto her secret.

"Tell me." Dammit.

"Look." Darlene pointed to the side of the path. Trees grew thick and heavy beside us. Heavy underbrush concealed the tree roots, throwing down leaves and rot from its wastings. A small space could be seen between two bent and broken trees, exposing a gap in the shrubs and bushes.

Of course. They left the path, same as I did once, with Stammer chasing. Back then, Stammer and I had foraged through the thick underbrush, making a new path with our tramping. This time, there was a clear path, and Connie had taken it with Stammer.

"We're going after them." Darlene gave my arm a tug. "C'mon."

I balked. Some things you don't wanna see. "Go where?"

Darlene gave me another tug, but I didn't budge.

"Where does it go?" I really didn't want to know the answer.

Snorting is a girl's way of being a boy. It tells you a limit's in sight, either in patience or propriety. Darlene snorted.

"Trust me."

Gauntlet thrown. Darlene wasn't giving up her mystery unless I crawled through the underbrush with her.

I shrugged my submission and followed.

We hit a clearing soon after. It stretched far and wide, with a road running alongside. I stopped dead in my tracks. I recognized the clearing. It was where I met up with Stammer that time we tried to get circus work.

"Are we going to Connie's fields?"

Darlene snorted again. "You could say that. Stammer is."

I had to snort, too. That or cry.

I set the pace after that. Darlene managed a stumble-run to keep up. Her skirt was sent flying by the wind. Soon, we were at the stand of trees where Stammer and I once crouched to scout out the circus.

The circus grounds were deserted. The bleachers were left behind in the rubbish-strewn field. Candy wrappers and old papers were trampled into the dead grass. A few grackles flew overhead, but none bothered to land. The pickings had been picked long before.

I lay hidden in the trees. Darlene flumped down beside me.

"You see 'em?"

I shook my head. "No. You?" I hoped her answer was *No*, too. I thought it useless to consider the alternative. No matter how happy I was to be included, I didn't want to see Stammer and Connie together. Well, I did in a way. A sad, sick way. Maybe I could submerge myself in this new hurt and hope it hurt less than losing my family.

"I see 'em!" Darlene wiggled beside me. She woulda risen, but I laid a restraining hand across her back.

"Don't. Let 'em be."

"You're right. We can watch from here."

Behind the bleachers, two heads could be seen through the wooden slats. One had hair of sandy brown, the other black. You could tell they kissed 'cause Darlene made a sharp intake breath and swore.

"Holy shit."

My swearing was much more rigorous. I kept it inside, though.

Darlene rolled on her back and hugged herself. She gave a sigh that was half-content and half-jealousy.

"You think it's nice to be kissed?"

I wasn't sure. I didn't want to say it, but I'd seen and felt a wide range with regards to kissing. Nevertheless, I hadn't established authority on it.

"Maybe."

"I think it would be swell." Darlene sighed again.

I kept my eyes on the two behind the bleachers. They seemed to have a fun struggle with each other as their bodies kept bobbing and swaying. No matter.

"What's that?"

"Huh?" I took a second to shake off my musings. "What are you talking about?"

"That."

"Where?" I looked at Darlene.

"There." She was still on her back and reached a hand to point straight at the sky.

I followed her gaze. There was a rag caught in the trees above us, fluttering yellow in the breeze. A chill rolled over my insides as I saw the rag move.

Darlene lowered her hand, puzzled. She squinted at the small cloth. "Maybe it's a handkerchief."

Maybe it was. I grabbed a rotten stick as I stood. The stick's length was perfect for poking. The leaves rustled and shook as I jabbed at the branch above us. The rag tore off and tumbled down to my feet.

"What is it?" Darlene propped herself on one arm to get a better look.

Good question. I reached down and picked it up. Yellow, little flowers, rust-coloured stains.

It was Dot's underwear.

24

I needed to get to my room fast. Problem was, Gram was in there. Who woulda expected that?

No one was around when I tiptoed up the stairs. The bar was empty. All the seats were tucked in, and the floor was clean. Even the glasses that had piled up on the counters were gone. That shoulda been my first clue about Gram.

The steps creaked like usual as I snuck up. Nobody poked their nose into the hallway as I walked through. The couple boarders left were at work. All good so far.

I heard singing when I got to my bedroom door.

"Gram?"

There she was. Opening the door even wider didn't change what I saw. Gram was smoothing clean sheets over my bed. Her dust rag still lay on top of the dresser. And the dresser was clean. Too clean. Dot's tea set was put away somewhere. That twanged a hurt inside.

"Ellen?" Gram startled and gave a smile that didn't quite reach her eyes. "How was school today?"

I swallowed my swear words at having her there. "It was fine, Gram. How are you feeling?"

The room darkened for a second as a cloud passed by outside. Then, it lightened again. Gram lightened with it.

"I'm well. Can you help me spread this quilt? I'm almost done here."

"Sure." Anything to move Gram along. I was happy she was out and about. Much more so than I'd expect, I'll admit. But I needed my space.

Gram put the final fluff on my pillows. "There."

I eyed the door, hoping she'd move to it and leave.

Seems Gram didn't wanna talk much either, as she gave me a quick hug and disappeared down the hall.

So, where was I?

Dot's panties felt crusty when I pulled them out of my pocket. I got a waft of leaf rot as I spread them on the dresser. The yellow fabric was faded and ripped. I wondered how long they'd been out there. I had a question in my head I couldn't quite answer yet.

Was this the underpants from the church, or what Dot wore when she disappeared?

I knew the easy answer. We found them near the circus grounds. Easy answer. I never liked easy answers.

The rust stain looked like old blood.

I didn't wanna think of how that stain got there.

Dot's drawer had its usual stick when you opened it. Gram had tucked the tea set in there. Rag Rabbit was squished down low beside Dot's socks. I almost rescued him for myself. I didn't.

I put Dot's torn underwear all the way in the back of the drawer. I moved some of the clothes to cover it. Now that Gram had breached the drawer, I didn't want any sudden discoveries. Lord Baby Jesus knows that my hiding skills needed improvement. Else, how did Grandpa find those cigarettes?

Darlene hadn't questioned when I told her the yellow rag was from the circus.

"I bet some clown left it." I held the rag pinched between two fingers, away from myself.

Darlene twisted her lips, like she tasted dirt. "You can have it. I don't need a souvenir of that show."

I wondered what Darlene had seen at the circus after Dot, Stammer, and I left the show. Was she thinking of something ugly or just plain scary? I was itching to ask but didn't want to perk her interest in the rag I held. Made me ache even more to remember missing the Big Top show. If we'd stayed, maybe we'd have come home with the same memory Darlene had, all three of us, instead of just two.

I made a play of dropping the rag away from us. I picked it up as soon as Darlene was distracted with watching Stammer. Neither of us really wanted to see Connie with him, as far as I could tell.

Now that I had brought the rag home, I wondered what to do with it. I should tell Gram and Grandpa. They'd wanna take it to the police. Right thing to do, I know. But I couldn't stand someone pawing through Dot's belongings again. I hadn't protected her from the start. They had the dress already. I don't see why they needed every piece of Dot to solve things. Some pieces I wanted to keep, to make it up to her. I knew she wouldn't have liked someone seeing her underwear.

Grandpa was in the kitchen with Gram when I went down. His newspaper was spread out over the table. His voice rumbled throughout the room as he read aloud. Nice to see him there. His usual choice was to lower himself into the words while he drank at the bar.

"Looks like good weather tomorrow." Grandpa looked up to share his smile with Gram. I guess he keeps it locked in a box otherwise. I tried not to get used to the sight.

Gram reached over and laid a hand on Grandpa's. "I might do some canning tomorrow. The blueberries out back look ready."

"That would be grand." Grandpa's smile made his moustache all wispy. Parts of his lips showed through, like they were still hiding from a predator.

Gram busied herself with the dishes. Grandpa's smile stayed. Gram's didn't.

"Ellen. How was school?"

I swear, the only thing grown-ups know how to greet you with is asking about school.

"It was okay."

"You see how nice the hotel looks today?" Grandpa caught Gram's hand as she went by. She paused in her shuffling of dishes to give him a pat.

I looked at the cupboards. Gram had emptied them and laid all the pots and dishes on the table. She was scrubbing them all down. A small stack of dirty cloths were piled in the sink.

"Looks like lotsa work done." My comment stirred up Grandpa.

"You should see the parlour. Head-to-toe spick and span." Grandpa mused and shook his head like he just got a Christmas present. "Spick and span."

Gram gave a smile and kept wiping. "I'll be moving on to cooking next. Anything you want for supper tomorrow? I think we can finish the last of the chicken tonight."

Grandpa laid his newspaper flat on the table. His eyes moistened, and he reached for his handkerchief.

"No. No. I got about all I need. Whatever you'd like to make is fine with me."

"I guess we could kill another chicken." Gram started restacking the dishes in the shelves. "That would leave more than one meal now that the boarders aren't so many."

Grandpa nodded. "I'll get on it after the paper."

The butcher knife was already in Gram's hand before we knew it.

"Where are you going?" Grandpa said it. If he didn't, I was gonna.

"I got time right now. Best do the plucking while there's still daylight." Gram gave the knife a small whet with a sharpening steel.

Another nod from Grandpa, slower this time. "Alright."

I could feel Grandpa's eyes on me. I looked up. Grandpa was staring. His eyebrows raised higher as he motioned me towards the door with his chin.

I didn't move.

Grandpa cleared his throat. "Ahem."

Gram was already out the door.

"Ellen." Grandpa raised his newspaper and gave it a small shake into reading position. "Why don't you join your Gram outside and help with the chicken."

Alright.

Gram didn't look like she needed my help. Her lips were thin as she held the struggling chicken over a wood block. One chop with the butcher knife, and its head rolled on the ground. Gram didn't let go until the chicken's body stopped leaping. Her forearms were coated in blood. She was splattered from her apron to her shoes.

I leaned over the chicken head in the dirt. Its eyes and beak lay open, tongue hanging out. I gave it a tap with my shoe. Nothing. No life left.

"Excuse me." Gram reached past me to pick it up. She dusted off some dirt and tossed the head into a basket she held.

"Gram, what's it feel like to kill?"

I don't think she expected a talk like that today. She looked me dead-on for a few seconds before shaking her head.

"It feels awful."

"Then why do it? Why kill?" I knew my answer. I just wanted to hear hers.

Gram paused, holding the basket. The chicken's wings hung over either side. A trail of chicken shit gobbed over and fell at Gram's feet.

"It's a way of preserving life in others." Gram said no more. She opened the door and stepped inside.

I don't understand grown-ups no more than I understand other kids.

25

Gram had been canning all day. She barely said two words to me when I came home for lunch. Her face was pinched and her hands busy as she sliced onions into a bowl. Jars stood stacked in rows on the kitchen table. One small space was undefended. I pulled back a chair as Gram leaned over to put a plate of sandwiches in its place.

"Here you go. What would you like to drink?"

"Milk, please." It felt good to have Gram hosting my appetite.

The sandwiches were pristine. Not a meat slice sloppy or out of place. A small bowl of coleslaw lay within easy reach. Gram already knew it was my favourite. Its spoon perched across the lip of the bowl.

Gram motioned towards the bowl. "That's fresh today. Make sure you leave some for Grandpa, though." She wiped her hands on her apron as she moved back to the stove. A pot of rubber and canning lids bubbled hot in a steamy haze.

I munched in silence. Gram didn't attempt to break it. The ones who would were long gone.

Gram did spare me a hug before I left for school again. Her arms tightened around me, and she laid her head on mine. My nose wrinkled as I hugged back. The briny tang of pickles clung to her hair and clothes. I worried that the scent was catching. I could picture the taunts at school. Polack. Pickle Breath. It was the last thing I needed.

Darlene was waiting by the front door as I came out. She brushed her skirt off and stood expectantly.

I didn't know what to do at first, but then I remembered. Connie always led.

"You wanna go watch the boys play ball?" I wanted to. I hoped Darlene felt the same.

"Sure." Darlene still made no move.

Looks like I was in charge of this ship. Right.

Stammer wasn't in the field with the boys when we arrived at school. He and Connie were sitting on the school steps.

Darlene made to go for them, but yelped when I gave her sleeve a tug. "Don't, Elly. You an idiot or something?" Darlene pulled her arm free, and gave me a glare. I forgot. In sight of Connie, I was still low chicken in the pecking order.

"Sorry."

Darlene rubbed her arm. "It's okay." She took another look at Connie as she said it.

They were cuddled up close, Connie and Stammer. Connie had her head bent low. She tucked a hair strand behind her ear as she giggled. Stammer had his face turned towards her. His hair stood up shocky, like Connie's giggles were giving him a charge.

Thank God for the boys. They broke up that love fest the minute they saw it.

"Hey, Stammer's smooching Connie."

Connie pulled away with a start. Her face was flushed. A small crowd of boys gathered around them. Darlene and I emboldened ourselves and pushed right into the thick of things.

"You gonna get married, Stammer?"

"I bet they done it already."

"Sure they have. Look at Connie's face."

One boy took to strutting and crowing. The others chortled with appreciation. Connie shrank behind Stammer. Her face got pinched, like someone had stepped on it. A curtain of hair fell over her as her shoulders began to shake.

I wasn't in a pleasing mood. Like-minded with the boys, I felt bold enough to join in: "Show us your face, Connie."

The sound of my voice startled her. She looked up with a flash of anger that stabbed at the crowd. I swear we all took a step back. The space around Connie grew bigger and still couldn't contain her anger. It was directed at me. The boys, she left alone. Different species, different rules. But I was someone she could pin down and press. Deep. Into the dirt.

"You little shit piece." Connie's lips worked at each word like she was chewing gristle. "You want Stammer so bad, you follow him everywhere."

There was dead silence after Connie spoke.

The breath had gone out of me. I gulped, but the air didn't seem so clean. Didn't feed me the words I needed to fight back. I shrunk into myself.

"Ya know, she does follow Stammer a lot."

"Always hiding in the outfield bushes."

"Hovers around his desk."

The boys murmured to one another and raised a collective voice. The hounds had scented fresh meat. I was doomed. Stammer remained silent during the storm. His raised eyebrows went higher as Connie stood.

"She wants him so bad. She's a slut." Connie curled her hands into her chest. "She wants him soooo much."

Grins and hoots followed Connie's pantomime. A few mimicked her voice, "Soooo bad."

Darlene was behind me, blocking my escape. She didn't budge as I took a step back. Her allegiance had changed. Again.

"Elly's got a fire in her belly." Darlene was pleased to add to the beating.

My thoughts deserted me. The words circled and pummelled me. I went under.

"What's going on here?"

Mr. Oswin stood at the top of the steps, wiping coal soot off his hands. His look found me as I was drowning, and I grabbed at him with my eyes.

"Elly, are you okay?"

Nothing you can say to that when the hounds surround you.

"Uh huh."

One by one, my pursuers left off the chase. The crowd dwindled to just Connie, Stammer. and me, all perched below Mr. Oswin.

Mr. Oswin shot a suspicious look at Connie and Stammer. Connie smiled and sat back down on the stairs. Stammer looked away. Nobody said a word. The only one eyeing around was Mr. Oswin, and his eye wasn't pleased. I had the relief of knowing my subterfuge of indifference was not airtight. Grownups usually operated on a different level, never minding the kid fights being played out below them. Mr. Oswin might be one of those rare breed adults who paid attention to what people were really saying. An interesting thought that would need more reflection. Later. Much later. Right now, the moment was for watching.

"Alright. As long as you're okay." Mr. Oswin stepped down the stairs, passing between Connie and Stammer.

I nodded.

Connie smirked at me, then held her contempt in when Mr. Oswin turned. Mr. Oswin's face registered a flash of something. A recognition? His eyebrows seemed to swell and hover low over his eyes a moment. I'd seen that look before on Mr. Oswin. It was his coaching look. Someone had missed the ball somewhere and was gonna get it.

Stammer sat up straight. He flushed but held his head level. His eyes were on the ground, though.

"It's too nice a day to be sitting around." Mr. Oswin crossed his arms as he spoke. "You bring your glove, Stani?"

"N-n-no, sir."

"Why don't you go borrow one? We've still got a few minutes before school starts."

"Yes, sir." Stammer jerked to his feet. Just like that, he was off to the field.

Mr. Oswin didn't move away like I expected after that. He continued to consider Connie and me. It's hard to be under a grownup's gaze when you don't know what he's thinking. No choice but to wait.

"You girls looking for something to do?"

Connie scowled and shook her head.

Mr. Oswin's question was an offer of some sort, and I was curious. "Do you need help?"

"I could use some. We got new books that Mr. Dionne ordered. It'd help to have someone stamp them and get them set on their shelf."

Books. A long time since my thoughts had been on books. Thinking about books was like someone raining lollipops all over me. Pages to turn, words to read. New books were the best, as you can read the words all glossy on pristine pages. I love old books, too. It's silly to think that the words get all used up after the first reading. They're just as good, and maybe even better, having rolled around awhile in someone else's mind. Books. Mr. Oswin was offering me time with books.

"I can help."

Mr. Oswin nodded. "How about you, Constance? It'd be nice to see what your father picked out for the class."

Connie's face flattened. "No, thanks."

"Suit yourself." Mr. Oswin pointed the way up the stairs. "If you change your mind, we'll be in the school."

"I won't." Connie stood and adjusted her skirt. "Like you said, Mr. Oswin. It's too nice a day for sitting around."

Nice words, but Connie had a way of bringing menace to a kitten. I shivered at the threat.

Still, books!

I followed Mr. Oswin up the stairs. He held the door open for me to pass through.

The honk of a truck stopped us both. Mr. Oswin shaded his gaze as he looked out to the road by the school. I squinted, but I could only make out a plume of dust. A truck came in sight through the road dust haze. It honked again and turned into the gravel path that led to the school. The driver waved at the field of boys as the truck rumbled past.

The honk was answered by a holler. It was Stammer. He came running from the field to meet the truck.

The truck stopped in front of the school steps. Stammer's Uncle Ward got out of the driver's side. He held out his arms to Stammer, who ran full tilt into them.

"How are you, m'boy?" Uncle Ward's voice was guttural and wet with tears.

Stammer didn't answer. His shoulders shook as he held on tight to the hug.

Nathan stepped out from the passenger side and leaned on the hood. His eyes were soft as he watched Stammer with his uncle. I thought I was the only one who noticed him.

I was wrong.

Stammer took a step back from his uncle. "Where's Nathan? I thought he came with you."

"I'm here." Nathan shifted his stance. His eyes flicked at the students gathering.

It took two strides for Stammer to reach Nathan. He grabbed Nathan around the waist and squeezed tight.

Nathan startled in Stammer's grip. He lifted a hand like he didn't know it belonged to him and patted Stammer gingerly as he eyed the crowd. It took one sob from Stammer to relax the set in Nathan's stance. He leaned his head on top of Stammer's and enveloped the boy in a tight embrace.

"I'm here too, m'boy. I'm here, too."

Uncle Ward joined in the embrace.

Mr. Oswin walked down the steps to the truck. He cleared his throat as he approached.

"Good to see you, Ward."

Uncle Ward broke from encircling Stammer and Nathan. He ran a hand through his hair. "It's good to be seen, Ozzie."

"You in the clear, then?"

Uncle Ward winced at the words. "For now. I've been released on condition that I stay in the area. There wasn't anything to find on me, other than the distillery. I coulda told them that."

Mr. Oswin grimaced back. "Seems society always wants to sniff out a wrong."

You'd think there was a code in those words. Uncle Ward nodded as he shot a glance at Nathan. Nathan looked everywhere but back.

"You want Stammer for the afternoon?"

"That would be nice, Ozzie. I think we'd all appreciate the time together. It's been rough on the boy."

"I'll tell Miss Oswin that Stammer's gone home for the day." Mr. Oswin held a hand out to Uncle Ward. "You take it easy. I may drop by later to see how things are."

Miss Oswin showed up at the top of the steps with the school bell. She raised it high, but paused mid-swing. Within the folds of her face, a frown appeared.

"It's okay, Karen." Mr. Oswin put an arm around Uncle Ward's shoulders. "Mr. Wojek is here to pick up Stani."

"It's still school time, Mr. Wojek." You could hear the teacher in Miss Oswin's voice. I was interested to see if it would work on grown-ups, too.

Uncle Ward released a breath, nice and slow. His face held patience and impatience all mixed together. He put his arm around Stammer's shoulders.

"I know, Miss Oswin. School is important. But there's a time and place for learning. There's also a time and place for family. This here is my family." Uncle Ward gave Stammer a tighter squeeze. He included Nathan in his gaze. "And we're going to spend some time together."

Not much you can say to a man declaring his intentions. Either you agree, or you don't. Miss Oswin seemed to agree.

"Alright then."

Mr. Oswin gave a nod, and our teacher smiled back.

It looked all settled for Stammer to leave, but a teacher is a teacher. I think Miss Oswin had one more lesson to teach.

"Before you go, Stanislaw…"

"Y-yes, ma'am?"

"Make sure you're early tomorrow. We'll go over what you missed this afternoon."

Stammer nodded. "Yes, ma'am."

"Ellen or Constance can help you if one of them is willing to come in early, too."

I don't know who gulped first, me or Connie. For some reason, I think it was a tie. Connie and I both nodded and spoke in unison. "Yes, ma'am."

Uncle Ward held the door open for Stammer and Nathan to get in the truck. He walked at a jaunty pace to the driver's side, giving the crowd a wave as he got back in. Stammer had a big smile on his face as he sat between his uncle and Nathan. He also waved as the truck backed up the gravel road towards the highway.

I kinda hoped he was waving to me.

Connie gave a sigh beside me. I guess she hoped the same.

Who knew that Mr. Oswin was a friend of Stammer's uncle? I had never seen them talk, though I remembered Mr. Oswin helping Stammer look for his uncle after we lost Dot.

And who knew that Miss Oswin had her eye on me, Stammer, and Connie? Made me wonder what else grown-ups actually saw without saying much in return.

26

The afternoon sun stretched across both students and desks, but the schoolroom felt as cheery as a funeral. Well, maybe not that far gone; I know what that feels like. Still. Funny how the one who makes your day can unmake it when he's not there.

Stammer was at home with his uncle. I was with Connie and some books.

At least there were books.

Connie and I sat on the floor by the bookshelf. Miss Oswin had put us to work together, as we'd both finished the afternoon's work. Connie sighed as she twirled a piece of hair. Every few minutes, she'd inch up onto her knees to peer over the desks. The boys pretended not to notice.

I was arm-deep in a cardboard box of new books. The crisp white scent of new-printed pages gave me shivers. I could smell it through the brown paper wrapping that hid each new treasure.

"You wanna open one?" I held a brown-wrapped book to Connie who twisted her lips in response.

"Eww! No. It's dusty."

True. There was a fine layer of cardboard dust on each book's wrapping. I brushed the grains off with my hand and started work on the edges of the package.

The book slid easily out from the wrapper. It was *Volume 2.*

"An encyclopedia set!" I forgot myself and blurted out my joy.

Connie rolled her eyes and sneered. "How exciting. Now we can read all day."

Some moments would be ruined by a comment like that. Not this one. It was too interesting. Too important. I traced over the script on the cover. *Encyclopedia Britannica: Volume 2*. I had found a whole book of B's. Da's and my birds were in there somewhere.

The pages stuck as I cracked the book open. I had a chore of it just easing the pages apart. It took more than a few tries to get close to Birds. When they finally appeared in their full-colour glory, I was spellbound. And the words! They flew in descriptive swirls, leaving feather plumes of prose weaving around me as I sat entranced. Facts and fancies of birds surged and spilled all over the pages. Eggs and nests, skies so blue to soar in. I felt Pa's hand guiding mine as I ran a finger under the words I read.

"Ellen?"

Miss Oswin stood over me. How long had she been trying to get my attention? I was alone on the floor. The box sat beside me, still unpacked. Connie had long deserted and sat at her desk, head bent over some work.

"Ellen. It's almost time to go home."

No words came. I looked down at the book I held in my lap. I hadn't fully surfaced yet. Miss Oswin musta seen something in my face, 'cause she crouched down as low as I ever seen her. No mean feat for a body her size.

"What book do you have there?"

I tilted the binding up, but otherwise stayed still.

Miss Oswin read each syllable out like it was its own word. "*Encyclopedia Britannica*. Are you enjoying it?"

I nodded. Still no words of my own came in answer. My mind was too full of the book and pictures that lay in my lap.

"Would you like to take it home with you? For the night, I mean."

A thousand, thousand butterflies of pages flapped up and away from the book I held. All the colours kaleidoscoped into a hum around me, that held me and hugged me. The words sang like honey and sweetened the world as I spoke.

"Could I?"

"Miss Oswin." A deep rumble of a voice cut off Miss Oswin's answer. "That is a new book for our school. It's meant to be used by all students. Here. In this classroom. Not just by one student, but by all."

Miss Oswin flinched.

So did I.

Connie's desk jostled. I flashed a look at Connie, but she kept a determined face over her paper. It wasn't her words that speared out. Mr. Dionne stood over Miss Oswin. I hadn't seen him come in, wrapped up as I was in literature.

Miss Oswin stood, meeting him at the same height. "Maybe we could overlook it just this once."

Mr. Dionne grimaced. "And what about the next time she asks?"

I didn't correct Mr. Dionne that I hadn't asked. Correcting a grown-up who's in charge is a risky move.

Miss Oswin stood taller. She gestured at me and the book I held. "If she asks again, my answer is the same. I'd prefer to encourage her. Books look pretty on the shelf, but that fails to serve their purpose. Books are meant to be opened and read."

Mr. Dionne harrumphed. "We didn't buy books for them to be carted away the moment they were unpacked."

"Books are meant to opened and read." Miss Oswin crossed her arms as she repeated herself, then uncrossed them quick. Maybe she'd stepped over some line with Mr. Dionne.

The longest stare I ever saw came outta Mr. Dionne. He finally spoke, giving me wink. "It looks like we have a little reader on our hands. If you really want to take the book home with you, I think we can grant you this favour."

I looked back at the book in my hands. The birds lay flat and dull on its pages.

"Ellen, Mr. Dionne is speaking to you."

I screwed up my cheeks in approximation of a smile I didn't feel. "No, thank you, sir. I think it best stay at school."

Mr. Dionne held my gaze like he was searching for some sass. Then he nodded and leaned on Connie's desk. "Suit yourself."

Miss Oswin gave a nod as well. "Time to tidy up, Ellen. You can shelve the rest of the books tomorrow."
"Yes, ma'am."

"No dilly-dallying, though. You'll have plenty of time to read once you're done."

"No, ma'am."

Mr. Dionne raised a hand to regain Miss Oswin's attention. "We'll have time to go over the rest of those reports tomorrow, Miss Oswin."

"Thank you, sir. I'll have them completed by then."

"Constance?"

"Yes, sir?"

"I want you home straight after school. No dilly-dallying on your part either."

Connie gave a quick scowl that froze when Mr. Dionne tucked his thumbs in his belt. "No, sir. I won't."

Mr. Dionne left soon after. It's hard to know whether some grown-ups are being nice or just biding time to police the wrongs outta you.

Connie walked out of school with Darlene. I was on my own again. The sounds of shrieks and scrambles echoed around me in the path through the woods. I was one of the last students on the trail, and I followed the fun without feeling any.

For a moment there, holding that encyclopedia, enjoying those birds, I had felt Da. He wasn't so close nowadays. His face blurred in my mind. What with me growing and feeling older, I didn't know if the spirit of Da would recognize me either. The last he'd seen me was more than a couple turns of the world around the sun. Maybe it spun his ghost out. Mam was fading too, though not as fast. Dot's shape was easier. I'd woken every day to her tumbled hair and morning grin for most of my life.

Sometimes, I think I block Mam and Da on purpose. A ghost can be nosy and know things about you that you don't want to know even about yourself. They're living in a small room with you, watching you, while you can't see them back. They get to peer into all your business.

When Mam was alive the last few months, we lived in a small room together. I know what it's like to try and hide secrets and have them ferreted out just the same. Mam would hush us at night and tell us to go to sleep. I'd breathe deep and long until I heard the door open and shut soft. Then, we'd know Mam had gone. Dot would sit up sometimes when she was still awake. Mostly she was not, and it was me who watched for Mam's return.

Mam would come back much later. She'd edge the door open, like she was making a prison break. I could hear her voice call gentle to see if we stirred. I'd never answer. I didn't want to break her heart with my knowing.

The men Mam brought home looked kinda like Mr. Dionne. I'd squint at them through my eyelids. Loud, dark, looming. All suits and bigness in their voice. They wouldn't hush, though Mam pleaded with them for quiet.

They'd mostly groan and swear. Sometimes they'd make Mam cry out. It sounded like fear, joy, and pain mixed all together. Once I couldn't help it and sat up with a holler. Mam looked out from under the man who pinned her and told me to ease myself. It was okay. To go back to sleep.

I did. But not before hearing a man's voice ask how much for me.

Mam cried after that one left. Her breath was shuddery and came in gasps. She looked like a ghost curled up on her bed. That was the last man I saw come to our room. We stopped eating so well soon after.

Mam's crying came harder, then softer and tireder. Her dying was out in the open. No longer a secret from me. Dot continued like it was no concern of hers, Mam thinning-out and coughing. I knew better. I likely caused it.

27

No one was in the bar when I got home. I'd gotten used to a head or two leaning back on their seats to peruse me before turning again to their drinks. I'd usually hunch my shoulders and climb the stairs as quick as I could. Same with seeing a boarder in the hallway. Most would nod but once in a while, a boarder, Henry, would ask me things about myself. He'd lean against a wall, all curious, dangling his shaving kit over one shoulder. His bathrobe was ratty, and he had hairy legs. I'd dodge his questions by mumbling. Still, it never deterred him.

We were down to one boarder, lately. That one. Henry. My luck, he was coming through the hall just as I hit the top of the stairs.

"Well, little Elly! How was school today?"

"Fine."

"You learn anything useful? Any science or nature?" His questions were usually served with a leer. Since knowing Billy Harner, I'd come to recognize that look.

"Some." Vague was best.

"Chemistry? Physics? A-na-to-my?" He affected the lean, so I knew there were more questions coming. His leans were getting bigger, taking up more and more of the hallway, blocking my path.

"I gotta go to the bathroom."

"Well, that's something to do with anatomy." Smirk. A big one. Not surprising. I had let myself in for that one.

"I gotta go."

"You come tell me later about your anatomy lesson." Henry laughed and gave my arm a quick tap.

The man's jokes were getting harder, the longer he knew me. I seen him sometimes with Billy Harner, so I had a wonder over it.

"Yes'um." Thank Baby Jesus, he moved so I could pass. I really did have to go to the bathroom.

The door was shut when I got there. When I jiggled the handle, it wouldn't open. Knocking didn't help. No one answered.

"Grandpa?"

I took a sniff, but couldn't detect any Grandpa residue. Usually you could tell when he'd been in there. He'd sit for an hour and let his inside smells seep out. I had to hold my nose mostly after Grandpa was through.

"Gram?"

No answer either. I'd run out of people to call, as the boarder was tramping down the stairs. Nothing for it but to pick the lock. One quick flick of my fingernail in the doorknob and I'd be in. I was rather proud of that trick. Had tried to teach Dot, but she didn't have the dexterity for it.

The door swept open over a puddle of pink water on the floor. Steam misted the mirror and clung to my clothes. The tub sat claw-footed in the wet air. Gram was in the tub. Her head lolled to one side. One arm was flung out, dripping red drops. The drops fell into the puddle on the floor, causing a bulls-eye of crimson to spread. Gram didn't move.

I screamed.

28

Things blurred some after that, so I'll tell what I remember: Henry came running back up the stairs followed by Grandpa. They both craned over me, saw Gram, and shoved me aside.

I hit the doorknob with my hip. It stung. Like hell. I couldn't clear the tears from my eyes. I looked down, and my socks were wet. They had been brown from a day in shoes. The pink didn't show on them, but I could feel the blood. Gram's blood. I had stepped in the puddle. I peeled them off and flung them down the hall. Didn't help as now I stood barefoot, and the puddle was seeping out the door.

Grandpa and Henry scrabbled with towels, all the while bumping into each other. There wasn't enough room for two of them, even with Gram in the tub.

The boarder yelled directions, while Grandpa kept crying "Oh God."

They managed to hoist Gram out of the tub and onto the floor. Water sloshed everywhere as they did, pinking up Henry's shirt. He didn't seem to notice, or maybe he did but didn't care. He leaned down and wrapped a towel round Gram's hand and wrist. Blood seeped through quickly, then stopped and didn't drip.

"We're gonna need a doctor." Henry's voice had a strain in it. His hands were tight around the towel and Gram's wrist.

Grandpa *Oh God*'ed a few more times and nodded.

Gram moaned and fluttered her eyes, which gave Grandpa some relief.

"Shh. Don't move, Grace." Grandpa patted her hair, smoothing it back. "We're here. We'll take care of you."

Henry looked up at me, thrusting his chin out towards the hallway. "Elly, we need you. Your Gram's gotta get to a hospital. Go find us a ride. Maybe Mr. Dionne or someone."

I didn't move. I swear I heard Henry mutter under his breath, "Dumbass kid." Didn't prick me at all. I was too numb.

"Elly. Go find us someone." Henry gritted his teeth into each word. His heavy-scowled stare woke my muscles, and I hopped back into the hall. I ran. Down the stairs. Out the door in my bare feet. Right into Mr. Dionne coming up the hotel steps.

He grabbed me to keep me from falling.

"Whoa, where's the fire?" Mr. Dionne's gaze took in my bare feet and all the rest of me.

Words didn't come, just shuddering breaths.

"What's the matter, little one?" Mr. Dionne held on to my arms and crouched to my level. "You hurt?"

That unlocked my chest. My air and words stormed out. "Gram's sick. Real sick. She's bleeding. Grandpa wants you to drive her to the doctor."

Mr. Dionne kept hold of me, but his shock registered in his brows. They raised real high.

"Can you drive Gram? It's an emergency."

"No." Mr. Dionne gave me a pat on the back and released me. "No, I can't."

I stumbled a step before regaining my balance. "What?"

"I can't. My car's done in right now. The engine's broken."

Mr. Dionne held still as he said it. He'd used his car this afternoon at the school. I wondered what coulda broke in the past hour.

"But you were at our school!" Usually I'd leave a grown-up alone, but this was Gram.

"And when I left, the engine boiled over. I wouldn't trust it on the highway." Mr. Dionne stood back. "Sorry, kid. Maybe someone else can help."

I looked around, but didn't recognize any of the cars or trucks nearby. I started to pace. Slow at first, then frantically. I was failing Gram. And Grandpa. I was failing them both.

Nobody I knew. Nobody around. I sunk down and sat in the dust of the street. Curled up over my knees and hid my head.

"Where's your shoes?"

Someone talking to me. I let the words hang there, as I breathed deep in my arm cave.

"Elly?"

Time to surface.

Stammer crouched in front of me when I lifted my head. He had a lean-in, hold-back look to his shoulders, like he wasn't certain if he should stay or go. His knuckles were white from squeezing together.

Stammer.

His eyes were soft, though, and he reached a hand out to give me a shake. "Hey. I said, where are your shoes?"

My tears flooded. My body shook. The best I could warble was, "Gram's sick. We need a ride."

My crying musta been enough, as Stammer stood and gave a shrill whistle.

"What's the howdy, Stani?" Nathan soon stood over me.

"Elly's Gram is sick. They need to take her to the next town."

Nathan nodded. "That's fine. We can help. I'll get the truck and pull it up to the hotel."

Stammer pulled me up by my hands. "Can you stand?"

I nodded, not daring to meet his eyes again. He'd see too much of my gratitude if I did. It'd scare him off, for sure.

"Watch for glass. You shouldn't be out in your bare feet." Stammer set off back down the street to our hotel. It felt good to follow.

Mr. Dionne was still at the hotel, standing in the doorway. His face was red, like he was tired and angry at the same time. "I'm telling you, the car isn't working."

"For Christ's sake. It's the blood, isn't it?" Grandpa stood jabbing a finger at him. Spittle came out with each word he barked.

Mr. Dionne paused at that, like Grandpa hit a nerve, then he firmed his face. "No, it's not the blood. I can definitely stand the blood. It's the car. It's not working. It'll conk before we get two miles down the road."

Grandpa's eyebrows heaved upwards. "Please. We're desperate."

"It's not happening." Mr. Dionne's crossed arms gave signal to Grandpa that arguing was a waste of time. Gram's time.

"Aw, shit." Grandpa cast a hand up to shoo Mr. Dionne away, but thought better of it. "Can you at least watch Elly while I find someone who can?"

Mr. Dionne parted his lips before answering. It wasn't a smile, exactly. "I could do that." He nodded, all neighbourly. "That, I could do."

Grandpa nodded back and started walking towards the church.

"Grandpa!" I found my voice, but it still shook.

Stammer added his own. "Mr. Johnson!"

We had to run, as it seemed Grandpa's bad ear was in charge of his thoughts at the moment. It wasn't until I tugged at his sleeve that he noticed and turned.

Grandpa's face was streaked. Dirt, blood, tears. Something else was there, too. Tiredness. His cheeks sagged, and I swear he choked back a hiccup.

"Grandpa, I found Gram a ride."

"This true?" Grandpa lowered his chin at us.

Stammer stood tall. "Yes, sir. Nathan has the truck over by the hotel right now."

We all looked to see Henry and Nathan marshalling Gram into the truck cabin. Nathan was reaching from inside the truck, hands round Gram's shoulders, like he was hauling her outta water. Henry braced her legs and swung them in.

"Mr. Johnson, room for one more!" Henry waved while holding the passenger door open.

"I gotta go, Elly." Grandpa gave me a quick hug. "Mr. Dionne's responsible for you until I return."

"Yes, sir."

Grandpa chewed his lip a moment. "Stani, can you stay awhile, too?"

I didn't need babysitting, yet here Grandpa was setting a handful of people to watch over me. Mr. Dionne, I could do without. Stammer, though. Maybe I wouldn't get so huffy about him watching me.

"I can stay." Stammer's shoulders went back as he vouched for himself.

I snorted, which put Stammer into his usual hunch again.

Grandpa ran at old-man speed towards the truck. He hadn't changed into shoes. He still wore house slippers that flip-flopped with each step.

Stammer and I followed behind, keeping pace easily.

Henry helped Grandpa into the truck cab before slamming the door. He gave the door a couple taps. Nathan gave a thumb's up, then drove off. Through the truck's back window, I could see Gram's head lolling against Grandpa. You'd think they were two teenagers being driven to a dance.

"Well, they won't be back for a while." Mr. Dionne nodded at his own words.

"Yep." Henry looked down at his shirt and the blood smeared across it. "Good Lord. I gotta change before my date."

Stammer kept turning his head back and forth from me to the men.

"What's wrong, Stanislaw?"

"Oh, nothing, Mr. Dionne." Stammer held his breath before letting it out. "I'll be right back."

"Take your time. We got things under control." Mr. Dionne gave a thumb hitch towards the hotel that made me grimace. A superintendent is bad enough at school. All tight with rules. I didn't want to imagine how strict he'd be with me at my own home.

Stammer, though. He promised to stay. Here he was, taking to the road faster than a speed racer. Watching him go tore a hole inside me. I'd hoped for his company while my grandparents were gone. Not that I'd spill my inner-most pains to Stammer if he did stay. Still, it hurt to know the potential was lost as quickly as it had come.

Henry gave Mr. Dionne a handshake before turning back to the hotel. His heavy steps soon faded inside. That left Mr. Dionne and me. He squinted at me, sizing me up. I'd expect that look from a kid in the playground.

"Have you done your homework yet?" Mr. Dionne raised his eyebrows as he spoke. Grown-ups and their school questions. Sick of them.

"Not yet. I just got home."

"Let's go inside. I can help you with your learning."

"Yes, sir."

I didn't know if my thoughts could manage the focus. It was math studies. Had to give it a try, though.

"*Elly!*" Stammer came up the road again, this time in company of an older woman. Miss Frieda Witt was with Stammer. I hadn't seen her since Dot's funeral. Mr. Dionne gave a frown, like he saw someone sitting in his favourite chair.

"Elly!" Stammer was out of breath when he arrived. "I brought Miss Frieda. She's gonna stay with you until your grandparents get home."

"I came as soon as I heard." Miss Frieda's cardigan had an unraveling end that hung down by her knees. Her skirt was dirty with grass-stains. She didn't look like she'd washed in ages, but she smiled me a big smile. I couldn't help but smile back, though I knew not many grown-ups liked her.

You could feel the dislike from Mr. Dionne. His legs stood wider, and he thrust his chin out again.

"Ellen's grandfather asked me to be in charge of her."

Miss Frieda frowned. "No offense, Mr. Dionne, but a young girl is best cared for by a woman."

"I was about to take Ellen back to our house, Miss Frieda. My wife and I are fully capable of looking after her." Mr. Dionne huffed out his words. I half expected steam to rise from them.

"That's very kind of you, but Elly would be best looked after here in her home. Besides, you got your own family to take care of, Mr. Dionne."

Mr. Dionne glowered, but forebore saying another word. He leaned like he was gonna take a swing at Miss Frieda, then re-steadied himself. "It's no problem for us to take in Ellen."

Miss Frieda paled and thinned her lips. "Elly will be well-looked after. She'll be *safe* with me."

That seemed to take some air outta Mr. Dionne's persistence. He gave a scratch of his neck. "Well, I guess women know best in these situations. I'll have Mrs. Dionne come around to see if you need anything." Mr. Dionne gave a look at his watch. "I've got to get home, anyways."

Miss Frieda crossed her arms. "Good idea."

We three watched Mr. Dionne get in his car. He nodded to us as he pulled away.

"Always the opportunist." Miss Frieda gave her head a shake before turning back to us. She looked Stammer and me up and down and shook her head again. "Time to feed you kids. Stani, you might as well stay with us for supper."

"I should be going." Stammer fidgeted and rubbed the front of his shirt, but didn't tic out his words.

I think my face fell, 'cause I was suddenly looking at my bare feet. They were grime-coated and wet.

Miss Frieda musta noticed them, too. "Elly, let's get you inside and cleaned up." She put an arm around my shoulders and started to lead me back inside.

"Well... I'll see you later." Stammer still stood, watching us go.

"You sure you won't join us? I bet there's something good to eat in the kitchen, and I know Elly could use the company."

I could. Nice of Miss Frieda to see it.

"Alright. But I can't stay too long." Stammer caught up to us and held the door open.

Miss Frieda gave him a nod and a "Why, thank you, Stan," as we passed through.

Stan. First time I'd heard him called that. The way Stammer straightened himself said it was a first for him, too.

29

Henry was coming down the stairs as we walked in. He eyed us as he stood at the bottom step.

"Bathroom's a mess. You don't wanna go in there." Henry shifted from foot to foot. "I'd keep the kids away until someone cleans it up."

Miss Frieda nodded. "I'll deal with it."

"Good. Just saying. Well, I won't be home until late, Elly. Don't wait up." Henry waggled his eyebrows at me.

I looked to see its effect on Stammer, but he avoided my gaze. Stammer found the floor very interesting at that moment.

"We won't wait up." Miss Frieda tightened her grip on my shoulders and gave me a little shake.

Henry gave a small laugh. "Heh. Good to hear."

Miss Frieda didn't even wait to see Henry leave. She marched me to the kitchen and plunked me down in Grandpa's chair. Stammer sat gingerly in my spot. He rested his elbows on the table, then changed his mind and put his hands in his lap to fidget.

"Now, y'all just sit right there while I see what Grace had planned for dinner. Miss Frieda felt the oven door for heat and opened it wide. She shook her head slow at what she saw.

"Leave it to Grace to have a full chicken roasting when she planned to off herself. At least it settles what I'm gonna feed y'all."

I couldn't help it, but my throat rattled a sob out at Miss Frieda's words. She looked up sharp at the sound.

"Oh, honey. I didn't mean it that way." Miss Frieda stood and leaned against the counter. "It's just that I known Grace a long time. She always heads into anything with full-on preparation. She's a special one, your grandma. It's why your grandpa married her."

I nodded, but couldn't hold back another shudder. I was getting as bad as Stammer with my shaking.

"She's been his rock for many a year, through good times and bad. Lord knows he went through some bad." Miss Frieda kept still a moment longer before bringing a corner of her cardigan to her eyes.

"M-Miss Frieda, I think I oughta go h-home after all. M-my uncle will be wondering when the truck doesn't show up." Stammer's face was red. He pushed back hard from the table, scratching out a protest from the chair. His hands fluttered as he stood, then settled into his pockets. "Thank you for the offer of s-supper but I n-need to go."

Miss Frieda stared before nodding. "You do what's best for you, Stani. Say Hi to your uncle and tell him I'm glad that nonsense is mostly done."

Stammer gave a short jerky nod. "I w-will. He'd be pleased to hear that."

"Tell him I'm still a customer if he starts up again. He'll know what I mean."

"I'll t-tell him." Stammer peeked at me and drew himself straight. "Bye, Elly. Hope your grandma is okay."

"Uh huh." I barely moved my lips in acknowledgement. It burned he wouldn't even stay for supper.

"You take care, Stani. Come back if you change your mind." Miss Frieda leaned back down to the oven. "Lord, there's even veggies in here. Smell that pot chicken. Mm-mm."

Stammer left without another word. The kitchen remained quiet except for the banging of cupboard doors as Miss

Frieda looked for plates and cutlery. I let her fumble around as I was in no mood to help.

I will admit, Miss Frieda is a good dinner companion. There were no questions about how was school or how much homework I had. She seemed more interested in what I was doing with myself after school. When she heard about my bird book, her eyes lit up.

"That must be a sight to see. All those birds." Miss Frieda chewed before speaking again. "You got a favourite?"

I sat back in my chair. I hadn't thought of that. I mean, I had in a way. I had picked out birds that matched different people in my family. Dot was a chickadee, 'cause she'd always chirped and sang. Gram was a purple finch. That was easy, on account of her purple yarn squares. Grandpa? He was a grosbeak. His build was all squat, brawnier than the rest of us. Mam was a robin, as that picture had the bird sitting on a nest. I had never figured what Da was. Sometimes he was a hawk when I pictured him in uniform. Other times a gray jay, all darting and proud, when Mam sat telling stories of his courting her.

"Maybe a sparrow?" I surprised myself at the sound of my voice. Wavering, climbing up the scale to treble when usually it hung lower and calmer.

"A sparrow! That's your favourite?" Miss Frieda guffawed, and a fleck of chicken flew out onto her sleeve. "That's the brownest of brown you can have for a bird. And tiny. What you see in a sparrow?"

What did I see in them? It wasn't obvious at first. I had to think.

"I like sparrows 'cause they can stand the cold. They can find seeds where you don't think any food is. And they can make a home outta anything." My voice got stronger as I rambled off things I knew about sparrows from years of watching. "And they sit all fluffed together, so no sparrow is left out. And they call out greetings to each other when they meet." A mix of reasons, really. Mostly 'cause they were hardy birds. They could live anywhere and outlast anything. But they still needed company for friendship and warmth. Same as me.

Miss Frieda smiled wide, showing a gob of chicken in her teeth. "Cute," was all she said.

After supper, we left the dishes in the sink for later.

"We got bigger chores to tackle." Miss Frieda scrounged around one of the tall cupboards before pulling out a mop and bucket to fill. "I'm gonna need your help with the bathroom. You seen what it looks like?"

"Yes, ma'am." I sure had.

"Well, how bad is it?"

I thought carefully how to explain. "You know when you cut a chicken's head off? How much blood there is?"

"Yeah?"

"Well, think of a lot chickens. Maybe a dozen of them, all cut open, tied together, and held over the tub."

Miss Frieda clucked her tongue. "Lord, as bad as that, is it?"

I nodded.

"We'll have to do it together, then. I can't do it, myself." Miss Frieda stripped off her cardigan and rolled up her sleeves. "I got issues of my own."

That didn't bode well, but Miss Frieda had been nice so far. I didn't want to disappoint her. I firmed up my stance and nodded again.

"Your feet are filthy, Elly. We'll get you cleaned up after."

Clumping up the stairs, I'd forgotten about my socks. There they were, lying in a pink, sodden heap in the middle of the hallway. Henry musta stepped 'round them on his way down.

"Ew. These yours?" Miss Frieda lifted a sock up with the handle of the mop.

"Yes, ma'am. I got them dirty and took 'em off."

"That explains the bare feet."

The sock slid off the mop handle to rest against the wall. Miss Frieda used the handle to give the other sock a swoop to join its mate. "We'll clean those later."

The bathroom door was closed, with a puddle seeping from underneath. Miss Frieda paused before opening the door.

"Jesus Holy Mary Margaret!"

The mess was worse than I remembered. I gulped back a gorge chunk that had suddenly thrown itself against my throat.

Blood. Everywhere. Splashed on the floor, the walls. Streaks even coated the mirror, casting a red hue over my face when I peered at it. The tub was full of dark, bloody water. I'd never seen a horror movie. I don't think I ever will.

Miss Frieda stared and swore again under her breath. "I hain't seen this much blood since..." Her face creased with a memory, and she gave her belly a rub.

"You okay, Miss Frieda?"

"Fine as can be, considering. Best get to it the way nature meant us." She stripped off her blouse and shimmied out of her skirt. Both she discarded to one side of the hall, away from the puddle. She stood in her underwear, her breasts sagging against her chest. "Take your pants and shirt off, Elly. It's just more work if we get them dirty."

I never been naked with a grown-up before. Well, excepting Mam. Even with Billy, I had some clothes on. I took my time getting undressed as I was nervous, but it was kinda energizing once I stood beside Miss Frieda, ready for scrubbing.

Miss Frieda gave the floor a good swipe to clear us space to work. Her mop hit something metal and sent it spinning to the middle of the room. It was the knife. Miss Frieda gave me a quick glance as she used a bloody towel to pick the knife up. She folded the towel over and over, hiding the knife in its depths, shaking her head and muttering Gram's name as she did. She tucked the knife and towel in the one corner of the room free of the mess.

"Is that the…" I couldn't finish my thought. Miss Frieda cut me off.

"We'll give the floor another round of scrubbing once we're done the tub and walls." She gave me a rag and directed me to clean the mirror.

The tub sat full of Gram's blood. I couldn't look at it. Miss Frieda noted my shiver and took a peek into its murky redness.

"Ain't you people got a chain to pull that plug out?"

I scrunched my eyes as I tried to remember. Dot had pulled the plug chain off and used it as a skipping rope for her bunny. "No, ma'am. It broke a while ago."

I heard a heavy sigh come from Miss Frieda. She leaned over the tub and peered into its depths.

"Well, time to dig for treasure." She plunged her arm full deep into the bloody water and shifted around. Her tongue tip poked out as she concentrated. A tug and a lift, and she held the plug high, letting the red drips fall back into the tub. A sucking sound slowly built as the filthy, rose-red water drained.

"*Voilà!*"

I started to clap, but remembered the cloth in my hand. It was dingy yellow, with rust stains. Small flowers dotted it everywhere. I almost dropped it.

"Where did you get this?" I spread the rag out to get a better look.

"Just there, perched on the sink. Grace musta been tidying up before she… well…"

Gram had used this rag. Even more important, Gram had seen this rag in my room, hidden in the drawer. Had brought it to the bathroom where she had tried to kill herself.

Gram had known about my hiding Dot's underwear.

30

Grandpa came home late that night. I woke to the sound of murmured voices down the hall. When I peeked out my door, I saw Grandpa and Miss Frieda standing opposite each other with arms crossed. The few whispered words I caught had both sharpness and my name in them.

"You need help."

"We're just fine by ourselves…"

"Elly's a growing girl."

"Go on home…"

"It's what Grace would…"

I eased the door closed and scrambled back to bed. Grandpa and Miss Frieda brought back bad memories of Mam and Da getting cross. Da didn't leave for war on the best of terms with Mam. My name had figured a lot in those conversations, too. Mostly in terms of my determination to learn baseball from Da. Mam had won, and I never got that glove.

In the morning, Miss Frieda called me down to breakfast. Grandpa had stomped through earlier, then down the stairs. He was leaving the bar when I made it down.

"Morning, Elly." Grandpa gave me a side-hug and continued out the door. Grandpa smoking? Above the reek of cigarettes, I could smell his anger and fear for Gram, like a sourness on his skin. Best stay clear of him for the day.

Breakfast was the same as supper, but it was still good. When it came to tidying up, Miss Frieda had the dishes put away all wrong. At least they were put away. Gram could fix the order when she came back.

"Hello? Anybody home?" A deep rumble voice called out from the front of the hotel.

Miss Frieda and I kept pace as we went to greet the visitor. When she saw who it was, Miss Frieda put a hand on my shoulder.

Father Don stood in the doorway. When Father caught sight of us together, he frowned. "I came to check on the family. Is Carl around?"

I could feel Miss Frieda's hand tightened as she answered. "He's just stepped out. Do you want me to pass him a message?"

A loud "Ahem" announced some discomfort of Father Don's. "No. That'll be alright. I'll tell him myself, when I see him." Father Don peered at me from under his brows. "How are you, young lady? Getting ready for school, I see."

Again, questions about school. I nodded, and hoped my smile was pleasant enough for the Lord.

"She's almost ready to go. I've got her fed, school lunch prepared, and she's just headed upstairs to get her things."

More throat clearing accompanied Father Don's look. It's like a whole symphony of words was stuck in his throat, waiting the conductor to signal. He finally clasped his hands together and smiled. "Well, it looks like everything's taken care of. You did Grace a great favour, Frieda. I'll wait for you and Ellen, then."

I don't know what Miss Frieda's face said, but her hand gave my shoulder another sharp squeeze. "I still have supper to make."

Father Don lowered his chin. "Let's leave that for Carl to do. I think he may need some time alone with Ellen."

"Goodness. I wasn't trying to muscle in on their family."

"No one says you were." Still, Father Don's snort punctuated his words. "Ellen, best get your things. School's about to start."

I took the stairs two at a time as I rushed to get my book bag. On my way back, I could hear Father Don's gravelly voice from the bottom of the stairs.

"Resist the tempt…"

Both looked up as my weight caused the top floorboard to creak. Miss Frieda gave a smile, even as her eyes glistened.

"I'm ready." I felt the situation, whatever it was, warranted my speaking first.

No one accompanied me to school. Miss Frieda gave Father Don a handshake and me a hug. She was soon traipsing down the sidewalk, muttering to herself. Father Don nodded his farewell.

"I'll see you soon." I wondered what he meant, as it wasn't Sunday. I watched Father Don follow in Miss Frieda's wake, then I made my own way to school.

Darlene was nowhere to be found. We had spent the past days before school talking over our Shakespeare soliloquys. Today was the first day she hadn't shown to walk with me. Although she was more girly than I usually liked, I missed her company. Especially today, since I was walking into the schoolyard carrying Gram's shame. Gram had tried to off herself. More than just Grandpa and me knew. It was going to be a hard entry back into school with my family grief out in the open.

A crowd had gathered around the school stairs. They were a mix of boys and girls huddled close. One or two kept vigil along the group edges, as if expecting an enemy from somewhere.

One small boy looked in my direction and pointed. "She's coming."

That caused me to suck my breath. The enemy they expected was me. No choice but to keep putting my feet in front of each other. It was a long, quiet walk.

The clot of kids spread out as they watched me approach. Their faces showed eagerness, like hounds scenting blood. I half-expected baying. Darlene was standing at the front of the crowd. She took a couple steps forward and linked her arm in mine.

What?

"How's your grandma?" Darlene spoke more to the crowd than me.

"Okay, I guess."

A boy shook his head and leaned towards me. "Is she really okay? We heard she almost died." He rubbed his wrists as he spoke.

"Yeah. What happened? Stammer won't say." Another boy jerked a thumb towards where Stammer sat on the stairs.

Stammer gave a shrug, but kept watch on me, too.

"C'mon. Tell us." Connie spoke up from beside Stammer.

The admission price to the kids club was my grandma's private pain, and the ticket was to be written in her blood.

Fair enough.

"There was blood…" My voice cracked. I almost lost my nerve.

"Yeah?" Most faces looked eager. One or two looked like they were already thinking of sicking up.

"Lots of blood. Everywhere."

"Oh, man!" One boy started jumping up and down on the spot. "How'd it happen?"

"I don't know. I didn't see. All's I know is I saw my grandma in the tub, and it was full of blood. Her blood."

"A real live blood bath!" Darlene went pale, but stayed by my side.

"Did you see a knife?"

I swallowed, remembering the glinting metal lying on the floor. In hindsight, I recognized the knife. It was Gram's special one for killing chickens. Now that I thought of it too, I didn't see what Miss Frieda did with the knife once we were done.

"Well?" Darlene tapped my back as if to fix my stall. "Did you?"

"Yeah," I admitted.

"Do you have it?" Darlene kept her hand on me. There was no escaping. Might as well give 'em what they wanted.

"No," I continued, "but I saw blood everywhere. On the floor, the mirror, the walls. It even flowed out the door." I was painting a red storm of a picture.

The kids ate it up like licorice.

"How much blood can one person have?" Connie scowled, like she doubted my words.

I wondered if I'd stepped too far, both in the telling for my sake and the traitoring for Gram's.

"A lot." Stammer spoke up. "I read there's at least a gallon of blood in the human body."

I threw Stammer a grateful smile. He nodded back.

Miss Oswin rang the bell for school to start. The crowd of kids swept me up in the current of movement up the stairs. I was smack in the middle, rather than my usual prowl along the edges. I was pleased, yet not. I hadn't sold Dot out like this when she disappeared, but Dot was a kid. What happened to Dot was still too scary to think about. It coulda been anyone of us kids, but it was Dot. Somehow, Gram's story didn't strike the same personal fear in my schoolmates. Instead, it was a joy ride of macabre. Grown-ups were supposed to die sometime, anyways.

Everyone moved quietly to their desks as we came in. It was only then that I noticed Miss Oswin wasn't alone at the front of the room. Mr. Dionne sat beside her desk, arms folded in front of him.

"Class, please take your seats." Miss Oswin motioned a shush at the little ones who were still fidgeting. "We'll start when Father Don arrives."

I gave Darlene a nudge. "What's going on?"

"Don't you remember? We're doing soliloquys today. Remember? We've been practicing them together."

Ulp.

I hadn't remembered. I had only half of it memorized and planned on doing more on it yesterday. I'd only remembered our school recital coming up, not Miss Oswin's test today. I forgot, and I was sunk.

Darlene sat up tall at her desk beside me. Usually she was the hunched one, trying to hide her dunny confusion at learning. Today, I looked like a slinking lizard in comparison. The best way to attract a teacher's notice is by showing you don't want to. I sat up straight, but too late. The damage was done.

Miss Oswin's eyes lit on me. "Ellen, would you like to be first today?"

No, ma'am. May I please go to the bathroom and never come back? What can you say to a question like that? I said the only thing that would forestall my doom.

"Yes, ma'am."

"Thank you, Ellen. When Father Don gets here, please come up front."

Father Don's arrival came moments later. We heard the tromping of feet on the stairs and the bustle of the door being jarred open. Father's Don's heavy breathing was punctuated by a few "Have mercy's." When he saw us all turned to watch him, he broke into a big smile.

"Good morning, students." Father Don's warmth spread out with his words. A few students around me relaxed their shoulders and grinned. Maybe I wasn't the only one who would be fumbling for words today.

"Good morning, Father." Like clockwork, the whole class greeted him back. I always wondered how students knew how to time our greeting together.

"Miss Oswin, Mr. Dionne, thank you for inviting me."

Miss Oswin motioned to a seat beside Mr. Dionne. "Thank you for coming to judge our contest, Father. Once you take your seat, we'll begin."

Father Don squished himself into the chair beside Mr. Dionne, elbowing him in the side in the process. Mr. Dionne winced, which caused a few giggles from the back rows. Hard looks from both Mr. Dionne and Miss Oswin quickly shushed them.

A nod from Mr. Dionne, and Miss Oswin began.

"This past month, the senior students have studied William Shakespeare's *Twelfth Night*." Miss Oswin peered behind at the grown-ups as she spoke. "The students have been working hard, and each has chosen a soliloquy to present today."

One of the small boys in the front row dropped a pencil, causing all the grown ups to look.

"I want everyone to be on their best behaviour during this. No fidgeting, no pushing each other, no playing with pencils." Miss Oswin gave a stern look to the boy. He slid down in his seat, so I could no longer see him.

Miss Oswin gave a satisfied nod and continued. "What you don't know is that I've asked Mr. Dionne and Father Don here to judge your soliloquys. Whomever they choose as the winner will receive a prize."

There were a few nudges and mutterings at that announcement. Darlene leaned forward with her lips parted.

"Mr. Dionne has graciously donated a book by Enid Blyton from our new library additions." Miss Oswin held up a book for all to see.

I was impressed, but not everyone was. A few groans leaked out from the seats behind me.

"Ellen, will you please come up to start us off?"

Geez. I had been so entranced by the possibility of winning a book that I forgot I wasn't going to win it. I was about to meet my doom.

The walk to the front went quicker than I thought, but my vision wavered with each step. My stomach decided it didn't like supper for breakfast. I managed to coax it into some semblance of peace by the time I reached the front of the room.

"Ellen, which soliloquy have you prepared?"

Which one? None of them, actually.

"My *Twelfth Night* soliloquy is spoken by Orsino in Act V. '*Why should I not, had I the heart to do it.*"

Miss Oswin nodded. So far, so good.

I managed the first four lines before I stalled. No words came to my mind, and I fell silent. My hands felt sweaty, and rubbing them on my pants didn't improve the situation.

"*Since you to non-regardance…*" Miss Oswin's voice startled me outta my staring dumbly at the class.

"*Since you to non-regardance cast my faith,*" I repeated. And so she helped went with every line until I got to the "*That screws me*" line. For some reason, it triggered my brain, and I rambled the rest out without thought of pause or punctuation.

The applause was polite, even for kids.

"Thank you, Ellen." Miss Oswin shook her head and motioned me to take my seat. A few boys nodded at me as I sat down.

"You screwed that up nice." Connie's voice tickled as she patted my shoulder. "Good job."

Huh?

I guess if I'd aced it, the bar would be too high for the other students. Hadn't thought of it that way.

Connie was called next. She walked to the front, not daring to look at Stammer. I watched Mr. Dionne's face as she approached. He leaned forward and didn't blink once, like he had a rabbit in his sight. Surprising thing was so did Father Don. By the time Connie stood at the front, you could see her legs trembling. I know mine would, being in the crosshairs of that line of grown-ups. I felt for her, but then I remembered her slow walking by Stammer's desk, and him reaching out to touch her.

Connie stood a moment, facing her Pa and the priest. Mr. Dionne nodded once, and she turned to face the class.

"My soliloquy is *O, what deal of scorn looks beautiful.*" Connie stopped dead cold as Mr. Dionne's throat cleared. She twisted her head round to look at him, and he waved her to go on.

"I forgot to say, my soliloquy is from Act IV of *Twelfth Night.*"

Mr. Dionne cleared his throat again.

"Act III." Connie's cheeks reddened.

The class watched as Connie worked her way through the first line. "*O, what deal... of... of...*"

"*Of scorn...*" Miss Oswin prompted.

Mr. Dionne shifted in his chair and blew out harsh through his moustache.

Connie stopped again. Her lips worked on a few more words, but no sound came.

Father Don reached out and patted Connie's hand. "It's okay, child. Take your time."

I don't think it helped one bit. Connie wrenched her hand free and ran back to her desk. She quickly sat down and huddled over her work.

No one spoke. Miss Oswin stood like she was gonna go comfort Connie, but Mr. Dionne laid his own hand on Miss Oswin. If my lip reading was right, I swear he said, "I'll take care of her." Miss Oswin had no choice but to nod and move on.

Each student after her fared not much better, but nobody charged off like Connie. Miss Oswin's sighs got louder with each prompt she gave. Mr. Dionne crossed and uncrossed his arms a lot. Father Don clucked sympathetically at times, else remained silent. Darlene was last to go. I never seen her leave her seat so fast. When she stood up front, her head was held high. I don't think Miss Oswin understood what it meant as she started her prompting early.

"Your first line is "*This is the air...*"

"Pardon me please, Miss Oswin, but I know my lines." Darlene cleared her throat and lifted her chin.

Miss Oswin's mouth made an 'O.'

"My *Twelfth Night* soliloquy is Sebastian's speech in Act IV." Again, Darlene cleared her throat and gave pause to scan the audience. Once assured of our attention, she nodded again.

We all looked back. Who had taken over Darlene's body?

> *"This is the air; that is the glorious sun;*
> *This pearl she gave me, I do feel't and see't..."*

And so it went for the whole soliloquy. Not one pause or mistake that I could pick out.

Darlene took her seat to the sound of long applause. Even the senior boys joined in congratulating her.

"Well." Miss Oswin leaned against her desk as the applause died. "That." She shook her head like she'd seen the baby Jesus come marching into town playing a trombone. "That was excellent, Darlene."

In the end, it was no surprise that Darlene won the book. If you'd told me yesterday Darlene would win, my eyes woulda popped out. Darlene hugged the book close when she received it. Her grin was half-triumph, half-disbelief. When she sat back down beside me, I could feel her happiness vibrating off her.

"Thanks. Never won no school thing before. Couldn't a done it without you." Darlene placed the book between us on the edge where our desks touched. "Wanna see what I won?"

I admired Darlene's book. Held back my jealousy, too, as I opened it and touched the crisp white pages. I hadn't practiced much with Darlene, seeing as we were fully focused on Stammer. Well, maybe just I was focused on Stammer. Still, she gave me credit in her victory. I'd take it.

When recess came, the girls gathered around Darlene as she read out some of the book. Her reading was awkward at times, but got better with each page she tackled.

I only had a few more bloody questions to answer about Gram. Seems like I'd satisfied curiosity enough. I was mostly let be and could join in where I chose. I tested the waters and moved around a bit to the few groupings around the stairs. When the boys came from playing baseball, I tried their group out with no ill will. People seemed to take it as matter of fact that I was one of the crowd.

The only exception to this was Stammer.

31

Stan. The older boys were calling him that now. The new nickname was trickling down to the younger kids, too. Connie had been the first to say it.

Connie was saying it over and over, apparently. Everyone was whispering about how Stammer and Connie were an item.

No matter.

Darlene didn't want to hang after school, even when I dangled us following Stammer and Connie.

"I gotta go." Darlene had a smile as she patted her book bag. "I can't wait to see Ma's face when I show her my book prize."

"You wanna do something after?"

"Nah. I'm gonna be busy tonight. Ma's got me helping the ladies with the baseball tournament. We're baking pies for it."

I was tempted to ask if I could help, too, but I'm not much interested in baking. Especially when someone else's parent is involved. I pictured Darlene's ma being kind and all, but the inevitable questions about Gram would probably surface. Even worse would be the *You-poor-dear* looks thrown my way, like crumbs for a duck needing fattening.

"S'okay. I'll see you later, then. I got stuff I gotta do, too."

"See ya tomorrow? Walk to school?"

"Sure."

Surprising how easy it was to fall into a routine of being included. I barely blinked an eye that I was being asked. Darlene's ponytail bobbed behind her as she ran down the path from school. Her grin still lingered in the sun-dappled spots between the trees. Although I was alone, the day felt warm because of it.

Stammer and Connie walked home behind me. I could hear Connie's giggle. I could feel the steam coming off her words.

"Oh, Stan."

That's all it took. Just one sigh of hers, and I was off. Running. Not wanting them to sense any motion or thought of me. I ran down the same path Darlene took and made a wide turn at the road. I was headed away from the hotel. Last time I'd come this way, I'd scrambled with Stammer through the roadside bushes. This time, I ran straight down the middle of the road full speed.

I didn't know where I was going until I got there.

Stammer's house.

No worries that Stammer would be there. He was far behind with Connie, likely headed to the circus grounds for another ride. Or so the older boys hinted.

The truck was parked beside the house. I walked in the dirt grooves worn deep in the earth. Long grass fronds brushed my pant-legs as I paced close to the house. The harsh burr of cricket chirrups continued unabated as I peered through a dirty cracked pane. I shielded my eyes from the sun, but could see no movement beyond the streaks of soil on the glass.

No one was inside.

I felt a rub at my leg and looked down. Stammer's ginger cat was pacing around and through my legs. One of his ears was torn, the other missing, a clot of blood matted in its place.

"Nice kitty." The cat was easy to catch and pick up. His legs stretched long as I lifted him from the ground, but he settled easily into the crook of my arm, purring and kneading his paws on my shirt.

"You get in a fight, kitty? D'you win?"

Cat perked his massacred ear forward. His body tensed and pushed off my embrace to drop to the ground again. He padded away quickly as a figure came into view.

Stammer. No Connie, just Stammer.

"Hey. What are you doing here?"

I looked around for somewhere to hide, despite having already been spotted. The grass wasn't long enough. It was too far to duck behind the truck. Stupid reaction, I know. But I panicked.

"I said, what are you doing here? You gone deaf?"

I was in an awkward spot with limited options for escape. My best chance was to distract him.

"I thought you were with Connie."

Stammer frowned. "I was. But she… and then I…" He scuffed a shoe in the dirt. "Aw, never mind. You didn't answer the question. What are you doing at my house?"

I sidled to put the truck between us. Stammer held my gaze and followed to stand on the other side of the hood.

"Well?"

"I…" Heat flushed my face and my throat tightened. What was I doing here? I didn't even know, myself. All I could feel was that the place had drawn me like a bird to a feeder.

"You looking for me?" Stammer waggled his eyebrows and jerked a thumb at his chest.

I couldn't help but smile. "Maybe."

"Well, here I am. What do you want?" He crossed his arms and leaned on the hood. His eyes never left me.

"To say hi?" I copied his stance and gave my own quirk of a grin.

"Huh." Stammer stood up. "You couldn't say hi at school?"

I shrugged.

"I mean, all this time, you keep walking by, saying nothing but looking. You couldn't have once said hi?"

"What?"

"Ever since I kissed you. No. Ever since we kissed. Your lips were in on that deal. Don't deny it." Stammer pointed at me and wouldn't stop. His finger jabbed with each word he barked. "You were there just as much I was, and you can't pretend it never happened."

"I didn't."

Stammer snorted. "You did, and you still are."

"I said I didn't."

"I mean, what would it have hurt for you to just stop and talk after. Even just to say 'Stammer...' Oh, don't keep shaking your head at me. I know you call me that, too."

"Okay, I do."

"Just to say even if once, 'Stammer, it was nice but I don't think of you that way. So, let's go back to being friends.' Argh!" Stammer paced as he let out a long growl.

"I told you I was sorry I ran."

"Yeah, you did. But you never even mentioned our kiss."

"Stammer..."

"Would it have killed you just to even talk to me?"

"Stammer..."

"What?"

Stammer had come to the front of the truck. I have no idea how it happened, but so had I.

"Stammer..."

"I said, what?" He scowled, then his eyes widened as he noticed how close we were.

"It was nice."

"Oh."

"Real nice."

They say you never forget your first kiss. I was still trying to forget mine. God take Billy Harner and shove him down in Hell. They never talk about the rest of them though. How there'd be times you'd lift right up outta your body and laze-float high above while your lips sucked and grabbed at another's.

Stammer's second kisses were just as good as his first.

32

It was a kiss I didn't want to stop inhaling. I wanted to stay in it with Stammer as long as I could. Who wouldn't? I mean, it made up for quite a lot. In that moment, I could forgive Stammer for many things. His going with Connie, his ignoring me, even his not chasing me when I first ran. He made it clear he'd been waiting for me to speak first about the kiss. Couldn't change the past, so I'd have to start with the future.

I couldn't erase Billy. Billy with his greasy hands and smirk of a smile. I had a weak moment when I joined him in the outhouse. I still remember giving in to him, though my stomach roiled at the smell of his teeth. He had a kiss that started soft enough, but ended with his tugging and sucking my lip, tongue pressing into me, probing mine.

Billy managed to get a hand down my pants. I didn't know if that counted for anything. I didn't have anyone to ask.

I kicked hard at his knees and wrenched myself away, scraping my own knees. I was panting after, some from the fighting, some from the surge I'll admit Billy made me feel.

Billy licked his fingers after.

I cried.

That's how I got the cigarettes. Billy musta been as frightened of my squealing as I was of him bragging. I still couldn't figure out if our boarder, Henry, knew. He and Billy were friends.

So far, I don't think Gram and Grandpa knew. Grandpa woulda tossed Billy out on his keester. At least, that's what I hope would happen if Grandpa knew.

Never no mind that stuff now. Stammer overlaid that memory with his own.

It was a good, good kiss. But at some point, Stammer and I had to exhale.

33

Stammer broke off first this time. My pride was okay, as he did it nice and gentle. He rested his forehead on mine and took a shuddering breath.

"I can't."

I let my own breath out. "What?"

"I said I can't." Stammer took a step away from me.

I stumbled forward with the release of his embrace. "What?" It was the only word I could get out. My stomach clenched, and my mouth couldn't form any other.

"I'm still going with Connie." He shoved his hands in his pockets. He was closed off again. No look at me, no smile. Just back to walling me out.

"I see." My hands didn't know what to do. They fluttered from my head to my chest, before finally settling on wringing each other for comfort.

"It's quite… intense, y'know?" Stammer had the indecency to look me straight in the eye right then.

I didn't think my blush would ever go away. Stammer's eyes went wide, then he quirked an eyebrow, like we were sharing a secret I wanted to be part of.

"Go away, Stammer. Just go away." My voice rose with each word.

"It's my house. You're the one trespassing."

"I said, go away!"

"Aw, c'mon. Don't be like that. We're still friends, aren't we?"

I felt used. Worse than Billy Harner, 'cause this time I expected something in return.

"Just take your stammers and go stammer somewhere else. Just leave me alone." My fury vented itself and settled into a sob. A big, racking sob. I stepped back so Stammer wouldn't be within reach to comfort me. More to keep me from accepting it.

Stammer thinned his lips. His face went flat like marble. Lord Jesus, his cheekbones stood out like chisels, and his eyes were as blue as jay feathers.

"I tried." He shrugged the words out and turned away.

"Stammer…"

A gunshot sang out from nearby. Stammer and I looked to the fields where it still echoed. We both tensed, knowing it came from the direction Dot was found. Stammer's uncle appeared in the distance, carrying a shotgun and walking towards us along the pilgrim's trail. Stammer relaxed, but I didn't.

I had only a moment before Stammer's uncle came near. Only a moment for me to tear down Stammer's wall. My heart was pounding. I had something to say, but I didn't know how to say it.

Uncle Ward came in from the fields while I paused. He held his rifle nestled in one arm and carried a dead grackle by its claws. Its wings flop bounced with each step he took.

"Stanislaw! Come help me."

The moment was gone.

I watched as Stammer ran to meet Uncle Ward. Stammer took the bird, and they both walked back.

"It was after the cat. Put it on the dung hill. One of the animals will finish it off."

"Yes, sir."

"Go find Nathan and tell him I'm about to go."

"Yes, sir."

Stammer broke out in a run.

"Ah, Ellen. You must be happy today."

I nodded.

I felt the exact opposite, but you don't point that out to grown-ups. It tends to keep unwanted conversations going.

"It'll be nice to have her back. I'm sure you've missed her."

"You mean Gram?"

"I thought your grandfather told you we're picking her up today."

I nodded again, as I didn't want to rat out Grandpa for not including me.

"We'll be back just after supper, so keep an eye out."

Stammer came back as I was about to leave. He came trotting right up beside me. I flinched. I couldn't help it.

"It's not your bird."

"Of course I'm not your bird. I never was."

"No, not you." Stammer scowled. "The bird. It wasn't your circus bird."

"Oh, the drongo!" I'd forgotten about it. The last time we saw it was the day we found Dot.

"It's been around here a lot." Stammer pointed at the trees beyond the property fence. "Hanging around with the grackles. It's bigger and shinier than them."

I turned to look, but couldn't see any sign of movement in the trees or air above. "When did you last see it?"

"Yesterday. When Connie and I..." Stammer blushed hard and met my eyes. "He's still around, your bird. You just have to keep an eye out for him."

If it was a girl speaking, I woulda thought there was a hidden message there. Since it was Stammer, I knew he just meant the bird. I nodded. "Thanks. I'll keep watch."

"I'm headed to the hotel. I can give you a ride back, Ellen." Stammer's uncle twirled the key ring as he spoke. He nodded at Stammer. "You wanna come for a ride to town?"

Stammer shook his head. "I should stay here. I still got my chores to do."

"Suit yourself."

I let Uncle Ward shut the truck side door as I slid into the passenger seat. The window was open, so I leaned an arm on the edge and gazed out.

Stammer was still watching.

"Stammer?"

"What?"

"Thanks. And see you tomorrow."

He nodded and grinned. "See you tomorrow."

I didn't look back as Uncle Ward drove us onto the main road. I didn't have to. I felt things were good enough.

34

Grandpa was sitting in the bar when Uncle Ward and I walked in. Blue-tinged air swirled overhead and seeped out the door into the hallway. The smell of cigarettes and unwashed man was powerful enough to make my eyes water.

Uncle Ward smelled it, too. He walked into the bar and clapped a hand on Grandpa's shoulder. I don't know how he did it. My own eyes were drowning. I even needed a sleeve to cover my nose.

"You ready?"

Grandpa grunted. "In a minute."

"They won't wait much longer than an hour."

A shrug accompanied Grandpa's scowl. "Alright."

Uncle Ward sniffed loudly beside Grandpa. "Just saying. When's the last time you washed? You are picking up your missus, y'know."

Grandpa took one more drag on his cigarette before stubbing it out. "I haven't. Not since I found her." He held Uncle Ward's eyes until the other man nodded.

"I see."

"Guess it's time I did, though." Grandpa gave a push back from the bar, stood, and stretched.

"We got time if you make it quick." Uncle Ward looked at his wristwatch.

Grandpa didn't smell any better when he passed me. I was glad he didn't give me a hug. He was a bigger fan of side-hugs than full, but his smell woulda killed me nonetheless. Grandpa clumped up the stairs, and soon the sound of water in the pipes from the bathroom creaked through the house.

I left Stammer's uncle to wait by himself. I had too many fidgets and worries that needed attending.

For the first time I can remember, the kitchen was empty. No Gram bustling and moving things about. The stove was silent and cold. A few dishes lay scattered here and there. I suppose Grandpa had been foraging during the day. I picked a couple dishes up and placed them in the sink.

"Ellen? We're headed out now." Grandpa called from out in the hall.

"Okay."

I could hear Grandpa and Uncle Ward murmur in the hall, then the door close behind their voices.

The house was quiet except for a couple of creaks as the water pipes relaxed into waiting. I don't think I'd been alone like that in a house before. Outdoors in a field, sure, but within four walls, I don't think ever. Even in my bedroom, there'd always been someone a room or two over, ready to come if called. I was in charge of myself. I guess that's what grown-ups dealt with all the time.

My thoughts started swirling. Kissing, fighting, being left out and left alone, dying. Seems the emptier the space around me, the more my thoughts raced. I picked up a few more dishes and stacked them for washing. I grabbed the dishcloth and wiped down the table and counters. The stovetop needed cleaning, too.

No one had checked the chickens today. I wondered if they'd been seen-to yesterday. I grabbed the feed and went out the back door.

The chickens came out of different nooks and crannies when they heard the door open. The rooster gave a crow as it flew down from his perch on the outhouse. All the chickens gathered at my feet, clucking angrily and pecking at the few seeds that fell as I opened the feedbag. Soon they were busy gorging themselves, no longer interested in holding me hostage.

The chicken coop had a few eggs. I gathered them, using my shirt as a basket, and carried them back into the house. Being busy held back my thoughts some. It eased and faded both the pains and the pleasures of the day. I hadn't thought of chores that way. Maybe Gram did.

"Halloo?"

Miss Frieda peered round the edge of the doorway, like she was frightened a wolf might spring at her. She relaxed into a smile when she saw me.

"You home alone, Ellen?"

"Yes, ma'am."

"I heard your Gram was coming home today. I stopped by to see if you need any help."

I grinned and made a show of wiping my hands on the dish-towel. "Thanks, Miss Frieda. I think we're doing pretty good, though."

Miss Frieda raised an eyebrow as she looked around the kitchen. "Looks clean and tidy. You do this?"

I nodded, still grinning. I was like a young bird showing its parents it knew how to fly.

"Wonderful job. You thought about supper yet?"

She had me there. I cast a frown at the cold box, trying to remember how much chicken was left.

"Not to worry. I brought something for you and your grandparents." Miss Frieda stepped fully into the room. She had oven mitts on and carried a dish. "It's my special casserole."

It was a good casserole. No, it was a great casserole! Miss Frieda spoke some about how she made it. I found it interesting to hear a grown-up talk and not about school. I'd never thought about the steps you need for cooking. Maybe Gram would show me the recipe for those biscuits.

"My mama taught me this casserole. I make it any time extra hugs are needed."

I thought about that as I chewed. Food as a comfort, both in the making and enjoying. "Can you teach me how to make it?"

Miss Frieda's eyes widened. "I would love to. It's a recipe that needs to be shared. I've worried it might fade away when I do."

I nodded as I continued to eat.

Henry soon joined us. His sighs of comfort as he ate gave reminder that Miss Frieda was an excellent cook. I thought so, too.

Miss Frieda didn't eat. She just sat watching us enjoy. Her fingers traced circles and maybe a heart or two on the table surface as she mused.

"You make this a lot, Miss Frieda?"

Her voice was soft in replying. "Not much call for a big casserole like this, or any of my cooking, for that matter." She traced another heart on the table. "I once made this for your grandfather."

My ears perked up.

Miss Frieda continued to trace a heart, then draw letters in it. "We were quite the friends back then, your grandparents and me."

I looked over at Henry, but he was busy chomping and chewing.

"Went everywhere together. They were an item even back then, but they always made time for me."

I didn't know if saying something would keep the story going, or just being quiet. I chose the latter, pretending interest in my plate.

"First time Grace felt her mood sit heavy on her, it worried me and Carl both. Grace stayed home a whole month back then. We didn't have any sight of her. Her parents barely said a word 'bout how she was doing."

There was a catch in Miss Frieda's breathing. I kept my eyes on my plate, not daring to break into her notice.

"Who wouldn't of worried together. Seemed only natural, me her best friend… taking care of Carl while she was sick." Miss Frieda shuddered. "I been paying for it ever since. I bled out all that mistake long ago, but feels like I'm still bleeding."

"This is delicious." Henry scooped another forkful of casserole into his gobby mouth. He smacked his lips. "Wouldn't mind eating like this all the time."

Miss Frieda looked up at the same time I did. Her eyes glistened though her lips smiled. "Much appreciated. I can drop off another sometime."

Henry's words were garbled with casserole, but you could still make 'em out. "I'd like that. A lot."

I pondered on Miss Frieda sitting beside him. She had only one ratty cardigan, as far as I saw. Her face was creased with worry that even now sagged around her smile. Sad eyes. Sad, sad eyes. I couldn't help but wonder if I was looking at a faraway version of me.

"Anyone here?" A voice called from the hallway.

I leapt up, hoping it was Gram and Grandpa, and went running. I wanted to leave my sad thought back at the table with Miss Frieda.

I stopped dead in my tracks. It wasn't Gram and Grandpa.

"Hallo, missy! I didn't expect to see you here!"

It was Samson the Strongman.

35

Samson had his bags plunked down beside him. Their worn leather and travel stickers showed he'd travelled far before landing here. His shoes were polished, though worn. He tilted his head as if listening to some high-pitched sound from me.

I realized I was squealing with delight and shut my mouth. I continued to grin, though.

Miss Frieda pushed by me, and reached out a hand. "You're that man from the circus. I never did thank you for the help you gave the children."

Samson reddened as his own hand engulfed Miss Frieda's. "It was nothing, ma'am. You did the main part of it by taking them home."

"You're from the circus?" Henry stood at my side, wiping his mouth with a napkin.

How could you not know he was with the circus? Even though he was dressed in regular people clothes-excepting his tie, of course, that was a riot of colours-he still stood larger than any other I'd seen crammed in our hallway.

The man nodded. "I am, but not for the moment."

Miss Frieda nodded, too. "Makes sense, seeing as you're here, and they're not."

"Yes'm." Samson shifted in place. "I'm Andrew, by the way. Andrew Fisher. Andy. I heard this was the main hotel in town."

Miss Frieda took a quick glance at me. "It is. It's the only one, but the owners are away right now."

"Oh." Samson... Andy... made move to reach for his suitcases, but stood again. "Are they coming back soon?"

"They should be back real soon." I spoke up quick before Miss Frieda could turn him away. "Within the hour. You can wait in the parlour until they come." The Strongman. Here. Wanting to stay at our hotel. There was no way I was letting that opportunity pass. I eyed his arms as he reached for his suitcases again. They bulged through his suit sleeves. I wanted to touch one so bad.

"You hungry, Mr. Fisher?" Miss Frieda motioned towards the kitchen.

Samson nodded. "I am."

"Come join us in the kitchen. I made a casserole."

"It's worth trying." Henry smacked his lips and made a show of patting his belly.

"Don't mind if I do."

The hallway was crowded enough with all four of us, one being a sequoia giant of a man. The front door opened, and it became a regular parade.

Grandpa came in first, leading Gram. Stammer's Uncle Ward brought up the caboose. I never moved so fast since I used to greet Da coming home from work.

"*Gram!*"

"Easy, Ellen, easy. My arm still hurts." Gram wrapped her good arm 'round me as I hugged her waist. She was gentle and tentative, so I eased the eagerness outta my own hug. The strength of my missing her surprised us both, I think.

Grandpa harrumphed, so I broke with Gram to give him a hug. I didn't know if it was what he was hinting, but he seemed to take it as natural course once it began. He even stayed longer in the hug than I did.

"Andy Fisher, what are you doing here?" Uncle Ward spoke, looking like his eyebrows were going to float right off his head.

Samson shrugged and smiled. "Told you I might look the place up when I was done."

Grandpa shifted his glasses for a better look at Samson. "I don't think I've seen you before. I woulda remembered."

"No, sir. We haven't met, but I was with the circus that passed through."

At the mention of the circus, Gram paled and swayed on her feet.

"Lord, you men keeping a sick woman standing in the hall while you jabber away." Miss Frieda tutted, while the men dipped their heads in response. "Here, Grace. Give me your arm. Ellen, grab hold the other."

"No, I'm fine, Ellen." Gram straightened. Her bandaged arm poked out from her sleeve as she waved me off. "I wouldn't mind your help upstairs, though, Frieda. I understand you've been seeing to things round here."

Miss Frieda dropped her sight at Gram's words.

"No, no. I meant you've taken care of Ellen." Gram put a hand on Frieda's shoulder. "That's twice you've been there to help."

Miss Frieda laid her own hand on top of Gram's. "I needed to be."

Gram and Miss Frieda went up the stairs, arm in arm. Grandpa stood at the bottom, watching them go.

"Carl." Uncle Ward laid his own hand on Grandpa. "I need to make introductions."

Grandpa turned to see Uncle Ward standing beside Samson, who shifted his weight from one foot to the other.

"I already know everyone here, and there's casserole waiting in the kitchen." Henry ducked back down the hall.

"Carl Johnson, this here is Andrew Fisher."

"Nice to meet you."

"It's a pleasure, Mr. Johnson. Are you the owner of this hotel?"

"I am."

"I'm looking for a place to stay tonight. Do you have any room?"

Uncle Ward raised a hand to scratch his cheek. "Before you answer that, Carl, I think there's something you both should know about each other. And about how Andy and I are acquainted."

Samson—no, Andy—stared a long moment at Uncle Ward and nodded.

"Sounds like I may not enjoy this." Grandpa crossed his arms and leaned against the bannister.

Uncle Ward cleared his throat. "That's for you to decide." He looked at Andy who nodded once more.

"Carl." Uncle Ward's voice faltered as he shook his head. "You've suffered a lot of loss this past year, family being the main of it."

"Damn right." Grandpa shifted and stilled again.

"You never once accused me of being a cause of your loss, though things looked to the otherwise."

Grandpa nodded, else said nothing.

"Andrew here was the one who found Dot's body. I met him while we were both in custody on suspicion of killing your granddaughter. I'm supposing Andy just got released, as I told him to look me up when it happened."

"That's right." Andy's face strained with the grief of being trapped when you ought not be. At least, that's how I woulda felt in his place. Schoolyard pain can be useful for figuring out who's a fellow sufferer.

"I see." Grandpa stared hard at Andy, then pulled a kerchief out of his pocket and busied himself with his glasses. "Give me a moment."

Uncle Ward took that moment to notice me sitting crouched on the bottom stairs. "Your granddaughter is here."

Grandpa looked up sharp. "Ellen, go see if your grand-mother is alright."

Tossed from conversation. Just like that. I held my grumbles in and walked slowly up the stairs. Lingering at the top didn't help. Grandpa shooed me off and followed the men into the parlour.

Gram and Miss Frieda were perched on the bed in my grandparents' bedroom. Neither noticed me hanging at the doorway. They had the look of Dot and me with their heads together. Miss Frieda gave Gram a hug that Gram returned.

"Ellen!" Gram spotted me first and gave me a wave to come in.

"Glad you're home, Gram."

"I am, too." Gram held out a hand to Miss Frieda. "Frieda's been telling me how you cleaned the kitchen and…" Gram's voice trailed off, but I knew she thought of the bathroom.

"She's a big help." Frieda gave Gram's hand a squeeze. "You should be proud of her."

I found it hard not to smile at those kind words.

"I should be going, Grace. I'll come by tomorrow to visit."

"I'll be expecting you."

Miss Frieda left me alone with Gram. Neither of us knew what to say. I was the one who found her. She was the one who'd found my secret in the drawer. The silence between was more comfortable than the words we'd have to spill.

"You didn't have to hide it." Gram spoke first, cutting through the silence, leaving space for my dread to grow.

"I didn't mean to." Playing dumb wasn't gonna get me anywhere on this one.

"You should have come to me right away." Gram shook her head slowly. "How can I trust you if you do things like this."

That hurt hard. She was right, though. But I lost her trust way before that. I lost it when I lost Dot. "I woulda, but it was Dot's and I didn't think it right."

"What are you talking about?" Gram narrowed her eyes as she tilted her head.

"What are *you* talking about?" I answered back with a question. That's one thing I'd picked up from Da.

"Your underwear. I found it. It had blood on it."

"Oh."

"You been having your courses without telling me?"

"No! It's not like that. I mean, yeah, I've had them." I'd actually had 'em for a while now.

Gram's face took on a grey hue. "What do you mean it's not like that? What's the blood from?" She gasped as she thought through possibilities. "No. No. Please don't let it be that. Not like your mama."

I was stunned. "What are you talking about?"

Gram moaned to herself as she rocked. "I knew it. I knew it when I saw it. Not again. I won't let it."

"Gram?"

Her eyes were hard when she looked up. "You're not to have relations. Not here. I won't allow it. Your mama chose her path. I couldn't stop her. But you. You're too young."

My face musta showed confusion, 'cause Gram reached out and shook my shoulders. "No sexual congress. You hear me? It's enough your mama ran off with that man. I won't have you going down that path too."

The heat rose in my face. I hadn't done what she accused, but it had been close. Billy Harner had the know of that one. "Gram, it's not my underwear!"

That took the wind outta Gram. She worked her mouth as if chewing on this new fact. "Then whose is it? Oh."

I nodded. It's all I had left. My words were gone, and tears were threatening to spill.

"Oh. Oh." Gram folded her arms as she eyed me. "Whose is it?"

I wiped at my eyes and hunched over my hands. "Dot's. It's Dot's underwear."

"Oh."

"I found it by the circus grounds. Darl…" I took a breath. Best leave others out of this. "I was there and found it."

"Oh, oh, oh." Gram's shoulders shook.

"I didn't mean to hide it!" I couldn't help the wail that took over my chest. "I'dda showed it to you, honest. It's just I didn't want Dot picked over no more."

Gram continued to shake. She scrubbed at her mouth with her good hand as her face creased. "My dear child. Poor, poor dear child."

"I know! Dot's gone. It's my fault. I can't bring her back."

That caused Gram to look up sharp. "I was talking about you, child."

Gram's words were more than I could take. The tears flowed, and my sobs racked and racked my heart. I crumbled in a heap in Gram's lap. She rocked me back and forth as I shuddered out my pain.

"Shush. Shush. I'm so sorry. We forgot about you in all this. Shush."

Gram waited a long time 'til my sobbing eased. She tilted my chin to get a good look at me.

"I'm s-s-sorry, too, Gram."

"We're all sorry, Elly." Gram squeezed me tight. "We all miss Dot."

I squeezed back.

"We got some work to do, though." Gram's face was thoughtful. "Where'd you put Dot's underwear?"

"Back in my drawer to keep it safe."

"We have to take it to the police. And I'm sorry, love, but they'll want to talk to you about where you found it. It may be important. It may be something Dot's trying to tell us."

That sounded like a plan. To help Dot. Before telling Gram, I wanted to avoid the whole thing. Now Gram and me were in it together. Maybe it was Dot trying to speak to me, too, and I shut her in a drawer with the rest of my pain. Time to open the drawer. Time to help Dot. That I could do.

36

There's no telling how men will talk with each other when there's issues on the table. You'd think them the best of friends, only to see them grab for each other's throats. Or you'd hold your breath, expecting fire with their glares, then find them drinking and laughing minutes later.

When I came downstairs, Grandpa was drinking with Andy. He was even snorting at a story that Andy held forth. I hung at the doorway, hoping to hear what they talked about. Something to do with the Tattoo Lady and the Ringmaster, best I could figure. And a bed they busted together. A few weeks ago, I wouldn't have been able to fill in the details. Now, I could. Got me my own little snort to hear it.

"Ellen? How long you been there?" Grandpa looked up at the sound of me.

"Not long." I felt bold enough to go in the bar. I stood by Grandpa and snuck peeks at Andy and his arms. "Gram's resting. She said she'd have supper later. I was to offer some to you both."

Grandpa took another tip of his glass. He did that at times, when he wanted a peace.

Andy was not tuned to our signals. "How'd she hurt her arm?"

Grandpa took another drink and let the sentence hang unanswered.

"Ah." Andy took his own noisy gulp, as if to make up for his asking. His bicep bulged like a mountain with the lift of his glass.

"You want me to bring the food here?" I looked at Grandpa, but stood closer to Andy. He smelled of leather and sweat. Not a Billy Harner sweat, but one mixed with the wind of the prairie. He looked up at me, but shifted closer to Grandpa in his seat.

"We'll come to the kitchen. We're about finished here." Grandpa drained his glass. Andy paused a moment, then did the same.

I beat them to the kitchen. I wanted to serve them. I told myself it was to show Grandpa that I was learning, but a small part of me wanted to show off to the Strongman.

I shouldn't have bothered. Andy barely gave me a glance as he and Grandpa talked over politics and farming. Andy had grown up on a farm much farther south than here. His folks had sold their fields after a bad mix of weather and crops.

I'd long been done and left while they were still talking over articles in an old newspaper Grandpa spread out over the table.

The stairs creaked much later at night. I woke to hear Grandpa's voice in the room next to mine. I could hear him showing light switches and talking about room rates. Some heavy shufflings and thuds followed the door being shut. Grandpa's footsteps disappeared down the hall to his shared room with Gram. I stayed awake awhile listening for more, but the night noises soon settled.

So did I.

37

If you wanna find a chicken's eggs, you gotta think like a chicken. Fortunately, that's easy to do, as the chicken is a real stupid bird. The ones we got were even dumber than most. One of them would strut back and forth where her nest was hidden under the chicken coop, then suddenly dart under. You could hear her loud clucking as she shifted herself to lay.

Gram always tried to get them to lay in the coop. Most of them she was successful with, but there were always one or two holdouts. Chickens is stupid. They don't see that at least they're warm and dry while nesting in the coop. Gram and I was gonna get their eggs no matter what.

Gram hadn't been up to collecting eggs since Dot died. I'd taken that task on, mostly remembering it without prompting. I wasn't getting prompted anyways, so it didn't much matter. Grandpa never looked to see if our cold box had the day's eggs, anyways.

With Gram back, I kept the job. I'd gotten to know the hens better and could stand their pecks when I fed 'em.

Andy was joining us for breakfast, so we needed those eggs. He was enormous, and I supposed his appetite would be giant, too.

When I got to the kitchen, Gram was already setting out the breakfast dishes. The frying pan was set on the stove. Everything was in preparation for the meal, awaiting the eggs. Gram even had the egg basket ready, so I didn't have to use my shirt. I don't think she'd approve of the chicken shit stains if I did.

"Morning, Gram." I gave her a hug and kiss.

Gram smiled, and it almost reached her eyes. "Good morning, my darling. Breakfast will be ready as soon as you collect it."

"Yes'm." My stomach growled with impatience as I opened the back door.

There was a clot of blood and feathers on the doorstep. More feathers were scattered, with blood smeared across the front of the chicken coop.

Not a chicken was in sight.

"Gram?" I think my voice had a panic in it.

Gram came right away, wiping her hands on her apron. "What is it, Ellen?"

"The chickens are gone."

Gram paced the yard, tapping with her foot at a half-eaten carcass she found by the coop. "Looks like a blood bath."

I flinched at Gram's words. She didn't even pause after she said it.

"Who do you think it was?"

"Not who. What. Probably a fox or two." Gram went to the gate and found it swung easily. The latch hadn't been shut. "Gate's open." She cast a speculative eye at me and shook her head.

"It wasn't me, Gram. I swear." I hadn't been through that gate since after Billy's groping.

"No matter. We'll make due with some rashers today."

The rooster chose that moment to climb up the outhouse and scream his call. "Ur-ur-ur-ur-roooooo."

"At least the ole bird made it." I found it small comfort, as that rooster was more annoying than productive, but at least one creature had made it through the massacre.

Gram thinned her lips. "Some help he is. I don't remember hearing him crow once last night."

The rooster crowed again and was answered by clucking.

Three hens appeared outside the gate, bobbing their heads as they paced.

"That rooster just avoided a visit to my cooking pot." Gram nodded with satisfaction at the ole bird up high.

I ran to the gate and opened it again. The chickens scattered, then grew bold and strutted through. They clustered around Gram, pecking the dirt around her feet.

"I wonder where they hid last night."

Gram gave me an eye. "Good question. And if you find the answer, you might find us some breakfast."

That was as much a direct order as Gram would ever give. I grinned and saluted back. "Yes, ma'am!"

Gram's eyes crinkled with her smile that time.

There wasn't much space between buildings where the hotel stood. The bush was thick behind, though. I picked up a stick and poked a few bush branches back. I got lucky the third place I looked: A chicken startled from under the brush and darted between my legs. There was an egg where she had hidden. I'd have to come back for it after I wrangled that chicken.

The chicken ran between buildings and out onto the street. That hen musta been a Catholic, 'cause it headed right down the street to church. Time for me to teach it some prayers. Chickens can run like the dickens when they want. Still, I kept up until I got close to the churchyard.

There were two people crouched on the church steps. The chicken ran past and one shot up. It was Stammer!

"Hey! This your chicken?" Stammer gave a holler when he saw me approach.

"Yeah! Fox got into them last night. Gate was open." I almost didn't see Stammer redden as I was running fast.

But he did. And I seen it.

He glanced at Connie—of course, Connie would be with him—and said a few things, then jumped up to join me in the chase.

We cornered the chicken around the back of the church. It hid under the stairs. Stammer blocked one side while I made grabbed for its tail. I pulled out a few feathers and got a scratch for my troubles before I finally got a handle on it. It flapped its wings wildly as I hauled it out in the open. The chicken calmed once I'd managed to get a grip on it and tuck its head in the crook of my arm.

Stammer gave a wild grin. "That was fun! Let it go again, and we'll give it another chase."

I gave a peek at Connie. "I don't think so. Your girlfriend is looking for you."

Stammer followed my sight and grimaced.

Connie sat all folded into herself. Her legs were twined around each other. She gave a little wave, but mostly just stared.

"She's not my girlfriend." Stammer gave a wave back despite the denial. His hair flopped forward over his eyes as he gave his head a shake.

My breath caught despite my best efforts.

"You said she was, yesterday."

Stammer's stammer came back as he balled his hand. "I kn-know I d-d-did. But today, she's not." His eyes held mine even so. They were bluest of blues, like a summer sky.

"Oh."

"So." Stammer shifted as if to walk, but stood his ground. "You coming to the game this weekend?"

"I suppose." I paused, trying to think of what would keep the conversation going. Connie's glares were getting harder to ignore for either of us.

"Would be nice to see you there."

I couldn't hide my smile. "Would be nice to see what the uniforms look like."

Stammer's shoulders straightened. "Yeah. They look real nice. We each got our names and our own number on them." He took another peek at Connie before looking back. "I'm number six," he added.

"*Hey, Stammer!*" Connie's yell had more annoyance than friendly in it. "C'mon, Stammer! I don't have all day."

"I thought you said you broke up with her."

"Stammer reddened again. "I guess more like breaking up. She don't know it yet."

"Oh."

The chicken chose that moment to shit in my hand.

"Oh. Geezus!" Crap of a chicken. Shit.

Stammer laughed. "You may wanna get cleaned up before tomorrow."

"No doubt." I shook my head, like getting shat on was no big deal. Really, I wanted to strangle that chicken. "Well, maybe see ya tomorrow."

"Right." Stammer turned and walked back to Connie.

Connie smiled and patted the space beside her on the church steps.

I forebore waving, considering one hand was full of chicken, and the other, full of shit.

"Elly?" Stammer turned halfway between me and Connie.

"Yeah?"

He looked at the sky, as if thinking something over.

I was about to turn again.

"It was me," Stammer yelled out, catching my attention again.

"What?"

"It was me. I left your gate open last night." He dipped his chin and grinned wide, then turned back to Connie.

I stood rooted until the chicken tried to flap and make a break for it. I grabbed it tighter and trotted back to our hotel.

Stammer left the gate open. Stammer in our backyard. Last night.

Well, I'll be.

38

Gram was right. Some things you just gotta get through. I don't know if that wisdom came with the opening of her vein. Or was it hidden inside her the whole time, and she forgot for awhile? No matter. Some things you just gotta get through.

Talking to the police that afternoon was one of them. I don't know of anyone who likes talking to the police. Except maybe their wives and kids. Maybe their parents. No. I bet even their parents feel nervous, like the child they raised now had all power over them, and if they'd done the child wrong while growing, well, that child could turn around and arrest them. Throw them in jail forever if they wanted. Police could throw anyone in jail if they wanted to, even judges, 'cause a judge can't stop an arrest, only reverse it much later once it's done.

I wanna be a policeman when I grow up.

The police that came to the house were the same as we talked to when making our first report of Dot. Neither of them was as nice as the one who told us news of finding Dot's dress. No cap in hand this time.

The policemen looked me up and down suspicious-like. I guess I deserved it. I mean, I'd withheld evidence that might have solved the case early, so they could go home and intimidate their families. But I had held it back, and here they were on a Saturday, stuck in a parlour, interviewing a child about another child's underpants.

It didn't help that Gram insisted on being there for the interview. She kept '*Oh dear*'ing and dabbing at her eyes while I spoke.

"That about does it." One of the men flipped his booklet closed and tucked his pen back in his pocket.

I heaved a sigh of relief.

The other one looked sharp at me as I did it, so I turned it into a cough instead. I guess no matter the age, we're all suspicious in the eyes of the law.

"She didn't mean to keep it." Gram's voice wavered, but her determination to say one last piece showed in her raised hands. "She didn't know how important it was."

"Well, now she knows." The hard-eyed policeman gave me a final withering look as he adjusted his hat.

"If you see anything else, you let us know right away." The other one, the note-taker, was more forgiving. He'd written down my words the first time. Maybe he remembered how lost I'd seemed. Maybe he had kids of his own.

"I will. I promise."

I don't think the word promise means much to police. They gave each other a quick look before the note-taker muttered, "Just leave it."

Grandpa stood in the doorway to the parlour. He made way for the police and escorted them to the front steps. I could hear their murmurs for a couple minutes before they finally left and Grandpa returned.

"They're going back to where Elly found it. They're going to take another look."

"Sweet Lord Jesus, please help them find something." Gram's breath shook. "All these bits and pieces, and still no knowing what happened."

Grandpa scowled. "We know what happened. Just not who did it."

That set Gram off again. She covered her eyes with her handkerchief and rocked. "Oh, dear Jesus. Oh, dear Baby Jesus."

Grandpa softened his glare and took steps to Gram's side. "Well, now. It'll be fine. They'll solve it, Grace. Just give them time." His face spoke worry along with his words.

Gram managed to look up, showing a curtain of tears on her face. "It's a hard wait, Carl."

"That I know, dearest one. That I know."

I sidled my way out of the room while they hugged.

Andy strolled in as I was sneaking out. He tipped his hat when I tried to pass.

"Afternoon, missy. You going somewhere?"

That stopped me in my tracks. "Just going out. Why?"

"No reason." He kept looking, though, like he wanted more words from me.

"You going somewhere?" I was happy to oblige.

"No, but maybe later." Andy took a quick look back out the door. "Say, you wanna show me around a bit?"

That perked me up. In more than one spot. "Sure. When'd you like to go?" I didn't even question that there wasn't much to see in a one-street town. You could pretty much look up and down the street, and your tour would be done. Still, a walk to school might be nice.

"How about now?"

"Okay." I had my shoes on already. I looked down at my jeans. Reasonably clean for showing someone around. Then I took another look at Andy.

He was still peering out the door.

"Who you looking for?"

Andy startled, like I was a mouse in an elephant cage. "No one."

A kid knows a lie when they hear it, even from an adult. That false rise to the end of Andy's words was a dead giveaway.

I lost interest though, since it wasn't me his words were rising about.

"What'd you wanna see?"

"I dunno. Maybe just around." Andy gave the same foot shuffle I'd seen Stammer do.

I thought a moment longer as I rested my eyes on Andy's face. "Ohhh." I almost smacked myself upside the head right there. "How about I show you some of the school grounds. There's a big baseball game there tomorrow."

I swear, Andy's ears perked up. If he had a tail, he woulda wagged it. "Okay. If you want." Studied nonchalance in an adult sounds the same as in kids. He was hooked. Bad. Time to find the one who had hooked him.

I was right. Andy spent barely two seconds looking at the rest of the street. The church, the store, the few houses, nothing held his attention. The moment I mentioned the path leading to school, he practically pointed in that direction and ran.

With age comes wisdom. In my case, I now had a bit of age, and the whole adult world was spilling out secrets left, right and center. My guess is those secrets were always there, going on right under my nose. You just had to know what to look for. No thanks, and yet thanks, to Billy Harner. That bastard.

It's odd walking through the path back to school, at least on a non-school day. And with someone who barely fits on the path to begin with.

"Watch that branch."

"Ow." Andy rubbed his face and snapped the wayward branch off and threw it into the bush. "You kids always go this way? I'm surprised the whole school isn't blind."

"Hee hee!" I couldn't quite suppress a giggle. "We're a lot smaller than you." True, grown-ups did use the path too, but they usually stayed in the middle. Andy seemed determined to walk by my side. His arm swung and occasionally tapped mine as we paced. I wondered if he needed a hand to hold. His face was scrunched, like he was thinking over a dangerous thought.

Past the bend, the school and field appeared. I stopped in my tracks. What had happened here?

Andy gave a whistle. "Whewww. Nice baseball diamond."

"It didn't look like that yesterday."

The school itself looked the same. The field, however, had been manicured and pampered until it was ready for lunchtime with the Ladies' Church Auxillary. The grass was shorn with straight, white lines painted down new dirt paths marking all the bases. A proper pitcher's mound had been built up. The most startling thing was the fence at home plate: short, chain-linked, and separating two benches from the field.

We had a true, dyed-in-blue baseball field! Stammer hadn't mentioned it. I wondered if I was the first kid to know. A mower and tools lay scattered around one of the benches.

"Mr. Oswin must be here today." I was stating the obvious, but I still didn't know if it was the right obvious that Andy wanted.

"Oh? Maybe we should ask him if he needs help." Andy's stride lengthened.

I had a hard time keeping up. Yup. I had taken Andy to the right obvious.

Andy didn't call out. I did. Least I could do, since he'd been so nice.

"Mr. Oswin? You around? Mr. Oswin?"

No answer anywhere. He wasn't around back the school either.

"Elly? What are you doing here?" Miss Oswin stood at the top of the school stairs. She wore pants and had her hair back in a kerchief. Not like a teacher at all. More like one of the store clerks on their days off. I wondered how young she was. Having kids, whether they're your own or not, must age a person until you can shake them off and let out your inner face.

"Hi, Miss Oswin. I'm just showing Mr. Fisher here around."

Miss Oswin smiled. "That's good. For a minute there, I thought I misread the date, and more students were coming."

"No, ma'am. Just me."

Miss Oswin came down the steps. Neither her nor the building shook as she did so. She seemed to have lost weight with shedding of her school clothes. She looked brighter, too. The thought bore minding that people were different than their jobs make 'em. I wondered who else wasn't the same when not working. Connie's dad maybe. Billy Harner never worked, so he was exempt. The priest, maybe, but he worked all the time as the Lord's servant.

"Are you Mr. Fisher?" Miss Oswin's look had a speculative tone, like when she'd seen Dot and me that first day.

Andy removed his hat and held out a hand. "Yes, ma'am. Pleased to meet you. Call me Andy."

"It's a pleasure, Andy." Miss Oswin's hand was engulfed by Andy's, but reappeared fine. Miss Oswin squinted as Andy fiddled with his hat. "You from the circus?"

Andy ducked his head. His eyes shifted, then he firmed up. "Yes, ma'am. I mean no, ma'am. I was, but I'm looking for other things to keep me occupied."

Miss Oswin nodded. "I think you know my brother."

"I believe I might."

"He had a maintenance job for a few days when your troupe was here."

"I seem to remember him." Andy's legs jiggled, though he stood his ground.

"He mentioned you." Miss Oswin gave a smile that opened her eyes up more.

"He did, did he?"

"He did." Miss Oswin took a breath as if about to plunge into a deep swimming hole. "My brother tells me everything."

Andy held eyes with Miss Oswin, but it seemed like it was a secret code being passed and not a thing of lust. "He does, does he?"

Miss Oswin noticed me staring and shook her head slight at Andy.

Andy looked at me quick. "Elly here a student of yours?"

I watched even closer with my name now in the conversation. I wondered what was under the layer of words.

"She sure is. One of my best students."

"I'll say. She's gonna be a fine woman you can trust." Andy gave my shoulder a pat.

Miss Oswin smiled again, but this time at me. "She is already."

I don't know if other people can see me blush. I sure feel it when it happens. I shrugged my shoulders, as if to deflect the nice they were throwing at me. It felt good, though.

"Ozzie's gone to pick up more supplies from the store. He'll be back soon. Would you like to wait for him here?" Miss Oswin gave a thumb to the new benches by the field.

"I think I might." Andy put his hat back on before eyeing me again. "Elly, you mind telling your Grandpa I won't be back until close to supper?"

The bell for school might as well have rung. I was being dismissed.

"Sure. You know your way back through the path?"

Andy gave below his eye a rub. "How could I forget?"

I left them both talking at the school steps. As I got to the edge of the field, Mr. Oswin's car turned from the road into the schoolyard. I watched as Mr. Oswin got out and joined his sister and Andy. Both men shook hands, then embraced. Andy followed Mr. Oswin back the car's trunk where they lifted boxes out.

Miss Oswin waved once from afar, then went back up the stairs to school.

39

We had a new word to live with when Gram came home. The doctor, who looked her over and sewed her up, gave out his judgment. *Melancholia.* He held her overnight in his small hospital just to make the word stick. It sounded like a Ukrainian name to me, like Gram had changed cultures and now ate nothing except perogies and cabbage rolls.

The truth was much harsher. Gram had been branded with an illness you had to outsmart into leaving. To fight the sadness, you had to busy yourself, keep moving so it lost interest in you and fell behind. You could never truly be sure it had gone, either. The sadness was like a stray cat you shooed from the barn, only to find it had snuck back in through a window left open. At least, that's what I supposed.

Sadness wasn't a disease that you could catch, as far as I know, but from what I seen, people treated it like it was. Best way was to hide having it. Gram was sunk in the water before we even began that dodge. People ain't stupid. They'd already suspected she'd been sick when most the boarders left the hotel for more dependable living quarters. When Miss Frieda was seen coming back and forth from the hotel, well, that set them thinking and talking. And, in our town, talking wasn't any good.

The word *Melancholia* beat Gram coming home. I heard it first in the schoolyard, the day before Grandpa went to pick her up. I paid the word no mind, as I didn't think it had anything to do with me. I was done with sad words, with Gram being sick, so my usual curiosity was sleeping.

Gram had a new name to keep her company. Melancholic Grace. Now forever scarred with a name she'd earned by carving into her wrist.

Gram was on a pill for her disease. Grandpa grumped about how we couldn't afford it.

"It's a waste of money, Grace." Grandpa took his glasses off for cleaning when he talked about money. "We have the hotel to think of. We're running close enough to broke already."

"I'll only take it when I need it." Gram put the bottle down on her night table, like it was only meant for when she was bored or had a spare moment to relax. I watched that bottle. I even picked it up and shook it when no one was around. It emptied fast. Gram was bored a lot those first few days.

The worst of it wasn't Gram's new love of sitting and staring. No. Our trouble with Gram was the trial of getting her out the door and into life. She was right back to where she started before cutting a hole in her arm. Listless. Except this time, she was smiling to herself mostly. And humming.

Grandpa got her out of the house for Sunday church, though.

Just barely.

The street went quiet when we stepped out. At first, I thought people were staring at Andy, whom Grandpa had invited along. But I was wrong.

Connie's mother gave a small wave from across the street, but didn't go any farther. A couple other families looked hard and huddled together like geese as they passed us by. Gram didn't notice. She gave a vague smile as Grandpa tucked her arm under his. They looked small together, with Andy's massive form behind them, smaller than usual. Maybe I was growing bigger, but it felt like the recent week had diminished them.

Things got easier by the church.

"Good morning to you, Grace." Father Don's voice boomed out from top of the stairs. He usually waited for people to approach him, but this time, he came down and took hold of Gram's hand.

"How are you feeling today?"

Gram blinked a few times like her brain was still warming up. "I'm fine, thank you, Father."

"Good. Good." Father looked around, spotted Connie's mother and gave her a wave. "Mrs. Dionne. Look who it is. Mrs. Johnson is back."

Connie's mother nodded. "I see that. Welcome back, Grace. We're looking forward to your baking again." She made no move to join us, though.

People got words and sympathy when someone's sick with their heart or cancer. Same with an infection, though they keep their distance. For Melancholia, maybe there's sympathy, but there's no words. Only silences and distance like they're afraid it's catchy. Maybe it is. I don't know.

People were friendly inside church, though. Maybe people feel they gotta be nicer 'cause the Lord Baby Jesus is right there on the cross, watching them. Or maybe the mean ones just delay going inside church as long as possible.

Stammer's family was sitting in their usual spot. As I passed, Stammer reached a hand out to stop me.

"Hey."

I couldn't hide my grin. Andy saw, 'cause he gave my shoulder a pat as he went by.

"Hey, back."

"You coming to watch us play today?"

I was going to refuse. I felt weak saying yes, but I said yes, anyways.

"Yeah, I'm gonna."

"Great!" Stammer gave my arm another squeeze. "Maybe you'll walk with me there?"

"Uh, yeah. Sure. That'd be nice." Holy Margaret. I looked up at the cross by the altar. I had a lot of thankful prayers to give today.

I followed Andy towards our pew. He lagged behind Grandpa, motioning me to pass. Andy didn't come join us in our pew like I expected, but paused halfway, in the middle of aisle.

Mr. Oswin was on the other side of the aisle, opposite where Grandpa settled in, near the front. Miss Oswin liked to sit up close, maybe 'cause it kept her from seeing us kids another time. Mr. Oswin always looked like he'd prefer the back.

Mr. Oswin stood up and took a step into the aisle, facing Andy walking up towards him. Mr. Oswin's hands were folded, like he was waiting for something. His face was bright, as bright as I'd ever seen it. His clothes were all pressed and clean. Matter of fact, he was dressed in a suit, not his usual tattered shirt no tie. All that was missing was a boutonniere, or whatever they call that flower a man pins to his jacket.

I couldn't quite see his face, but Andy stopped before Mr. Oswin. They both nodded a greeting. Then they sat down together beside Miss Oswin. She shifted to make room.

The Dionnes came in last and shuffled in to their usual spot in front of us. Connie eyed me as she sat, sneaking me a small wave while her parents settled themselves.

"What are they, multiplying?" Mr. Dionne's voice rasped harsh as he looked across the aisle.

I tried to catch what he was looking at, but he'd already turned back to his wife.

"Shh, dear. We're about to start." Mrs. Dionne whispered her admonishment and ducked her head at the angry look Mr. Dionne gave.

"I know, and I don't need your explaining." Mr. Dionne settled himself with a few more harrumphs.

For once, mass was quick. It went faster when I had something to worry about, whether Gram was gonna fall asleep or not. I wasn't used to being the one with sharp elbows. Gram didn't complain. She didn't sing along, either. Maybe my thoughts were occupied with Stammer. I think Connie's were, too, as she watched closely when Stammer went up the aisle for communion.

Father Don closed the mass with a prayer for all our community, and for health and prosperity. I think his eye lingered on Gram as he spoke. She paid him no mind as she nodded to herself. Her chin dipped until I elbowed her again.

"Before we go, I'd like to remind you all to come and support the baseball game today." Father Don raised his arms wide to include all of us. "The boys have practiced extra hard with their coach. It's their first game, and they'll get a chance to show off those nice uniforms the Auxiliary sponsored."

People murmured and nodded. The game had been on the town's mind for more than a few days.

"Mr. Oswin, would you like to say a few words as their coach?" Father Don rarely gave someone else the chance to speak in church. As the baseball team's coach, Mr. Oswin was worthy of that honour.

Mr. Dionne muttered to himself as Mr. Oswin stood.

"Well, our boys are looking pretty good there. We're as ready as we'll ever be." Mr. Oswin rubbed a hand on the back of his neck as he talked. "Much thanks and gratitude to the ladies of the church. The uniforms look awful nice. We'll be proud to wear 'em. We hope to see you at the school. First pitch is two o'clock."

Mr. Oswin gave Father Don a nod as he sat again. Short and sweet. Father Don gave his staunch look of approval before continuing.

"I understand you set up a regular pitch and stands."

"That's right." Mr. Oswin half stood. "We got the chain link donated by Mr. Dionne, and he also gave us the stands left over from the circus."

Mr. Dionne nodded as a few polite claps rang out.

Father Don waved his hands as if to stop any ruckus.

I looked up, but the Lord Jesus seemed just as content with the noise as he did with silence. I wondered what position Jesus woulda played if he was a baseball man. Maybe first base?

"We'll see you all at two o'clock," Father Don continued. "And as a reminder, bring your appetite, as the Ladies' Auxiliary will be selling pie and lemonade."

Baseball, pie, lemonade, Stammer. Stammer, Stammer, Stammer.

I gave one more look of thanks to the Lord Jesus on the cross. The day was turning into a mighty fine one.

40

Stammer and I were going to the game together. Was it a date? Wasn't it? You never know what someone means until you ask. The problem with asking is sometimes you find out they don't mean things the same way you hoped. Until then, you at least have the possibility.

I didn't bother asking Stammer if it was a date. I didn't want any words getting in the way of things. Besides, him actually showing up was good enough for me.

I didn't see Stammer after church. He was gone by the time I got out. Gram, Grandpa and me were the last few to leave. Gram just sat in the pew, all folded into herself.

"How are you feeling, Grace?" Mrs. Dionne paused as her family went by.

Gram's eyes twitched. "I'm feeling fine. Thank you for asking." Gram gave a tug on her dress sleeve. She hadn't taken her gloves off all service. Still, you could see the edge of the bandage poking out.

She looked up and smiled when more people murmured her name, else Gram stared at her hands. She'd been quiet the whole service. Her usual was to tut and nod when Father Don said something particularly noteworthy.

When we got home, Gram went straight up to her room. Being Sunday, Grandpa paced in the parlour, instead of visiting the bar. He daren't, outta respect for Gram and Jesus. We all knew Gram had no interest in catching him, though. Her mind wasn't focused on policing others. I didn't pay them much mind, as my own thoughts were on the afternoon. Time to get ready.

My jeans hung over the chair in my room. They were more brown than blue, as I'd forgone washing them while Gram was away. My other pair were no better. Seems everything I owned was brown. Even the Sunday dress borrowed from Gram held the feel of the earth. I thought of Connie and her twirl-skirts: how she looked like bubble gum you could chew, with her pinks and greens. I needed something brighter to wear if I was to attract and hold onto Stammer.

Nothing else to do but to bother Gram.

"Who is it?"

"Gram, it's me. Can I come in?"

There was a creaking and shuffling before the door finally opened. Gram stood there, already back in her housecoat and slippers.

"Of course, Ellen." She held the door wide enough for me to slip through and shut it again.

I balanced and bounced on my toes, wearing my brown dress, as Gram settled herself back into bed.

"Gram, I need to ask you something."

"Oh?"

I gathered my words for a rush. "Do I look pretty in this?"

Gram didn't answer right away. She tilted her head as she looked me over. "You do. But it's not the right colour for a girl."

"Oh." It was my turn to be brief. My heart sank, taking my confidence with it.

Gram lifted the covers and swung her legs over the bed edge. "What's the matter, Elly? Did someone say a mean word to you?"

"Not exactly." Not at all, as a matter of fact. No one had ever said anything about how I looked. It hadn't been a problem before. At least, not until I wanted Stammer to notice me.

"What is it, then?"

I caught Gram's eye with my own. "I don't want to wear this anymore."

Gram chuckled. "Is that all? We've been through this before. You know you can't wear your pants to church."

"That's not it." I shook my head at how wrong she was. "I mean, I don't want to wear *this* dress anymore."

Silence greeted my pronouncement. Gram sat waiting to see if I'd add more words.

I sighed. "It was kind of you to lend it to me, but…" I shifted from foot to foot. "Is there something else I can wear?"

Gram tilted her head, like she'd caught sight of a bird she'd never seen before. "You want to wear… a different dress."

I nodded. Several times. Short and quick. "Yes. Or a skirt or something." I'd seen Connie wear kiltie skirts. They sashayed pretty when she moved. "I want to look nice."

"I never thought I'd see the day."

"It's for the baseball game today."

Gram didn't speak.

I rubbed a hand over my mouth, but the words spilled out. "Stammer asked me to go with him."

"Lord Almighty, there's a girl somewhere in you, yet." Gram stood and stepped to her wardrobe.

I flinched at her choice of words as Gram opened the wardrobe with her bandaged arm. Maybe she didn't mean her words the way they sounded, like nobody believed I was a girl. Like Gram had a hard chore to make me look like one. I shook the thought away.

Hangers rasped as Gram thrust them back and forth.

"Here it is." She held up a skirt. "I haven't worn this in a long while."

It was navy blue, the same colour as my jeans when I'd first got them. It wouldn't feel too different, and yet it would be. A few pleats swayed as Gram held it up higher to inspect it.

"Could I wear that?"

"It might be too long." Gram laid the skirt on the bed. She tapped her chin with one finger as she thought. "Best get started on it."

I couldn't help myself. I ran at Gram and hugged her from behind.

Gram startled and reached an arm back to return my exuberance. "Now, child. Don't mention it. We'll get you all set."

Getting that skirt the right length meant standing still with pins poking into my legs. Gram was a careful seamstress. How she managed to talk with pins in her mouth, I'll never know. I keep holding back a gag, thinking about her swallowing one by accident.

"There." Gram stood back satisfied when she'd placed the last pin. "Now, take it off carefully, mind you. Don't go dislodging any of my pins."

I shimmied out of the skirt with only one pin scrape. Gram took the skirt from me and placed it on the bed. Her sewing basket lay in wait, needle already threaded, ready to give me my chances at Stammer.

Grandpa brought lunch upstairs so Gram could keep working. She waved it off, urging me to eat. Her needle flew as she fussed and hemmed.

"There. You go try that on." Gram held the skirt up. "Come back when you're ready. I want to see how it fits."

I brushed a few lunch crumbs off my lap as I stood.

Gram made a face. "Wash your hands first." She laid the skirt back on the bed and soon was settled with her own sandwich.

When I finally put the skirt on, it felt nice. It fit well and flared when I twirled.

Gram hummed as she tidied up her sewing basket. She looked up with a smile when I came in.

"Look, Gram!" I walked back and forth, turning quickly on my heels. The skirt dipped and swayed.

"Don't you look nice? Just like your mam." Gram sat down and pulled off her glasses. She wiped them as her eyes glisten. "Just like your mam."

Gram's words were as heartfelt as anything I'd ever heard her say. I hugged her again for it.

Then, I sat down in the parlour to wait for Stammer.

41

I know you're not supposed to act all whack-a-doodle if you're waiting for a boy, but I couldn't help it. I had a definite case of ants in my pants.

At first I sat prim and proper in the parlour. Soon, I'd swung my legs over the chair armrest and was kicking them in tune to my singing. Grandpa walked by on his way out and took a few steps back to scowl at me.

"Your Gram has to clean up any mess you make."

"Sorry, Gramps." I was feeling extra swingy. I gave my feet one more kick before I brought them to the floor.

Gramps. The new nickname didn't improve Grandpa's grimace, but I was too busy thinking of Stammer to note it.

One of the armrests had a spot of dirt on it. I licked a finger to rub it when I remembered Grandpa was still there.

"Ahem. Looks like you're old enough to do the cleaning in here." He squinted at me to punctuate the threat.

"Uhhh… sorry Grandpa." I stood to go outside. I figured it was the safest place to avoid having more housework put on me.

"Why are you in here, anyways?"

"I'm waiting for someone."

"Oh?" Grandpa shifted to block me leaving. "Do tell."

"We're going to the baseball game."

"That's not the tell I want. Try again."

I shifted, suddenly aware that I was swimming in new waters. Having a boy drop by when you're in dirty jeans is one thing. All dolled and gussied up while waiting put my afternoon in a different category. Considering how Grandpa banned me from the circus, I suddenly had a cold chill run through my chest.

"It's Stammer. You know, the kid with the stammer?" I figured downplaying Stammer's best qualities might get me off the hook.

"Oh. Ward's nephew." Grandpa straightened. "Why didn't you say so?"

And with that, Stammer had parental—well, grandparental—approval. I grinned, then pulled my face in to a respectable solemn. "He's playing in the baseball game, but he wanted us to walk there."

Grandpa nodded. "Make sure you're home before supper."

It was as easy as that. I had a feeling, though, if it was Billy Harner showing up, that the hotel would close, and I'd be locked up in my room for the night... or maybe for good.

Still, one more thing to check.

"You and Gram going to the game?"

A shake of his head gave me some relief. "No. Your Gram and I are staying home this afternoon. I've got some chores around here."

I couldn't keep the relief from seeping through my eyes. No grown-ups watching Stammer and me.

Grandpa musta caught my thought as he waggled his eyebrows at me. "I may show up later, though."

Drat.

I made an escape outside. Maybe Grandpa was joking, maybe not.

Still no Stammer, so I tucked my skirt behind me and sat on the steps to wait. A few people walked by, mostly adults going to the school. A few younger kids, too. None were interesting to yell Hello to.

My saddle shoes were dirty. I'd forgotten to give them a swipe. The inside edge of my skirt came in handy.

Stammer chose that moment to sneak up from the side. "*Boo!*"

I shrieked. Holy Margaret. I even acted different in a skirt.

"Stani, you scared me."

Stammer gave a deep, dark laugh. "I did, didn't I?" He gave a low whistle, too. "You look nice."

I know I blushed as Stammer's grin got wider. I felt it was time to distract him.

"You got your glove?"

"Yep, right here." He stood up and threw his shoulders back. "Whaddya think of the uniform?"

Stammer's pants were ragged as always, but his baseball shirt was fresh and clean, pinstriped in navy. He looked like a real baseball man.

"You look… nice," I finally conceded.

That got me another grin.

"You ready, Freddy?" Stammer leaned over and held out the crook of his arm.

"As ready as I'll ever be." I swung myself up to stand beside him.

"Shall we?"

We joined the small crowd moving through the path to school and soon stepped onto the open field.

So many people!

Cars and trucks were parked on the grass to the side. People milled around the school or peered over the fence onto the diamond. Young children ran, chasing each other by the stands. A few tables were set to the side, festooned with balloons and streamers.

Crack!

"Heads up!" Stammer gave my arm a tug to grab my attention.

I looked to where he pointed. A ball was soaring towards us. Stammer couldn't get his glove on fast enough as it whizzed by, then rolled on the ground into the bushes.

"Whew. That was an opposing team hit." Stammer nodded to himself. "I'm gonna have my work cut out for me."

"You playing outfield?"

"Yep, but I'm backup for first base." Stammer took a look at the path we came from. "Say, y'know, they don't allow people to watch from the outfield."

"Oh?" I guess I hadn't thought of where I'd sit to watch Stammer. I couldn't sprawl in the bushes like usual anyways, as I was in a skirt.

Stammer musta thought the same thing. "I'll be up to bat, though."

"There is that."

Stammer gave my arm a squeeze before leaving to join his team. I watched him go. The moment warranted another Holy Margaret.

"Holy Margaret."

"Pardon me?"

I looked up to see Father Don standing beside me. "Uhhh…"

Father Don smiled. "It's okay. You can pray to the saints, but make sure you keep it saintly."

I swear Father Don looked me over, then winked at me. That made me lose whatever words I'd brought.

"The team looks good." Father Don leaned over the fence to peer at our boys. His elbow nudged mine as he settled in. I felt icky all of a sudden. Standing with the priest was the last place I'd pictured myself on a day like this. On a date like this.

"Those uniforms sure make them look handsome. Don't you think?" Father Don turned to face me. "You girls did a lot of work to make the team come together."

"Uh. Thanks." I didn't feel particularly involved in that. Other than being bossed by Connie's mother for an hour, I hadn't given two hoots about what the team wore. I stand corrected. Now I did. Because of Stammer. I mused at his arm muscles as he swung three bats together on the side.

"You coming to sit?" Father Don plucked at my elbow.

I couldn't hold back a shiver at his touch. Grown-ups. Kids don't go controlling body space like that, not unless they mean to pop you one. "No thanks, Father. I'm gonna watch from here."

Father Don frowned. He crouched and put his face close to mine. "You could get hurt here. Why don't you come sit with me? It'll be safer in the stands." He took hold of my elbow as he spoke.

I had no choice but to follow.

Lucky for me, Father got waylaid by Connie's parents.

"What a wonderful afternoon, Father." Mrs. Dionne was full of smiles.

Mr. Dionne gave a nod to us both.

"It certainly is. How is the refreshments table going?" Father Don released my arm and laid a hand on Mrs. Dionne's instead.

"Just fine, Father. People have eaten half of the pies already." Mrs. Dionne pointed at a man walking by, carrying a dish. "You might want to get a piece now, before they're gone."

"Where's your grandparents?"

"Huh?" First a priest, now a superintendent speaking to me. Not at all the first date I imagined.

"I said, where's your grandparents?" Mr. Dionne laid his own hand on my shoulder. "I'm looking for Carl. I don't see him anywhere."

"Oh. They stayed home."

Mr. Dionne peered at me, like he was weighing the truth of what I said. He took another scan of the crowd. "Well, when you see him, tell him I'm looking for him. We've got some accounts to go over."

"You can find him at the hotel." Daring to refuse him, I know, but I was on a date. Messages could wait 'til after.

"I'll drop by later." Mr. Dionne looked at his wristwatch. "Maybe once the game is over."

I nodded and slipped away from the Dionnes and Father. If Grandpa was in money trouble, I didn't want to know at that moment. I wanted to keep my thoughts on Stammer.

The stands were full. I didn't recognize most of the people there. The opposing team had a lot of support. I scanned the faces, looking for someone I knew. Miss Frieda maybe, or Darlene. I didn't have many options, now that I think on it.

I finally saw Darlene and Connie tucked in the crowd way up high. Darlene waved and shrugged. There was no space near them. I couldn't see Miss Frieda anywhere. A few of the older girls settled into seats a few rows up. I glanced their way, but they ignored me. A couple years makes a big difference in school.

"Hey, Sugar." Billy Harner stretched out and waved at me from the front row. "Come join us?" Billy patted a small space between Henry and himself.

I shook my head.

Henry whispered something that made Billy laugh.

It also made my fists clench.

"If you change your mind, we'll be here. We'll take care of you." Billy laughed again.

I unballed my fists as I walked away. I wanted to hit Billy Harner so bad.

The only one I really wanted to sit with was Stammer. I made my way back to the place Father Don had shooed me from, close to the team benches. Andy was there, leaning on the fence, talking to Mr. Oswin. Neither looked as I scooted up beside them. I wasn't interested in what they had to say, anyways. They talked mostly about strategies and the game. Mostly.

Mr. Oswin went back to his bench, leaving Andy to watch the game.

"Miss Elly! You find your friends?" Andy leaned over as he spoke. I could barely hear him over the crowd cheering. Our pitcher had struck someone out.

"I wanna watch from here. What's the score?"

Andy gave a little headshake. "We held them off. Still no score, and we're up to bat."

Good. I hadn't missed seeing Stammer. I paid close attention as he jogged in from the outfield, hoping for a wave. Stammer headed straight for the batting helmets and bats, without once looking at the crowd.

Two batters got base hits on their turns. One stole third base to the roar of approval from the crowd. A few people booed, and others grinned good-naturedly at the sound. I wished I coulda played.

Stammer was up next.

I watched as Stammer strolled to the plate, swinging his bat back and forth over his shoulders. He settled into a crouch and gave a nod to the ump.

The catcher flashed a hand signal, and the ball came whizzing to the plate.

Stammer swung hard. His lineup was perfect.

Thwack!

I kept watch on Stammer as he twisted and looked up behind him. He kept looking and following, and his gaze travelled down to meet my own. His face had a look of surprise, and he yelled something at me.

That's the last thing I remember, as everything went dark.

42

"She's coming 'round ..."

"Give her room."

"Elly? Elly? Wake up."

"Oh Lord, look at the blood ..."

"Get those kids away ..."

"How is she ..."

"Elly?"

Words whipped around me, faster than I could catch 'em. And colours... sparkles... Dark, then sparkles again.

"Elly?"

Elly. That's my name. I couldn't ask who's saying it.

"We need a towel..."

Something pressed on my head. It hurt like hell. It didn't block the sparkles.

"Uhhhh..." Best I could do.

"She's waking up..."

"Elly? Elly."

"Uhhhh..."

Someone raised me to sit. They had a towel pressed to my head, best I could guess. I was on the ground, crouched over my legs. Someone's hand supported my back. My teeth felt rattled, and I tasted metallic in my mouth.

My head.

I woulda sold my head at that moment. Cheap.

It hurt like crap.

Ain't no poetry in a sore head. It just hurts. Like crap.

"Elly? Can you move your arms and legs? Elly?" Whoever it was pinched my fingers. Hard.

"Ow!" I pulled my hands away and jiggled my legs. Just to make them shut up.

"She's coming to."

"Let's get her to a seat." Someone pulled me up gentle, and guided my feet.

Words started clumping and making more sense. I peered through my eyelids, but it hurt too much. Everything was blurry. Grey-shaded figures loomed as I was pushed slowly into a sit. Someone opened my eyelids and peered at me. I thought it was Mr. Oswin, but I wasn't sure.

"That's a real bad knock."

"The bleeding's stopped."

I felt the towel shift on top my head.

"Yep. It's done."

I opened my eyes wider. It still hurt. I was on a bench. People surrounded me. One person leaned in to peer at me close.

"I'm so sorry." Stammer's face wavered as it came into focus. "You okay?"

I blinked, but Stammer's face was still hazy. "What?"

"I feel awful. Just awful." Stammer came into sharper view for a moment. His eyebrows were raised, like he was asking me a question.

"What happened?" I asked him one instead. I think I already knew, but I needed someone else to say the words. I still couldn't.

"You got hit by a ball." Stammer's face was replaced by Mr. Oswin's. Andy peered in close, too.

"What?" Their voices were blurry. Their faces were blurry. Everything was back to blurry. It hurt like hell every time I moved my head.

Mr. Oswin's face disappeared from view. "She needs to go home."

Home. I wasn't home. I was at the baseball game. I was watching Stammer. I got hit by a ball. What?

"I can take her."

"You sure?"

"I was going there after the game anyways."

Mr. Oswin's face leaned back close. "Elly? Elly. I need you to listen."

I nodded but winced. My eyes were getting easier to keep open.

"Elly? You've been hit in the head. You're at the school. Mr. Dionne is going to take you home now."

I nodded again. "Did we win?"

A smattering of laughter sounded. It hurt.

"She wants to know if we won."

More laughter as people's shadows cleared away from over me. Just a few remained.

"Elly, we're going to lift you to the car. I need you to put your arm around Stammer."

That I could do.

Stammer hugged me tight. I must admit, I kept lighter on my feet than I needed, just to wallow in his warmth. My head hurt like Hell, but Hell, I'd dreamed of him holding me, so can you blame me for getting some enjoyment outta my injury?

I was tucked inside a car and watched as the door closed. The slam jostled my pain.

Mr. Dionne slipped in beside me on the driver's side. He gave me a smile as he started the car. "Don't you worry, miss. I've got it under control."

There was a knock on my window. I turned to look and winced as my head pounded. Still, I could make out Stammer. He laid both hands on the window. I lifted a shaky hand and laid it over one of his. The pane of glass seemed to melt, and I felt his warmth wash through me.

The car started to move. I jostled back in my seat. Stammer started to pace beside the car, then run. His hand left a print streaked on the window as he fell behind. My own left flecks of blood there. My head throbbed. My heart, too. I turned despite the ache to watch through the back window.

Stammer was still watching as I left.

So was I.

43

I got a picture of Da tucked in my book of birds. I keep it tucked in the last pages, hidden special for myself. It's got no Mam or Dot in it, just Da and me. It's the only picture I got of family that's all my own.

I don't look at it much, as it's too painful to see.

Da's in uniform. He's crouched down and reaching to the side. Da's not even looking at the camera. He looks startled, with eyes wide open, like he can't believe he's with me. Like he can't believe he's got a kid. His lips are parted. I always wondered what he was saying, what he was trying to speak.

I'm between his legs as he crouches. I got a smile that's coming, but not fully there. Like I know there's a picture, but I'm not sure I wanna be in it.

Da's got his other arm around me. I look safe. I feel safe every time I check the picture, but it's as if there's only so much safe in that picture, and if I check it too often, I'll wear that safe out.

I need Da's arm around me. I know I've run outta safe moments with Da. He's moved on without me. Ma and Dot, too. But I still look at that photo, hoping he's here. I still need Da's arm, his leaning behind me, keeping me safe.

44

Mr. Dionne was a careful driver. He took it real cautious. Checked his mirror a lot. I remarked on it inside my head, but didn't say anything. Words still hurt to think. I know he was cautious though, 'cause I had my head turned towards him and watched him drive. I felt most comfortable resting my head facing him. My other side had a lump that burned any time it was touched.

"You still with me, Ellen?" He reached a hand out and patted my leg.

I didn't say anything. It hurt too much. I didn't move my leg either. It didn't seem important. My head lolled with each bump in the road. I felt like I was looking through a curtain at things.

The car stank like urine. I wiggled in my seat despite the pain in my head, wondering if the smell came from me. Another jolt sent that thought flying. I did all I could not to throw up.

We drove longer than we should have. School's not far from town center, even without the shortcut through the trees. I didn't note it at the time, but still, some part of me musta known.

The car moved onto bumpy ground, did a slow wide circle round, then came to a stop.

"Just a brief pause, then we'll get you home."

My stomach kept going. I vomited on my shoes.

"Oh, hey now. Hey there. What are you doing?" Mr. Dionne's voice was sharp and hard.

I felt his hand grab the back of my hair and haul my head back up.

"What do you think you're doing, you little shit? Can't you open the door?"

He let go of my hair and gave my head a shove back onto the seat. My head bounced with the strength of his push. I felt my neck spasm with a sharp jab that made me gasp.

Then he chuckled. "Well, no kisses for you today."

My vision wavered. I couldn't control my breathing. My mouth tasted like sharp acid. I scrabbled at the door handle, but couldn't find it.

"You looking for this?" Mr. Dionne reached over me and easily found the handle. He pushed the door open. "Get out."

Gladly.

As I moved to leave, Mr. Dionne seized my arm. "Don't go running."

A chill ran up my spine.

"It'll only be worse if you do."

I couldn't understand what was going on. Outside the car was a big grassy field. I'd seen it before, I'm certain. My legs were wobbly as I leaned out and swung my feet to the ground. My legs buckled as I stood. I had to grab onto the side of the car.

"Here, now. No falling." Mr. Dionne was at my side. His hand had a grip in my armpit, holding me.

"Thanks," I mumbled. Then I froze. I still had no idea what was going on. All I knew was Mr. Dionne scared me.

"We're going over here." Mr. Dionne held on tight to my arm as I stumbled behind him. The place we were was more and more familiar.

We came to a clump of trees with a small clearing inside it. I looked back to where we left the car. We were at the circus grounds.

"No!" My heart was beating against my chest, trying to get out. I knew somehow that I should be doing the same against Mr. Dionne, but my limbs felt like molasses.

"Stop struggling. I swear, you and your sister…" Mr. Dionne didn't finish the thought. He gave my arm a push. I fell onto the ground in the clearing.

I lay there a moment as Mr. Dionne looked at me. At least, that's what I supposed he did. My eyes were closed, and he was quiet. I could feel his feet on either side of my hips, though.

"You and Billy do it?"

What? The word formed, but stayed bubbled in the back of my throat.

"You like it with Billy? Billy's been bragging about you."

I couldn't get up and run. I curled into a ball on my side instead.

Leaves crunched as Mr. Dionne stooped over me. He grabbed hard at my arm and wrenched me back to face him. He laughed as my hands came up to block him. It didn't help me none. He soon had my hands grasped above my head as he lifted up my skirt.

I wiggled and tried to kick.

Mr. Dionne laughed again. "Hold still. It'll be over before you know it."

I kept wriggling, but he had me too firm under him. I felt my skirt lift, and cold air hit my crotch. My panties were wrenched down my legs and stretched over my boots, then ripped off me completely.

Mr. Dionne held my panties up with one hand and sniffed them. "You smell pretty good." He stuffed them in his pocket. "The question is… how good do you feel?"

"Please, please, please…" I could only get one word out, only one word, and repeat it. Please.

"Oh, I'm not gonna hurt you. I'm just gonna fuck you. Then, if you're good, I'll take you back."

"Please, please, they'll know." I couldn't get my threat full out. My words were still slow, and my head pounded with each breath I took.

"It don't matter. If you tell, I'll just say you're lying. You're dreaming all this, anyways." Mr. Dionne lifted a hand to my cheek. "Poor dear. Poor, sick dear."

I struggled, but he was right. Didn't matter. I couldn't get away.

Mr. Dionne was determined. He got as far as Billy.

I felt a finger intrude, and I gathered my voice and screamed. It earned me a hard slap. My cheek stung, but no matter. My head hurt worse. At least the finger was gone.

"Little bitch." Mr. Dionne shook me and pressed down with his hips.

I opened my eyes wide. As wide as I could.

Mr. Dionne was fumbling with his belt. He smiled as I watched. "You're about to have an education, my dear."

"Please."

"Say 'Please, sir' and I might stop."

"Please…" That earned me another shake.

"No 'sir'?"

I turned my head away. Tears came, and my vision blurred again.

Mr. Dionne let my hands go and stood. I couldn't see what caught his attention. His legs blocked part of my view. Then I heard something. I shifted my head for a better look.

A car was pulling into the circus grounds. It stopped in front of Mr. Dionne's car.

45

Mr. Dionne used one foot to flip my skirt back down. He picked up some leaves and scrubbed his hands with them. He edged his way through the thin trees out into the field.

He never looked at me or said nothing. Just left me lying there.

My wrists were sore from where he grabbed 'em. I lifted my hands to peer at what damage he'd done. They were red in streaks where his nails bit in, else not much to see. I touched the tender spot where my head pounded. My fingers came back red.

Voices carried up from the grassy field. I could hear arguing and slamming of car doors.

"*Elly? Elly!*"

"S-Stammer?" My voice came out as a croak. I turned on my side and watched the world dipsy-doodle, then right itself again. I felt like heaving, but my stomach had already emptied itself. I gagged a few moments until the sensation passed.

"*Elly!*"

I licked my lips, trying to moisten them. I tasted blood. My bottom lip felt bruised from where I bit it.

"*Ell-yyyyy!*"

"Stammer?" My voice was stronger now. I sat up slow, moving with the waves that threatened to knock me down again.

My motion musta alerted him, 'cause soon Stammer came crashing through the trees. He knelt in front of me, reaching for my knees. He put a hand to support my back, as I looked ready to slide flat again.

"You okay?"

I shook my head as tears welled up. "N-n-no." My own stutter startled me. I sounded like Dot when she bumped herself. The thought made me cry harder.

Stammer gathered me up for a hug and rocked me.

I wanted to keep crying, so his hug would keep going, but my tears came to an end. "I'm alright."

"He touch you?"

I shook my head. I was too embarrassed.

"Good."

I realized I had no underwear, and I was sitting with my knees lifting my skirt. I tucked my skirt in, but Stammer had seen.

He reddened. So did I.

"Well, then. I just wanted to check." He made movement to stand.

"Mr. Dionne took 'em."

"What?"

"My underwear. Mr. Dionne took 'em."

Stammer's face darkened. "So he was trying to hurt you."

"What'd he say?"

"That you'd vomited, so he came here to clean you up before taking you home. That you'd bolted as soon as he stopped the car. He was just trying to catch you and keep you safe." Stammer looked skeptical, but I didn't know whom he was skeptical of.

"Ah." Mr. Dionne's story sounded plausible, like it coulda happened, especially with the vomit inside his car. I lived the truth of it, though: Mr. Dionne tried to rape me. I looked up at the trees above us, remembering when I'd found Dot's missing underwear.

"Stammer, I need you."

Stammer reddened more and took a step back. "Ya don't say."

"No, I need you. You gotta do something for me." I turned my head to look where Mr. Dionne and Andy were talking. I needed proof of my claim.

"Okay, then." Stammer nodded and held a hand out for me to grab.

I pulled myself up, fighting another wave of nausea. The world span and swam, but I took a breath, determined to fight it.

"Help me down to the cars."

46

A flock of birds landed in the trees above us as Stammer helped me up. They settled a moment, then took off as one as we rustled through the bush to the clearing. Their caws filled the air while they circled overhead.

"Those might be your grackles." Stammer's breath flicked warm over my ear. He held my arm snug over his shoulder and braced my hip against himself as we walked together.

I almost fainted. Not because of my head.

"What are you doing here, anyways?" I looked Stammer over. His new uniform had a bloodstain on it from helping me up.

"I felt bad I'd hit ya. I ran after you to wave from the road as you passed." Stammer curled a lip. "The car was going the wrong way when I got there."

"Oh." Somewhere, somehow, Stammer had been with me. Following me, though I couldn't see him.

"Andy saw me running back. He's the one who got Mr. Oswin's car for us to use."

I coulda kissed Stammer right there and then if I hadn't just thrown up.

Andy and Mr. Dionne were arguing as we approached. Andy leaned on Mr. Dionne's car door as he raised his voice. His arms were crossed, and he was shaking his head. Both men stood straighter when they saw us approach.

I closed my eyes as we came near. I stumbled 'cause of it, but Stammer was ready. He lifted me off my knees and kept us going.

"*She blacked out!*" Stammer yelled it loud as we made our slow way down.

I winced at the words. Even sounds bothered me.

Mr. Dionne gave a nervous look at Andy and started 'round the car to meet us. "Is she alright?" I thought I could smell hot sweat roll off him as he came up. His suit collar was stained, and his face was slick.

"She's okay. She just can't remember what happened." Stammer gave me another hoist and adjusted his grip.

Mr. Dionne heaved a sigh.

I peeked through my eyelids. With everyone crowded around me, it was time.

"Uhhhhh…" My groan wasn't faked. I really felt like crap. I leaned harder on Stammer's arm, causing his grip to slide again.

"Can we put her back in the car? I can't hold her too long."

Andy motioned to the car he drove. "We can put her in there."

I groaned and nudged Stammer.

Stammer tightened his grip. "Uh, no. No. Not Mr. Oswin's car. She's all dirty with vomit."

"I can take her." Mr. Dionne's voice trembled. I could hear the high '*Thank the Lord*' in it, though the Lord certainly had nothing to do with Mr. Dionne's part in things.

"Fine." Stammer moved to the passenger door. "Would you open it?"

"Do you think that's wise?" Andy laid a hand on the door. "After finding them here, instead of…"

I groaned real loud to drown him out. Real loud. I don't know how no one figured I was a faker. "Ohhhhh…"

It worked. Andy stepped back to let Mr. Dionne open the door.

Stammer helped me duck my head as I was lowered in. The whole car stunk of vomit and urine. "Careful with her feet. There's puke on the floorboards."

"Phew. Don't envy you driving her." Andy waved a hand in front of his nose. "Smells like a bad cook's outhouse."

I opened my eyes. "Where am I?"

Mr. Dionne leaned in. "You're okay, Miss Ellen. You've hit your head."

"I don't feel so good."

"Just hold on. I'll get you home in a snap." Mr. Dionne closed the door. I could see him through the windshield as he strode over to the driver's side.

Stammer opened my door back up. "Where'd you smell it worse?"

I pointed at the glove box.

"Right." Stammer disappeared beyond the door a moment. "Don't go anywhere."

I saw Andy nod.

Stammer reached back in and over me to the glove box.

Mr. Dionne whipped open the driver's door. "What are you doing?"

"Getting her something to wipe her face." Stammer fiddled with the glove box handle. It opened after a few pulls.

"Don't do that. Here. I got something here you can use." Mr. Dionne produced a handkerchief from his pocket. I saw the corner of my underwear peek out.

"It's alright. I got something here." Stammer pulled out a cloth and held it out to me.

My eyes went wide at the sight of it. My nose wrinkled at the smell, and my stomach heaved.

"This it?" Stammer shifted his grip so he held the cloth by an edge.

My eyes teared up. I nodded.

It was Dot's urine-soaked underwear.

Mr. Dionne moved first. He sat down quick and pulled his car keys out. The car engine roared to life just as I stretched a hand to Mr. Dionne's jacket pocket. My underwear was just within reach. I lunged, even as another throb exploded in my head. I was suddenly, forcibly, painfully wrenched backwards.

The car engine thundered in our ears, and its exhaust heat near scalded our faces. Mr. Dionne spun his wheels a moment before they gripped and he peeled off. Dried grass showered the air as Mr. Dionne's car raced away over the field, back to the road. My head pounded with the reverberations of the car motor. The noise faded as the car drove farther and farther into the distance.

Stammer was sprawled underneath me. His arms were still wrapped around me.

"You okay?" Andy knelt on one knee beside us.

I looked at Stammer. He let go my waist and lay back flat on the ground. A groan escaped him as he rubbed his face with his hands. "Yeah."

"How about you, Elly?"

I shrugged. I didn't feel too bad. The headache was easing. Whatever energy had come with my lunge still coursed through me. I could stand without too much pain. So I did.

Stammer groaned again as the pressure of my body left him.

Andy studied the dust plume of the escaping car. "I'm gonna keep him in sight." He turned and studied me. "You think you can walk home?"

"I think so." My arms and legs weren't hurt. I was moving easier, though the pain in my head continued as a dull throb.

"Tell Ozzie I've still got his car." Andy jingled a set of keys in his hand. "And tell him to phone the police."

"I'm taking Elly home first."

Andy nodded as he got in the car. He drove off at a fast clip. A few rocks were thrown up as his tires spun into action.

Stammer sat up and watched Andy go. He adjusted his baseball shirt and made motion to stand. He shook his head at my offered hand. "You might get sick on me if you strain."

"I don't think so." I frowned, but conceded the point. He was right. My vomiting woulda made for a bad ending for our date.

"**H**ave another biscuit, Father." Gram held the plate out to Father Don.

"Don't mind if I do." Father Don paused over the offering before picking a particularly cheesy one. He tried not to cram it in his mouth, but I detected the intent from where I sat.

"These are heavenly." A few crumbs fell out as he spoke.

Gram pretended not to notice the mess on the rug below him. We were sitting in the parlour for one of Father's daily visits to Gram. She said it was just the medicine she needed, a rosary and a laugh. Father Don always asked about me, so I suspected his visits were to check how I was doing, too.

I could tell the Father liked coming to visit, mostly in how he eyed the door to the bar and headed there on his way out.

"You outdid yourself, Grace."

"Oh, no. These are Ellen's. It's her third batch."

Father Don lifted his half-eaten biscuit in salute. "Well done, miss."

I grinned despite trying hard not to. "Thank you, Father."

Grown-ups don't stretch out their smiles as much as kids do. Something about keeping decorum. I was getting older and wondered if I'd ever master that particular skill. Cooking on the other hand, I could do. I took to cooking like I was born with oven mitts on. And baking. Easy as pie. Father's compliment felt good. Gram nodded her approval as well, and my grin broke out full force.

Father Don brushed his hands off, ignoring the napkin Gram had placed on the armrest earlier. She winced at the crumbs, but regained her smile.

"I should be going." Father Don hoisted his bulk up. "Is Carl around?"

"He's in the bar." Gram gave a mock sigh. "Probably got a glass ready for you."

"Well, thanks for making time for me." Father Don held out a hand. He always pretended his visit was for his own soul. Gram liked that. I did, too.

Henry came downstairs as I was collecting dishes from the parlour. He darted a look at me and nodded tight as he passed by. He didn't often speak to me nowadays. If anything, he made room for me in the upstairs hallway if I happened to pass.

Billy Harner also treated me different. If Billy saw me walking down the street, he'd nip back into whatever door he was coming out of. I don't think I'd come face to face with him ever since he mocked me at that game.

I don't think anyone else noticed Billy's avoidance of me. I had my suspicions about Billy, though.

"Afternoon, Henry." I always called out, just to make sure Henry knew I'd seen him.

"Uh, hello, Ellen. How you been?"

"Fine, thank you." I usually left it at that.

Henry paused to see if I had anything to add, then scooted outside. I carried a few suspicions about both of them. They likely had something to do with Mr. Dionne.

"Anyone home?" Miss Frieda's voice rang out from the front door.

"I'm here." I stood in the hallway, carrying the plates. I'd have to go back for the teacups.

"Hello, Elly. Gram downstairs right now?"

"She's in the kitchen." I motioned behind me with my head.

"She up for company?"

"Father Don just finished with her. She might have some steam left."

Miss Frieda gave me a hug as she went by.

Laughter came from the bar as I trailed in Miss Frieda's wake. Grandpa was holding forth, tucked between Father Don and Andy. They laughed again, but cut off when they saw me.

Grandpa gave a grunt. "What you looking at, Elly?"

"Three wise men."

Grandpa snorted.

"Smart girl, that one." Andy tipped his glass at me. He'd stayed as a boarder, working for Grandpa in trade. "You do your homework yet?"

"Did it as soon as I got home." I didn't see why a strong man would be so concerned about brains, yet he was. He even helped at the school, now that Mr. Oswin was both maintenance man and filling in as superintendent.

Mr. Dionne was no longer in town. Good thing too, as I wouldn't be able to look at him without thinking of Dot. Thinking of how close I'd come to being with Dot. I still shake, Dot. I can't believe what you went through. I only had a taste of your last moments. Did you cry out for me when you realized you weren't going home? Did you cry out for Mam? For Da? I don't wanna think about your pain no more, Dot. You're my sister and all, but the thought of what you went through scares me, now more than ever. It could have been me.

It could have been Connie, too. In some ways, it likely was. I know that now. The next time I saw Connie, I couldn't say anything to show my sympathies, as she tucked her chin down and looked away. Seeing as how I knew about her bruises,

I thought she'd wanna share some words with me. I was wrong. Some secrets are too painful to let go of. Some secrets stay dark, even when the light comes shining, searching them out. The police came searching for Connie's father. I was the cause of it.

Mr. Dionne. The bastard had my underwear in his pocket. We'd managed to get Dot's back, but I lost my own in the process. The bastard.

I made no mistake that time when I came home. I told Gram right away what happened. I cried in her lap over the shame of it. I burned from the thinking of it for days after. How it ached that I hadn't grabbed my panties outta his pocket. Stammer's saving me had lost me that chance. I couldn't blame Stammer, though. Never did, not even at the start, even though I was in agony over it.

Having possession of my underpants turned out to be Mr. Dionne's undoing.

They found him a few towns over that same night. He was trying to make it through the border on a little-used road. He hadn't thought to discard my panties. Maybe he thought them a souvenir or something. Why else keep Dot's in the glove box of his car? I always wondered if Mrs. Dionne and Connie sat in that car, holding their noses and speculating why it smelled so bad. Then I remembered, they usually walked to church. You wouldn't see 'em in that car, just Mr. Dionne alone, driving around to the school or his fields.

I don't know if Mr. Dionne'll be convicted or not. Gram and Grandpa talk the case over like they're the Crown Attorneys. The police have got witnesses for Dot's underwear. Both Stammer and Andy saw it come outta Mr. Dionne's glove box. Turns out, Andy was right behind Stammer and had pulled us both out of the car before it roared off.

Mr. Dionne was sunk. So said the gossip I overheard. People still shushed about it when I came near. They shushed more and watched when Connie and I got close to each other, too. No one thought jailing Mr. Dionne was a forgone conclusion, though. Some even said Mr. Dionne would likely get off. The fact is, they weren't sure he was mean enough to do it. I knew he was. I couldn't discount their other argument. They didn't think he was strong enough to do it. His being the perpetrator hinged on the fact that Dot was found deep in a place you needed more than one person to open. The police only had Mr. Dionne on the docket. Mr. Dionne might argue his way outta being jailed, because he couldn't lift that distillery lid alone. How could he do it alone?

As I said before, I had my suspicions.

It took two trips to get the cups and dishes to the kitchen. The water warmed up nice over my hands as I filled the sink. Gram and Miss Frieda sat at the table, looking over recipes.

I wondered which ones, and if they'd teach me. Dot woulda liked to learn how to bake. I know she woulda enjoyed that time with Gram.

"Elly, someone's at the back door."

I shook my head at Gram's voice.

"Elly? Answer it, will you? It's for you." Gram and Miss Frieda tittered together as I looked over to where Gram pointed.

Stammer's face peered through the pane. He gave a gentle tap on the glass and waved.

"Go on, Elly. We'll see you in an hour." Gram smiled as she let me off my chores.

"Thanks, Gram." I dried my hands, opened the door, and joined him.

"Hey!" Stammer leaned in. I thought he was trying to kiss me, but Gram and Miss Frieda still watched from inside.

"Hey, yourself!" I moved my head so his lips brushed past my ear instead.

Stammer frowned until I motioned to the kitchen window. Then he nodded, understanding.

"Whatcha doing here?" I could see the bounce in his stance.

"I wanna show you something." Stammer lifted his face towards the trees behind the house.

I looked up but couldn't see anything other than leaves.

Our rooster chose that moment to crow. "Ur-ur-ur-urooooo..."

The leaves broke into black arrows that shot up in a rush. They circled overhead as we watched.

I caught my breath as I looked back at Stammer, partly 'cause I suspected I knew the birds. Mostly 'cause Stammer stood beside me.

"Did you see him?" Stammer leaned in closer.

I peered again at the trees, holding still so Stammer wouldn't scare. "Maybe. Did you?"

He nodded. "I saw them when they landed. He's with them, alright."

It was the grackle flock. I couldn't see, but I knew one of them had the blood red eyes that spoke of being different, of coming from far and still fitting in. One of them was my drongo. I could picture him, soft dark feathers and sharp senses, amidst the flock as they circled once more then flew away.

I watched the flock get smaller and smaller as it winged its way through the sky. I still missed Mam and Da. And Dot. Nobody was tucking me in bed at night now that they were all gone. But I'd found a new flock here to fly with in Gram and Grandpa. And Stammer. I was safe and not alone, just like my drongo.

The End

Acknowledgements

This book would not have been possible without the support of my publisher, Stephen Moran; my editor, e-formatter and all-around fab friend, Jette Harris; my paper formatter, Briana Morgan; my illustrator-cover artist, Brian Bullard; and my cover designers, Jessica Wynn (1st ed and Kelley Tate (2nd ed).

The following photographers' works were used as part of inspiration for cover art:

Bob Baker, Common House Sparrow featured in Cornell online bird guide
Alistair Ross Taylor, Spangled Drongo from Michael Dahlem's website, mdahlem.net
René Lortie, Gray Jay featured in rlortie.ca

Thank you to those who read my words, and both encouraged and inspired me: Family Claudio and Massimo, Mom, Dad, all my brothers, Brent, Kerry, Mark, Albert and Pat Bryski, Gido and Baba, Belinda Loschiavo, Jayne Halayda, Beatrice James, Dedeshya Holowenko, BK Lyon, Stephanie Hunter-Nisbet, Michelle Morrow, Tarquin Carlin, Romeo Kennedy, Sylvia Apostolakis, Tiberius Blaze, Lindy Lee, Christine Stanton-Hayes, KT Bryski, Melissa, Agnes, Charlotte, Tela, Eliza, Nicole, Fran, Annelisa, Mona, Sheila, Rhonda, James, Ernesto, Cam, Kara, Chris, Amy, Declan, Hermit, Stacy, Dave, Pharm, Ricardo, Karla, Jason, Shanon, Samantha, Tractus, Carl, and William Shakespeare.

Words, like people, need nurturing to thrive.
Thank you, muse.
Thank you to all who helped my words thrive.

About the Author

L. M. (Lisa) Bryski, MD, is Canadian (convenient, since her home is somewhere in Canada). She could reside most anywhere, though, as she spends considerable time living in her own head. Lisa is a real doctor, but doesn't play one on TV. She gets to wear a lab coat at work, and she likes to fix emergencies, not cause them.

Lisa has many proclivities, including a love of pancakes and all things breakfast. She enjoys reading and writing, and is very proud of her pronunciation of difficult words. Her humour is horrible, her punctuation abysmal, but she always finds a way to end her sentences with a period.

Book of Birds is Lisa's first novel, inspired by many childhood visits to Saskatchewan, a love of ornithology and the Marx Brothers movie, 'At the Circus.' Somehow, in Lisa's oddball mind, it all came together in the form of a book.

You can find L. M. Bryski on Twitter as @LMBryski. She also has a website, www.lmbryski.com, and can be reached by email, lmbryski.writer@gmail.com. Inquiries about the author may also be made through Moran Press at Moran-PressGroup@gmail.com.

Made in the
USA
Lexington, KY